Pr

"A smartly plotted thriller set within a well-imagined dystopian future. Highly recommended!"
THE WISHING SHELF

"Raphael Pond masterfully explores themes of technology's grip on creativity, the power of empathy, and the search for purpose in a fractured world. With rich characters and a narrative that rings with emotional depth, this novel confronts the struggles of identity, agency, and the fight to reclaim what makes us truly human. Prepare to be captivated by a story that challenges, inspires, and resonates long after the final page."
KATHRYN DARE, PORTLAND BOOK REVIEW

"A rollicking sci-fi adventure with memorable characters, Bell Tower takes the timely theme of device addiction to its logical conclusion."
ANDREW VERLAINE, AUTHOR OF *STIGMAPLAY*

About the Author

Raphael Pond earned a degree in professional writing at York College of Pennsylvania. While there, he also studied the philosophy of technology and its effects on humankind. Raphael currently lives in Salem, Oregon where he is a personal trainer by day and a writer by night. In the summers, he and his wife like to go on adventures in nature. They are always looking for a good hike, hot spring, swimming hole, or rock wall to climb.

raphaelpond.com

BELL TOWER

RAPHAEL POND

Bell Tower
Copyright © 2025 Raphael Pond

All rights reserved.
Print Edition
ISBN: 978-3-98832-131-2
Published by Vine Leaves Press 2025

No parts of this publication may be reproduced, stored in a retrieval system, or transmitted in any form or by any means, electronic, mechanical, photocopying, recording, or otherwise, without the prior written permission of the copyright owner.

This book is sold subject to the condition that it shall not, by way of trade or otherwise, be lent, resold, hired out, or otherwise circulated without the publisher's prior consent in any form of binding or cover other than that in which it is published and without a similar condition including this condition being imposed on the subsequent purchaser. Under no circumstances may any part of this book be photocopied for resale.

This is a work of fiction. Any similarity between the characters and situations within its pages and places or persons, living or dead, is unintentional and coincidental.

Cover design by Jessica Bell
Interior design by Amie McCracken

*For Empathy,
say these words:*

*When eyes meet eyes, we find
the prize—a reason
to live, a reason to thrive.*

*For Silence,
whisper these words:*

*Smile at your chances.
Chuckle at your tomb.
Laugh at your chances.
Cackle at your doom.*

*For Greatness,
declare these words:*

*I will myself with all my might.
I squeeze the dark and out comes light.*

1
A New Era

Sasha Sumzer grinned.

Before him, a bell tower slenderly rose into the sky. Sasha had memorized dozens of bell towers in America. He had visited each one personally. This bell tower, the one in front of him, was connected to a post office.

Sasha crossed the street and entered the post office. Inside, there were two lines. Sasha patiently waited in one. A few people gave him stares, curious stares.

He wore linen pants, a white t-shirt, and rose-gold sunglasses. By his side, he carried a black briefcase. And, more unusual than anything, he seemed genuinely happy in a generally unhappy time.

"Next!" a clerk called.

Sasha stepped forward.

"Hello, I'd like to speak to your manager, please."

The clerk rolled his eyes and yelled over his shoulder, "Hey boss!"

The manager came out and stepped up to the counter. Exhaustedly, he said, "Can I help you?"

Sasha opened his briefcase. Rows of cash glinted with minted iridescence.

"I would like to buy this property."

"You want to *buy* the post office?"

"Well, I don't really care about the post office. But it's connected to the bell tower. It's all one building, one property. If I want control of the bell tower, I must buy the whole property."

"What do you want with the bell tower?"

"You're not using it, are you?"

"No ..."

"Of course you're not!" Sasha laughed. "Every bell tower in America has been decommissioned for the last fifty years." Sasha leaned in and lowered his voice. "That's why I've been buying all of them—the tallest bell towers in the country."

"You want to *own* every bell tower? Why?"

"I'm going to ring in a new era—one of healing, one of great understanding."

A woman in the other line started raising her voice. She sounded worried, scared.

"Please, I need this package shipped overnight. You must ship it overnight."

The clerk replied to the woman: "I can't guarantee overnight, mam. Not without a surcharge. It might get there by morning. It might not. It's a fifty/fifty chance without a surcharge."

The woman started to cry. "I can't afford a surcharge. Please, is there anything you can do?"

"Mam, I'm sorry ..."

"Please! Just help me!" The woman grew angry, desperate.

A young man behind her blinked his right eye twice. Both of his eyes lit up with glowing white rings. He started recording the woman. He filmed her shaky head, her rising voice.

Sasha took notice. He stepped over to the other line. He put his hand on the man's shoulder and spoke in a low voice: "Why are you recording her?"

"Huh?"

"Why are you recording her? She's clearly distressed. She's clearly upset. Is that your initial reaction when someone is upset? To record them?"

The young man stepped back, releasing himself from Sasha's hand.

Sasha continued: "You were going to skezz her, weren't you? You were going to share the worst part of her day with the whole world."

The young man blinked twice. The glowing rings disappeared from his eyes. He looked at Sasha and said, "Who are you, dude?"

Sasha took off his sunglasses. His rust-red irises arrested the room.

"My name is Sasha Sumzer. I'm a meditation teacher."

"What happened to your eyes?"

Sasha turned away from the young man. He walked back to his briefcase on the counter. He took out a wad of bills, peeled one off, and handed it to the clerk in front of the woman.

"Please make sure this woman gets her package delivered overnight." Sasha turned back to the manager. "As I was saying, I'm offering twice the value of this entire property, plus a little extra for your troubles." Sasha smiled. "You can keep the post office. I just want the bell tower. I want full ownership of the bell tower and all its operations. If that sounds like a deal, I suggest you call a real estate agent and start digging around for a property deed."

Forty minutes later, Sasha had made his offer on the tallest bell tower in Albuquerque, New Mexico. When he was done, he stepped outside and pulled a piece of paper from his pocket, a to-do list. He crossed off one item and read the next: *Visit little brother.*

Sasha opened an app on his phone and ordered a car to pick him up. When the car arrived, Sasha got inside.

The driver said, "You going to the community college?"

"Yes. Thank you very much."

The car rolled along for several minutes. When Sasha looked in the rearview mirror, he noticed a solid, white circle in the driver's right eye. They passed a billboard. It read: *Don't Glow and Drive!*

Sasha coughed. "Excuse me, sir. I think it's illegal to glow and drive."

"I was using it for directions."

"But ... it's a straight shot from here to the community college."

"Alright, you got me." The driver blinked his left eye twice. The glowing, white circle dimmed and disappeared. "Sorry, I just get bored sometimes."

"I hear ya," Sasha said.

"You're not gonna report me, are you?"

"No, that's okay. We all need friendly reminders."

"What's your deal anyway? What do you do?"

"I'm a meditation teacher."

"So like, eat granola. Watch your thoughts pass by like clouds. That type of thing?"

"That's a fluffy idea of meditation. Real meditation, true meditation—it's terrifying."

"Terrifying?"

"It can also be violent. That's when you know you're really meditating."

"You're not like ... a serial killer, are you?"

Sasha didn't answer. He simply smiled.

The driver nodded.

"So, what are you doing at the community college today?"

"I'm visiting my younger brother. He's a professor there."

"Do you guys get along?"

"We haven't spoken in years."

"You trying to make amends?"

"We'll see. I have some exciting news I want to share with him."

"Exciting news, huh?"

"This morning, I bought the tallest bell tower in Albuquerque."

"A bell tower? Shit. I don't think I've ever heard one."

"Every bell tower in America has been decommissioned for the last fifty years. Do you know why?"

The driver shrugged. "'Cause you can see the time on your phone. Or through your Domes. No need for bell towers."

"Exactly. No need. But what if we still used them, the bell towers—not to signify time, but to signify empathy."

There was a pause. "I think you might be the weirdest customer I've had today, man."

Sasha laughed. "Can I ask you a question?"

"Sure."

"How old were you when you got Glow Domes?"

"Seventeen."

"Do you like them, enjoy them?"

"They're entertaining. Sometimes."

"Other times?"

"Other times, I feel like they're frying my brain."

"Do you intend to keep them? For your whole life?"

"Probably. Glow Domes are the new smartphones. They connect the whole world. Life is shitty with them, but impossible without them."

"I'm curious: When you die, will you have your Glow Domes removed from your eyes?"

"What?"

"When you die, will you have your Glow Domes removed? Or will you be buried with them forever on your eyes?"

The driver blew out a contemplative sigh. "You know what, I've never really thought about it, but now that you're asking, I'm gonna have my Domes ripped out before they bury me."

Sasha smiled with satisfaction. "And why is that?"

"I don't know. I came into this world as flesh and bones. I want to leave as flesh and bones. I'm not bringing Glow Domes to the afterlife."

"So in your heaven, there are no smartphones? No Glow Domes?"

"Fuck no!" The driver laughed. "My heaven isn't going to have *any* technology."

"How so?"

"In my heaven, I'm gonna be naked. Picking berries. Living off the land. Full hunter-gatherer type shit. I'm going to live in a lush, green paradise, kind of like Earth before we fucked it into oblivion. That's my heaven. How 'bout you Mr. Meditation Teacher? What's your heaven like?"

"Heaven for me ... is bells. Just the ringing and ringing of bells. Everywhere. All across the land. For everyone to hear. A celebration. A turning point. A new era."

"That sounds pretty. I mean, I think it sounds pretty. Like I said, I've never heard a bell."

"One day ... one day soon, my friend."

The driver looked at Sasha through the rearview mirror.

"Hey man, can I ask you a question?"

"Of course."

"You got any meditations for sleep? Like to fall asleep?"

"Do you have trouble sleeping?"

"Every night," he said. "Every night, I stay up late scrolling through my Domes. I sit there blinking my right eye hundreds of times, scrolling through stupid shit. Probably look like a cracked-out goblin in my own bed. It's bad, man. Sometimes I go hard. I blink and I scroll until my right eyelid cramps up. That's when it's time for bed. But by that point, my mind is so anxious, I can't sleep worth shit. So I'm asking: You got any meditations for sleep?"

"Hmm." Sasha thought for a moment. "I have a simple exercise."

"I'm all ears."

"Once you lie down in your bed, think about your toes. Then wiggle your toes."

"Toes. Got it."

"Then think about your knees. Wiggle your knees."

"Knees. Done."

"Wiggle your hips."

"Hips."

"Wiggle your shoulders."

"Shoulders."

"Wiggle your fingers."

"Fingers."

"Then wiggle your head."

"That it?"

"Then go back to your toes and do it all again."

"Alright, let me see if I got this. Wiggle toes. Wiggle knees. Wiggle hips. Wiggle shoulders. Wiggle fingers. Wiggle head. Then do it all again?"

"Yup. And keep doing it. Over and over. Until your mind is in your body."

"Huh," said the driver. "And this works? It helps people fall asleep?"

"More often than not, yes, it works."

"Interesting." The driver scratched his head.

"Something wrong?"

"Just wasn't what I expected."

"Did you think I was gonna tell you to eat a bowl of granola?"

"Ha!" The driver laughed. "Are you gonna bill me for that sleep meditation?"

"Free of charge." Sasha cleared his throat. "But my other meditations—my most powerful ones—those come with a price."

"You got a temple or something? A place where people come to you?"

"I own a meditation shop here in town, on the west side of Albuquerque."

"A *shop*? No temple? No church? But a *shop*?"

"My shop has no religious or spiritual affiliations."

"What's that mean?"

"It means: No chakras. No crystals. None of that fluffy stuff." Sasha looked out the window. "Your mind is an engine. It's a piece of machinery. It should have its own shop—a place for regular, practical upkeep."

The driver nodded. "I get it. It's like a gym for your brain. Stay all mentally fit and shit." The driver chuckled. "I could use that, man. Glow Domes are like candy for your brain. And my brain is fat as fuck!"

Sasha let out a big-bellied laugh.

"I'm serious!" said the driver. "My memory is fucked. I glitch out all the time."

"Glitch out?"

"Yeah, like, I'll be at the grocery store, trying to decide on ice cream, right? And then suddenly, I'll forget what I'm doing. I'll forget where I am, *who* I am. And then I gotta do this weird exercise where I try to remember my mom and dad's first names, like if they're real, then I must be real, and this grocery store must be real. And then I choose chocolate ice cream." The driver shook his head. "It's bad, man. I see it everywhere."

"You see people forgetting and remembering that they're human?"

"Yeah. You know it when you see it. It's like ... if a robot could catch rabies, and you saw the *moment* the rabies got to the robot's brain—*that's* what people look like when they glitch out in public. That's what happens when people go five seconds without using their Glow Domes." The driver grunted. "We're addicted, man. Straight up addicted."

"What do you intend to do about it?"

"About what?"

"This addicted world we live in—what do you intend to do about it?"

"*Me?* I'm thirty years old, man. I got another fifty to go, and then I'm peacing the fuck out of this planet. I'm going to *my* afterlife, *my* heaven, *my* nakedness and berries." The driver sipped from his mug. "Why? What are *you* going to do Mr. Meditation Teacher?"

"I don't believe in an afterlife. If I want my heaven, I must create it—here on Earth, in this lifetime."

The car stopped. "Well, here's the community college."

"Thank you," Sasha said. He opened the door.

"Wait, wait. Hold up."

"Yes?"

"You said your brother works here—at the community college?"

"Yes..."

"But you own a meditation shop on the other side of town?"

"Correct."

"So you all are brothers. You live in the same town. But you haven't spoken in years?"

"Correct."

"Some drama about to go down?"

"*Something* is going down this year. Something big."

2
Glow Domes

Inside the community college, Professor Smith stood before his class. He had sandy blonde hair and deep blue eyes. One of his eyes, however, had a rust-red freckle.

"Listen, everyone. Your essays from last week—they were not good. Many of you failed to answer the essay question."

His class stared at him blankly.

"The question was: How are people with Glow Domes fundamentally different than people without Glow Domes?"

He hoped someone would bite.

"Anyone?"

The class was silent.

Professor Smith pointed to a student. "Do you have Glow Domes?"

The student nodded.

"Get up here."

Professor Smith pointed to another student. "Do you have Glow Domes?"

The student shook her head.

"Get up here."

A moment later, two students stood at the front of the room. Professor Smith smiled to his class. "Here we have two people.

One is a Glower. One is a LowLight." He paused. "They are the same age. They are the same race. They grew up in the same town. And yet, their brains are fundamentally different." He paused. "Let's try an experiment." He looked around the room. "All I need is an object. A single object." He spotted one. It was a brick on the floor that he had used as a doorstop. He snatched the brick and held it high. "This is a simple red brick. These types of bricks are typically used in constructing houses or laying pathways. I, myself, have used it as a doorstop. And we, as a class, are going to use it as an experiment in creativity." He gave the brick to the Glower student. "Tell me, what are all the ways you can use this brick?"

"What do you mean?" said the Glower.

"Besides construction, how else could you use this brick to your advantage?"

The Glower held the brick in his hands. "Um, I don't know."

"Try!" said Smith.

"I don't know. It's just a dumb brick."

"Give me something. Anything."

"You could use it as a doorstop."

"That's *my* creative use of the brick. Give me one of your own."

The Glower stood there awkwardly, holding the brick, feeling uncomfortable.

"Your time is up." Smith grabbed the brick and handed it to the LowLight student. "Your turn. Tell me all the ways you could use this brick."

The LowLight student thought for a moment. "You could use it as a weapon. Bash it against someone's skull."

"What else?"

"You could lift it a bunch of times, like weight training."

"What else?"

"You could use it as a paperweight."

"What else?"

"You could use it to pound chicken meat."

"What else?"

"You could use it as a bookend."

"What else?"

"You could use it as a counterweight in a pully system."

"What else?"

"You could use the edges to draw straight lines."

Professor Smith nodded and smiled. "That's enough. Both of you take your seats." The two students sat back down. Everyone looked at Professor Smith like he was weird, mental, or in the wrong place. He did look very young for a professor.

"Anthropology," he said, "is the study of humans as they live in different groups. Today, in 2072, we have two major groups: Glowers and LowLights. As you just saw, a Glower could not think of a single creative way to use a brick. But the LowLight—she thought of several creative ways to use a brick." He paused. "Can anyone state what I might be implying?"

"That LowLights are smart and Glowers are dumb?"

"No!" Smith snapped. "That's too easy. Dig deeper. What could the LowLight do that the Glower couldn't?"

No one answered.

"Come on. Anybody?"

"Imagine?" a student answered.

"Yes!" Smith beamed. "She could look at the brick and imagine a different purpose for it. She could imagine a new use, a new path, a new way forward."

Professor Smith repeated the phrase in his head—*a new way forward*. He felt hopeful for a second.

Then he stared at his students, at the Glowers especially. All of them had the same look on their face, a look of emptiness. Smith had talked with other professors, other teachers. They all noticed the same thing, and every year it was getting worse. These kids had absolutely no desire to live. It wasn't their fault, but still, they had no spark, no drive, nothing.

"Glow Domes stunt your creativity," Smith said. "They shorten your attention span. They damage your memory. All of this is common knowledge. We see it every day. So why—why do three out of every four people decide to get Glow Domes?"

"To get an easy job," a student smirked.

"Ah yes, you mean a job at a Scrolling Center." Smith crinkled his nose. "A show of hands: How many of you plan to work at a Scrolling Center when you graduate?"

Most of the students raised their hands.

"Would you ever work in a Scrolling Center?" a student asked Smith.

"Ha! I'd rather cross the Sahara Desert than work in a Scrolling Center."

"Why?"

"Because I like work that actually feels like work."

A student in the back raised his hand. He had barely been paying attention all of class and he didn't really understand what Professor Smith had been saying, but he could understand the disdain in Smith's face, the disapproval in his voice. He asked Professor Smith, "What do you have against Glow Domes?"

"I have nothing against Glow Domes."

"Do you think they're good or bad?"

Smith crossed his arms. He took a deep breath.

"I think Glow Domes *feed* you information. But it's up to you to digest it."

The students stared at Smith.

"Listen, you guys are the next generation. You've been exposed to more information than any generation before you. By the time you finished breakfast this morning, you saw more photos and more headlines than your grandparents saw in their entire lifetime. But how many headlines did you actually digest? How much of that information did you actually process?"

The students looked at him funny.

"Have you ever heard the term, 'mull'? Does anyone know what it means *to mull?*"

A student answered: "To think something over. Ponder it for a while."

"Yes. To mull is to take an idea and examine it from many different angles. Look at it on face value. Test it for double meaning." Smith got excited. "Define the idea on a microscopic level. Define it on a macroscopic level. Play with the idea. Take the idea on a hike. Take the idea to a party.

"Give the idea different conditions. How would it grow in a small town? How would it grow in a city or a country? What would the idea look like between two people? Between a thousand people? What would the most righteous person say about the idea? What would the most depraved person say about the idea?

"What would the idea look like in different time periods? What would it look like in different cultures? Is the idea corruptible? Is it vulnerable? Can the idea change people? Or would people likely change it?

"Asking these questions—and countless others as you randomly interact with your physical surroundings over long periods of time—is the art of mulling. And mulling has produced some of the greatest achievements of humankind, both externally and internally." Smith looked around the room. "No matter what you guys do in life, never forget how to *think*. Never forget how to *mull*."

The sound system came on. Everyone heard five water droplets, each complete with a *ping* and a *plop*.

"That's our time, folks. Please rewrite your essays. Have them ready by Friday."

Students murmured as they left the room. Soon it was empty.

Professor Smith stood in silence as he looked around. His walls were covered with black and white photographs of great horned owls. Each owl looked out of its frame with a pensive, piercing stare.

Two years ago, a colleague told Smith that his classroom was too blank and too sterile, that he needed to fill it with his "interests." Smith didn't have many interests, but he did like birds, and owls were his favorite.

When Smith hung up the pictures, his colleague had asked: "Why owls?"

Smith had answered, "I like their eyes. I like how they see right through you."

Smith heard a knock on his doorframe. He turned.

"Sasha!"

"Hello, little brother."

"What the hell are you doing here?"

"I came to say hi."

"It's been *ten years*."

"I know. You should be happier to see me."

"I don't want you in my life, Sasha."

Sasha stepped forward. "Well, I'm here. I'm in your life. And I want your help."

"Ha! Help with what?"

"Building a new future."

"What's that supposed to mean?"

Sasha smiled. "Glow Domes ... Scrolling Centers ... We're going to take it all down, Hugo. We're going to raze it to the ground."

3
Axiom

Hugo laughed. "What the hell are you talking about?"

Sasha answered, "I want to take down Axiom."

"You want to take down Axiom? You realize you sound like a terrorist?"

"A terrorist wants people to live in fear. I want people to feel *alive*."

Hugo shook his head. "And how do you plan to take down Axiom, Sasha?"

Sasha smiled. "The meditations."

"Ah yes, the magical meditations!"

"I've been perfecting them."

"Oh, I'm sure you have."

"They're real, Hugo."

"Yup. They're as real as the tooth fairy and leprechauns."

"Don't play dumb. You remember that day."

"What day?"

"The day with the cold water. The day I disappeared."

Hugo turned away. "I don't care, Sasha."

"Excuse me?"

"I don't care about your meditations or your weird magic. I don't want any part of your plot against Axiom. I just want to teach my classes."

"And how are your classes going?" Sasha smirked.

"They're going..."

"Do you think your students are going to change the world?" Hugo stared at the ground.

"Do you?"

Hugo didn't answer.

"Do you?"

"No! Okay! No. I don't think my students are going to change the world. They're not going to do anything meaningful with their lives. But it's not their fault. It's not anybody's fault. It's just the world we live in today. Everything's automated. Real skills aren't needed. If you want a well-paid job, you have to work in a Scrolling Center. It's not ideal. But it's reality."

"You want to talk about reality, Hugo? Here's the reality: Sooner or later, they're going to replace you with a robot. They're going to replace you with *online learning*. And then what? You'll be out of a job. You'll have to get Glow Domes and work in a Scrolling Center. All day, you'll sit there with glowing white circles on your eyes. You'll blink left and you'll blink right. You'll mutter meaningless comments as you watch meaningless news clips. You'll do it day after day, year after year. And that big, academic brain of yours will *rot*—and you'll never speak or think as eloquently as you once did." Sasha crossed his arms. "How's that for reality, Hugo?"

Hugo groaned. "Why can't you just leave me alone?"

Sasha chuckled. "It's cute."

"What's cute?"

"That you changed your last name. *Professor Smith.*"

"Don't you dare, Sasha."

"What's wrong? You don't want everyone to know that you're a Sumzer?"

"Shut up!"

"Hugo Sumzer! Right here! Ding! Ding! Ding!"

"Shut the fuck up, Sasha!"

Sasha took off his sunglasses. "Look at me, Hugo. Look at my eyes. They used to be blue and beautiful, just like yours."

Hugo snatched the sunglasses and shoved them back onto Sasha's face.

Sasha continued: "You and I are royalty, Hugo. We could have inherited Axiom. But we didn't. We ran away."

"Yeah, and then I ran away from *you*."

Sasha paused to look at the owls on the wall. Then he looked back to Hugo. "Can I tell you something, little brother?"

Hugo sighed. "I guess."

"The very first bell tower—it didn't signify time. It signified Solosis."

"Solo-what?"

"Solosis—a soul-to-soul osmosis. You see, a long time ago, humans discovered Solosis—this ability to funnel one life through another. A super-empathy, if you will. It was so powerful and so healing, people never wanted to forget it, so they erected a bell tower. And every so often, they rang the bell. They reminded themselves to look each other in the eyes. And when they did, they would say a sacred phrase, one that unlocked a bond between two souls."

Hugo raised an eyebrow. "So you're going to bring down Axiom ... and change the world ... by ringing a bell tower?"

Sasha walked to the window.

"See that?"

"See what?"

Sasha pointed in the distance.

"That's the tallest bell tower in Albuquerque. I just bought it this morning."

"What?"

"I own the tallest bell towers in America—one in every major city."

"Why?"

"Because you can't attack a problem without offering a solution."

"Sasha, what the hell are you talking about?"

"I'm going to use the bell towers to ring in a new era, to revive the meditations." Sasha turned and grinned. "But first, we destroy Axiom."

"You sound like a nut job."

"Come on, little brother. What do I have to do to convince you?"

"I don't know. We haven't spoken in ten years. And now you show up, out of the blue, wanting to overthrow the biggest corporate conglomerate the world has ever seen."

"Okay, I get it."

"Do you?"

"Of course. You and I are family. We need to bond. So, let's bond." Sasha sat down as he straightened the sunglasses on his face. "How about one of our games?"

"Which game?"

"How about: Heaven's Bouncer."

"Who's the bouncer?"

"You are. You decide *who* or *what* gets into heaven. Ready?"

"Go."

"Fireflies."

"In. VIP lounge."
"Vape pens."
"Hard no."
"Cigarettes?"
"I'll accept."
"Memory foam mattresses."
"No. Only because it's heaven. We already have clouds."
"Baby ducks."
"Just baby ducks? No adults?"
"No adults."
"Do the baby ducks age in heaven?"
"No. They stay baby ducks."
"Then yes. Baby ducks are in."
"How about jewelry, specifically eyebrow rings."
"Yes. Totally."
"How about sports?"
"Do I get to pick and choose?"
"No. Either all of the sports or none of the sports."
"None. Sorry sports."
"How about breakfast food."
"In. In. In."
"How about sand?"
Hugo laughed. "Just sand? Not beaches or castles, just sand?"
"Yup." Sasha smiled.
"Sure. Fuck it. Welcome to the party, sand."
"How about shoes?"
"Fuck shoes. We have sand."
"How about donuts? Are donuts getting into heaven?"
"Only if milk comes too."
"How about heroin?"
"Definitely."

"How about meth?"
"Definitely not."
"How about lava lamps?"
"Only if they're eighty feet tall."
"How about eye contact?"
"Just eye contact in general?"
"Deep, meaningful eye contact."
"In heaven? Of course."
"How about smartphones?"
"No. No fucking way. No smartphones in heaven."
"How about... Glow Domes?"
Hugo didn't answer.
"Come on, Hugo. You're the bouncer. You decide *who* or *what* gets into heaven. And I'm asking: Do Glow Domes get into heaven? Into your heaven that you're guarding? Hm?"
Hugo stared at his desk. He took a deep breath.
"No."
"And why not?"
"Because I'd rather send them straight to hell."
"See!" Sasha beamed. "I know you hate them, Hugo. I know you hate them just as much as I do. So join me, little brother! I have a plan. I know how we can bring down Axiom."
"Honestly, Sasha, I believe you. If anyone is going to take down the Axiom empire, it's going to be you. But what does that mean for the masses? All the people in Scrolling Centers?"
"Scrolling Centers." Sasha chuckled. "When I was sixteen, Dad took me to a Scrolling Center." He paused. "I wish I could say it was a positive experience."

4
Scrolling Centers

Sasha sat in the middle of his bedroom floor. There were four candles in front of him, two to the left and two to the right. Directly in front of him was an hourglass. Inside the glass, sand slipped through the narrow passage and fell in a steady stream.

Sasha was practicing a pacing meditation. The goal was to start the hourglass, close his eyes, feel the length of an hour, and then open his eyes exactly when the hour was over. He couldn't open his eyes too soon or too late. He had to open them right when the last grain of sand fell through the hole.

From what Sasha could tell, he was about fifty-eight minutes into the meditation. He was so focused and so still, it felt like his skin was vibrating. He became one with time. He understood it, not as a number or a measurement, but as a feeling. And the feeling suddenly ended. He opened his eyes. The last grain of sand fell through the hourglass.

"I did it," Sasha said. "I did it!"

He grabbed the hourglass and ran out of his room.

"Dad! Where are you?"

Sasha ran down the stairs of the big Sumzer mansion.

"Dad!" He checked his father's office, but it was empty. "Dad!" He pushed open the doors to the big conference room. "Dad! I did it! I meditated for exactly one hour!"

Sasha's father was in the middle of a meeting. He sat at the head of a long wooden table, the sides of which were lined with Axiom shareholders. The shareholders gawked at Sasha with white rings in their eyes. Sasha was shirtless, holding an hourglass.

Bill Sumzer glared at his son. "Sasha, I'm in a meeting."

"But I did something cool. I meditated for exactly one hour."

"Are you still into that nonsense?"

"It's not nonsense."

"Can you make any money with meditation?"

"Meditation isn't about money."

"Well, my son, this meeting is about money. And money is more important than sitting around and counting your breaths all day."

The shareholders snickered. Sasha suddenly felt ashamed. A few minutes ago, his skin was vibrating to the tune of the universe, but now, in front of his father, he felt cold—cold and alone.

"Sasha?"

"Huh?"

"Can you quit standing there like a weirdo and let us continue our meeting?"

Sasha didn't answer. He lowered his head and left the room.

Later that day, Bill barged into Sasha's bedroom. He saw candles on the ground and immediately blew them out.

"What are you doing?" Sasha protested.

Bill grabbed the candles and threw them in a trashcan.

"Put on a shirt."

"Why?"

"We're going on a trip."

"Where?"

"It's time for you to learn about the family business."

Bill smiled. Sasha had noticed that his father had two kinds of smiles: fake or mischievous. Right now, he had a mischievous one.

Bill drove them to a nearby Scrolling Center. When they walked into the building, Bill held up his arms and proudly said, "Welcome to Axiom, where life revolves around the news."

Sasha looked ahead. He saw rows and rows of lounge chairs. In the chairs, employees laid back with glowing white circles on their eyes.

"These are your employees?" Sasha asked.

"Yes."

"Shouldn't they be working?"

"This *is* their work."

"I don't get it."

"Work is hard, Sasha. These days, nobody wants to work. They want something easy. And you know what's easy? Checking the news. Checking the headlines. That's all people need—a headline, something to react to."

"Why are you telling me this?"

"Because *this* gave us the idea for Scrolling Centers. Why try to motivate people to learn skills and work hard? If all they really want to do is check the news, let them check the news. Let *that* be the new work. Let *that* be the new lifestyle."

Sasha walked up to a Glower in a lounge chair. Every few seconds, the Glower muttered something.

"What are they saying?"

"They're giving their opinions."

"Opinions on what?"

"Sports, business, politics, entertainment. We feed them three-second news clips and they share their opinions on each one."

"But, that's not a real skill."

Bill chuckled. "There are seven billion people in the global economy, an economy that gets more and more automated every year. There simply aren't enough jobs or skills to go around."

"So you make up fake jobs? Fake skills?"

"Now you understand. It's all fake, Sasha. It's fake work. It keeps people busy without making them work."

"If no one is working, how does Axiom make money?"

"Subsidies. The government gives us money to employ college graduates. We help the graduates pay off their debt, which, in turn, helps the government."

"How does it help the government?"

"If it weren't for us, the student loan bubble would have burst by now."

Sasha waved his hand over a Glower's eyes, but the Glower didn't notice.

"What do you do with the opinions?"

"More opinions means more demographics. More demographics means better advertising. Better advertising means more money from ad companies."

Sasha vaguely understood this triangular relationship between the government, ad companies, and Axiom. What he clearly understood was that Axiom made loads of money by numbing people in sleek, black lounge chairs. It gave Sasha an unsettling feeling. When he looked at the rows and rows of Glowers, he wanted to shake them, to rile them—in the worst possible way.

"Aren't you excited, Sasha?"

"For what?"

"One day, this will all be yours."

"I don't want it."

"Excuse me?"

"This is lame."

Bill gripped Sasha by the arm. "This is *lame?*"

"Let go of me."

"Why don't you let go of your silly candles and breathing exercises."

Sasha squinted at his father. "You're an asshole."

"You need to grow up."

Sasha backed away from Bill. He ran down a hallway and pushed through an exit door. Once outside, he began to walk. He walked for a long time.

"Stupid Glow Domes," he muttered to himself. "Stupid Scrolling Centers."

Sasha stopped at a fast-food restaurant. He walked inside and went straight to the counter.

"Thirty burgers please."

A few minutes later, the cashier handed Sasha two big, heavy bags. Sasha grabbed the bags, left the burger place, and walked a few more blocks down the road.

Eventually, the pavement turned into grass, and the grass turned into mud. Sasha smiled. He saw his favorite place in the whole world—a wanderer camp.

"Hi Greg! Hi Donna! Hi Jennifer!"

Sasha handed out warm burgers. He knew most of the people by their first name. For the past year, Sasha had come here often to talk to people, to listen to their stories.

"Hey, Sasha!" an old man called.

"Frank!" Sasha beamed. Of all the wanderers, Sasha knew Frank the longest.
"What's up, Frank? You want a burger?"
"Oh sure, I'll take one."
"Here you go. Extra cheese."
"Thanks, kid."
Frank unwrapped the burger and took a bite.
"How you doing, Frank?"
"I can't complain."
"You want a new pillow?"
"No."
"You want a new jacket?"
"No."
"Is there anything you want, Frank?"
"No. I don't want stuff. More stuff, more stress, more problems."
Sasha looked at the deep-seated wrinkles on Frank's face.
"Frank, what's the most valuable thing you own?"
Frank tapped on the side of his skull. "My wits, kid. My wits."
"Yeah?"
"I could lose it all—my tent, my toes, my teeth. But as long as I have my wits, my light is bright and shining."
Sasha smiled. "I like that."
Frank took a big bite out of his burger.
"What's new in the world, kid?"
Sasha sighed. "I went to a Scrolling Center today."
"And?"
"And I think the world has lost its mind."
"I could have told you that."
Sasha shook his head. "How did it get this way, Frank?"
"What way?"

"Everyone is on their Glow Domes. Everyone is rotting their minds away."

Frank chuckled.

"What's funny?"

"*You*, kid."

"What do you mean?"

"You're the only kid I know who doesn't like Glow Domes."

"I just don't want to be numbed out all the time. I want to be sharp and focused. I want to be as fierce as a lion."

Frank smiled at Sasha. "I have something for you."

"What's that?"

Frank pulled papers out of his sleeping bag.

"I know you're into this stuff, so I got you these."

"What are they?"

"Apparently, they're meditations, ancient meditations."

Sasha stared at a page. It had a drawing of two people facing each other. Below the drawing was printed text.

"What's this meditation?" Sasha asked.

"This one is for empathy. It creates a cosmic bond between two people."

Sasha looked at the second page. It had a drawing of a person standing tall, shining outward in every direction.

"What about this meditation?"

"This one unlocks your fullest potential. It's the achievement of greatness."

Sasha pointed to the third and final page. It had a drawing of a person on their knees, clutching at their head in agony.

"What's this meditation."

"This one cleanses the mind. The reward is great. But the trial is brutal."

Sasha took the pages out of Frank's hands. He studied them more closely.

"Where did you get these?"

"Tore them out of a book at the library. Some book on ancient monks and secret societies. I don't know. They're probably bogus. But it's fun to imagine."

Sasha read the lines of text.

"Frank, can I borrow these pages?"

"Keep 'em kid."

"You sure?"

"Sure as sure. Just keep the burgers coming."

Sasha dug in the bag for the last burger. He handed it to Frank.

"Thanks, kid."

Sasha stood up. "I gotta go, Frank."

"You just got here."

"I know. But I gotta go home and study these."

"The meditations?"

"Yeah. I wanna see if they're real."

"They're probably not."

"I know. I just wanna see."

"What will you do?"

"Sorry?"

"What will you do if they're real?" Frank asked.

"I don't know. I'll figure it out as I go."

Sasha started to walk away.

Frank called out, "Hey, kid..."

"Yeah?"

"Be careful."

Sasha grinned. "They're just meditations. What's the worst that could happen?"

Sasha left the wanderer camp. He rented a bike and rode across town, back to his affluent neighborhood, his massive family mansion. He hurried upstairs and slammed the door to his room. Then he got out the papers and studied the second meditation.

It was called the Maxis meditation. Sasha read the text over and over. It described the Maxis meditation in detail—how to do it, how it worked, what it felt like. It said that Sasha had to pick something, something to *know*, something to *embody*.

"Hmm," Sasha said. "What do I want to *know*?" He paced his room for a minute. "If I could know anything, I would want to know how to fix this stupid world we live in. But how do I do that?" He scratched his head. "I know! I'll heal minds! Everybody has lost their fucking mind, so I'll heal minds! That's it! That's what I want. I want to heal every mind. I want to be a mind-healer!"

Sasha read over the Maxis meditation. The meditation had a secret phrase, one that unlocked the meditation itself. On the page, the phrase read: *I will myself with all my might. I squeeze the dark and out comes light.*

Sasha nodded his head. "Okay. I just focus on healing, focus on being a healer, and I say this phrase."

Sasha closed his eyes and sat upright on the edge of his bed. Very slowly he rocked back and forth.

"I *will* myself with all my might. I *squeeze* the dark and out comes light."

He felt sharp. He felt focused.

"I *will* myself with all my might. I *squeeze* the dark and out comes light."

He felt even more focused.

"I *will* myself with all my might. I *squeeze* the dark and out comes light."

Sasha was on to something—a clean, swift energy, a powerful focus.

"I *will* myself with all my might. I *squeeze* the dark and out comes--"

The door to his room flew open.

"Sasha!" his father barked.

Sasha stuffed the papers under his sheets.

"Did you see the wanderers today?"

"Yeah."

"Why?"

"I don't know. I love the wanderers. No smartphones. No Glow Domes. They're the only people on the planet who don't have their heads up their asses."

Bill crossed his arms and smiled.

"What?"

"I made some calls."

"To who? For what?"

"That wanderer camp you love so much—I'm having it demolished."

"What?"

"All the wanderers are being apprehended as we speak."

"What?!"

"They're being sent to a rehabilitation center. After that, they'll get Glow Domes. Then they'll be assimilated into Scrolling Centers."

"You're putting them in Scrolling Centers?"

Bill smiled sinisterly.

"But Dad, you're going to fry their minds. That's all they have!"

"I don't know why you're so upset, Sasha. I'm giving them warmth, food, shelter, and a well-paid job."

"But that's not how they want to live!"

Sasha started to cry.

Bill rushed at Sasha and grabbed his throat.

"Stop it!"

"Stop what?"

"Stop caring about the wanderers! And start caring about Glow Domes!"

"I hate Glow Domes!"

"Why? Because they pay for your clothes? Your food? Your education?"

"No. Because they make people shitty and dumb!"

"Excuse me?"

"It's true! People on Domes are dumb, Dad!"

"Glow Domes are the future." Bill seethed. "You will get Glow Domes, Sasha. You will become the future. You will take my place at the head of Axiom."

Bill let go of Sasha's throat. He began to walk away, but before he left, he turned back and said, "No more breathing exercises."

5
There's a Meditation for That

Hugo stood by the window of his classroom.
"Have you and Dad ever gotten along?"
Sasha didn't answer.
Someone knocked on the door. Hugo looked up.
"Ruxton! Come on in!"
Ruxton Riggins, age twenty-two, walked into the classroom. He had messy, black hair and ivy-green eyes.
"Hey, Professor Smith." Ruxton shook Hugo's hand.
"I'm not your professor anymore. You can call me Hugo." Hugo smiled. "How are you doing, Ruxton?"
"Hanging in there." Ruxton glanced at Sasha. "Nice shades, man."
"Thank you," Sasha replied.
"Ruxton, this is my older brother, Sasha. Sasha, this is Ruxton. Ruxton is a former student. He took my modern anthropology class last year."
"It was an interesting class," said Ruxton.
"Did you get a degree? Sasha asked.
"Na. I just audited Hugo's class because my girlfriend was in it."
"How is Sydney?" Hugo asked.

"She's okay."

"How's the diner?"

"It's okay. I'm still cooking."

"What do you cook?" Sasha asked.

"I make the best—I mean, *the best*—scrambled eggs. We're talkin' fluffed to perfection. Pure, cheesy perfection."

"I bet you'll make head chef soon."

"I doubt it."

Hugo noticed the black bags under Ruxton's eyes.

"Is Sydney still at the flower shop?"

"Yup."

"Are you guys still an item?"

"I don't know. She's pretty mad at me."

"What did you do?"

"A few days ago, we went on a date."

•

Ruxton looked at the menu. "I think I'll get chicken alfredo."

"Isn't this place cute?" Sydney said.

"I think you're pretty cute." Ruxton got out his phone and snapped a picture of Sydney as she posed across the table. Right as he took the picture, a man at the next table started mocking Ruxton. He held up an invisible phone and pretended to take pictures while grunting like a caveman.

Ruxton clenched his teeth.

"Hey," Sydney said, "Don't let him get to you. This is our night."

Ruxton breathed. He tried to keep his cool, but a minute later, the man at the next table turned on his Glow Domes. He aimed his stare at Sydney's skirt. He recorded her legs as he licked his lips.

"Hey!" Ruxton snapped. "Knock it off."

"I'll record whatever I want."

"You want to record something? Record this." Ruxton stood. He grabbed his glass and bit through the rim. As he chewed the shards, he stepped to the man and grabbed him by his lapels. "Record this, you creep!" Ruxton pursed his lips together and spat a load of glass across the man's face, like a shotgun spread.

Fifteen minutes later, Ruxton was in the back of an ambulance, rushing to the hospital to treat the cuts in his mouth. Sydney sat next to him, visibly upset.

"Why did you do that?" she asked.

"Because he was a shitty Glower."

"Why did you really do it?"

Ruxton sighed. "Because he deserves my nightmares, not me."

•

"Does that mean you and Sydney are done?" Hugo asked.

"I don't know," Ruxton said. "She helped me check out of the hospital. But she hasn't talked to me since." Ruxton paused. Then he said, very sadly, "I don't blame her. I'm not a happy person to be around."

Sasha cleared his throat. "You know, Ruxton. I might be able to help."

"Yeah? How so?"

"I'm a meditation teacher. I have a meditation that could help you and Sydney."

"How would it help us?"

"It will bond you and Sydney in a way you've never been bonded before."

"How much does it cost?"

"Free of charge."

"What do I have to do?"

"Well, you and Sydney would have to come to my meditation shop on the other side of town."

"And then?"

"And then I would lead you both into the meditation."

"And then?"

"And if you two commit to it, the meditation will open your minds. It will open your hearts. It will give you the ability to heal each other."

"That sounds too good to be true." Ruxton turned to Hugo. "You ever try this stuff, your brother's meditations?"

"No. I can't say I have."

Sasha extended a card to Ruxton. "Stop by my shop any time. Bring Sydney. If you two do the meditation, I guarantee—it will change your lives forever."

Ruxton took the card. "Thanks, uh, Sasha."

Sasha nodded.

Ruxton stood up. "Well fellas, I gotta go. Thanks for letting me vent."

"Off to work?"

"More like: Off to get faded."

"Ruxton ..." Hugo groaned worriedly.

"Don't worry, Hugo. *Tomorrow* I'll work on self-betterment. But *today*, I'm gonna get fucked up." Ruxton waved as he left the classroom.

Hugo turned to Sasha. "What the hell do you think you're doing?"

"What?"

"You're stealing my student!"

"Former student."

"Whatever. You're stealing him."

"He's an adult. He can make his own decisions."

"That's not what I'm saying, Sasha."

"What are you saying?"

"I'm saying I've built a life here, okay? These are *my* students. And I'm not going to let you fill their heads with crazy ideas about weird meditations."

Sasha smirked.

"What?" demanded Hugo.

"You're so tense."

"Because I'm still angry at you."

"It's been ten years."

"And I'm *still* angry."

"If only there were a way for us to bond, to open our minds and truly understand each other. Wait a second. You know what—there's a meditation for that."

Hugo shook his head. "I'm tired, Sasha. Please leave."

•

Ruxton left the community college and stopped by the liquor store. He bought himself a pint of vodka. Then he went back to his dingy apartment.

Once inside, he sat on the couch and stared at the coffee table. It had two items: a bottle of pills and the pint of vodka.

Ruxton held out his hand. His fingers trembled.

"Alright my friends. Time for your sweet relief."

Ruxton popped a pill into his mouth. Then he took two swigs of vodka.

Twenty minutes passed. Ruxton held up his hand.

"Still shaky, huh?"

He popped two more pills and took three gulps of vodka.

Another twenty minutes passed. Ruxton held up his hand.

"Better..."

Ruxton threw back a handful of pills. Then he downed the rest of the vodka.

An hour passed. He held up his hand.

Finally, his tremors were gone and his fingers were free—graceful, fluid, and free. He moved them through the air, steadily and confidently, like a composer commanding an orchestra.

"That's it," he said. "Here it comes."

Ruxton felt music swelling inside of him. He stood up and walked around his apartment in circles, waving his hands and swinging his arms, conducting a symphony that no one else could hear.

"Ah yes," he said. "The violins ... now the flutes ... steady with the tubas ... a little louder with the drums ... clarinets are coming in hot ... now everyone, get ready ... get ready ... wait for it ... wait for it ... brassy trumpets now!"

Ruxton threw his arms high. He felt like he could fly.

Then the crescendo ended, and he crashed onto his bed.

The pills and vodka hit hard and fast. He went from peak to sleep in a short little flash.

6

The Flower Shop

Early next morning, Ruxton tossed and turned in his bed.

He arched his spine like an arrowless bow. He balled up like a threatened caterpillar. He raked at damp sheets with his fingers, and he burrowed his face into holes that weren't there. He rolled away from heat, and he rolled away from cold. His bed was a prison cell, and he sluggishly ricocheted from edge to edge and corner to corner as a nightmare mopped his body across his mattress.

"Left or right ... left or right ... left or right."

In his nightmare, he had to decide soon.

"Left!"

He heaved upward, eyes wide open, breathing heavily.

After a long minute, his breathing slowed down. He got out of bed and went into the living room. On the coffee table, he saw an orange bottle. He grabbed it and shook it. Nothing.

This was the worst part of his day, the worst part of his daily cycle. Everything hurt, especially his head. The next few hours were going to be a grind, and he wasn't sure if he was going to be able to do it. But then he thought about Sydney. He thought about her beautiful hair. He wanted to fight for her; he wanted to make eggs for her every morning.

Ruxton took a shower. After he dried off, he stood in front of the mirror and held out his hands. His tremors were bad. But there was nothing he could do about them right now. He got dressed, got in his car, and drove to the flower shop. When he walked inside, the aroma of roses greeted his nose.

"Hi, Sydney."

Sydney Salazar was arranging flowers at the counter.

"Hi, Ruxton."

"How are you?"

"A little busy. Can you hand me three tulips from that cooler?"

Ruxton spotted the tulips. He carried them to Sydney as gently as he could.

"Thanks."

"You're welcome." Ruxton looked at Sydney fondly. She had frosty blue eyes and very distinct hair. It was silver and white at the same time, as if dipped in stardust. "I like what you did with the daffodils in the display."

"They're okay. Daffodils aren't my favorite."

"Which one is your favorite?" Ruxton asked.

"You should know this by now."

"I guess it slipped my mind…"

"A lot of things slip your mind because you're drunk and high all the time."

"Ouch."

"Too harsh?"

"Maybe."

"You know what's harsh, Rux? Watching you *eat glass*."

Ruxton hung his head low.

"What is wrong with you? I just wanted a nice night out."

"I know. It was that guy though, that Glower. He was being a real dick. I didn't like the way he was treating us."

"I don't like how Glowers treat LowLights either! But *eating glass* is not the answer. You disturbed *me* more than you disturbed *him*."

"You're right."

"Ruxton, if I'm right, that means I have all the answers. And if I had all the answers, I would know how to help you." Sydney choked up. "But I *don't* know how to help you."

"Hey, don't say that."

"It's true! I don't know how to help you. And you won't get help. You just keep popping pills and chugging some death wish."

"Sydney, please …"

"Do you remember two weeks ago?"

"What do you mean?"

"We were on your couch. You were a little loaded. I looked at you and said: 'Are you happy with us, like us, as a couple?' You said, 'Yes. Absolutely.' Then I said: 'Are you happy with yourself, with being alive?' And you got real sad. And you didn't answer." Sydney paused. "What the fuck am I supposed to do with that, Ruxton?"

"Sydney, I'm sorry. It's just … these nightmares."

"Ah yes, the nightmares, the ones you'll never talk about."

"I think I may have found a way to talk about them."

Sydney crossed her arms. "I'm listening."

"Well, not here. Not right now."

Sydney rolled her eyes and picked up her shears. She angrily cut through a stem.

"Sydney, hear me out."

"Maybe you should go."

Ruxton panicked. "Hugo has a brother."

"What?"

"Professor Smith. Our anthropology professor. His first name is Hugo. And he has a brother."

"What in the world does that have to do with us?"

"His brother is a meditation teacher. He invited us to his meditation shop."

"Meditation shop?"

"He wants us to try a meditation, one that might help us."

"Help us how?"

"I don't know. He said it would help us bond, open our minds or something."

"Or something?"

"I think we should try it!"

"Ruxton, I've never meditated in my life."

"No, but you've got soul."

"Soul?"

"Yeah, you work with flowers; you work with your hands; you create beautiful things. That takes mindfulness. You could probably meditate."

"Ruxton, I don't know."

"Can we please try it?"

Sydney sighed. She looked at her arrangement. "This is missing something." She motioned for Ruxton to follow her. They walked down a hallway. One side of the hallway had three big coolers. Inside them were beautiful arrangements. Royal red roses popped into view. Sunflower yellows mingled with blues.

"Did you make all of these?"

"This morning, yeah. I had two birthdays, three funerals, and one 'Just Because.'"

Ruxton winced. *I should get her more flowers. But what kind of flowers do you get a flower shop worker? Ugh, I wish I remembered her favorite flower.*

They walked out the back of the flower shop and into a fenced-in lot. There were two raised beds with homegrown flowers sprouting from each. Sydney stood at the corner of one of the beds, next to a group of golden-yellow flowers.

"I know you're trying to remember."

"Remember what?"

"My favorite flower."

Ruxton admitted his guilt with silence.

"It's this one," she said. "Solidago. I love solidago."

"Because it's like a firework."

Sydney nodded. "Like yellow sparks bursting in the air." She paused. "It's a filler flower, so it never gets much credit. But I don't know what I would do without it. I use it all the time."

A bumblebee flew around the stem, then landed in front of Sydney. She looked at the bee with sadness in her face.

"Are you thinking of your mom?" Ruxton asked.

"Yeah."

"She taught you how to pet a bumblebee."

"Yeah."

"How long has it been?"

"About a year."

"Have you tried petting a bumblebee since?"

"I've tried. But I can't bring myself to do it."

"How did your mom teach you? What did she say?"

●

Sydney's mom pointed to a bee. "Look at that one," she said. "He's a fat one, a real blimp." Sydney's mom smiled. "Let's try to pet him."

"We can pet bumblebees?"

"Yes. But there's a special way to do it."

"What do I do?"

"First, take a deep breath."

Sydney took a deep breath and exhaled.

"Now lean forward."

Sydney leaned forward.

"Tell the bee hello."

"Hello, bumblebee."

"Compliment his work."

"Good work on the flowers today, Mr. Bumblebee."

"Now, use the very tip of your finger to touch the fuzz on his back."

Sydney reached her finger forward.

"Slower," her mom said. "Pet him. Don't push him. Just pet him."

Sydney slowly petted the bumblebee. One stroke. Two strokes. Three strokes. It was the calmest, most delightful thing she had ever experienced.

•

"I can't do it," Sydney said. "I want to, but I can't."

"How come?"

"It just doesn't feel right."

Sydney bent down and clipped a stem of solidago; she carried it back inside. Ruxton followed.

Sydney stood behind the counter. She stepped side to side, eyeing her arrangement from different angles. When she spotted a hole, she deftly slid the stem into it. Glittery yellows splashed into other colors like a floral zest. The arrangement was complete.

Sydney asked, "What's Hugo's brother's name?"

"Sasha."

"And this meditation shop—is it far?"

"No. It's right here in town."

"Okay."

"Okay, what?"

"I'll try it. This meditation thing or whatever."

"You will?"

"Yes. But Ruxton ..."

"Yeah?"

"I need change. I can't watch you kill yourself. Especially after my mom."

Ruxton gulped. "Let's try the meditation and see what happens."

"Okay."

"I'll pick you up tomorrow morning."

Ruxton turned to leave.

"Ruxton ..."

"Yeah?"

"Don't get too loaded tonight. Be semi-sharp for the meditation tomorrow."

Ruxton nodded.

7
The Solosis Meditation

Ruxton picked up Sydney at the flower shop. Then he drove his car onto the freeway. As they cruised in the middle lane, Ruxton looked left, then right, checking all the drivers around him.

"Jesus," he said. "Everyone is on their Glow Domes."

They passed a billboard. It read:

Don't Glow and Drive!

Ruxton shook his head. "Can anyone just enjoy driving anymore?"

"Some people enjoy multi-tasking."

"Multi-tasking. That's the worst addiction."

Sydney shot him a glance.

"Okay," he said, "Maybe not the *worst* addiction."

Sydney stared out the window. "I read an article the other day. It said the national attention span is down to three seconds. Can you believe that? If something can't be explained in three seconds, it's not worth explaining."

Ruxton took an exit. He made several turns, then parked the car. They walked a few blocks before they found it—a blue building with gold lettering: *Meditation Shop.*

When they went inside, they froze. Sasha was leading a small class. He spoke with the voice of a lion.

"Okay, everyone. This is an old Taoist meditation. It's ten steps. Ready? One is Fun. Imagine a thousand tiny smiley faces. Imagine them swishing around in your mouth, giddily riding the waves of your tongue. Now, swallow the smiley faces. Feel them rushing down your throat. Feel them warming you from the inside out. Feel the smiley faces."

Everyone took a deep breath, then exhaled.

"Good. Now, number Two. Two is Shoe. Feel your feet. Gently press them into the floor. Feel stable. Feel grounded. Good... Now Three. Three is Tree. Imagine your legs as roots. Push your roots into the ground, into the soil. Pull the earth's nutrients up through your roots, up through your legs. Pull the energy up your thighs and into your pelvis. Good... Now Four. Four is Core. Feel your organs in your torso. Feel them churning and working like a clean machine. Good... Now Five. Five is Alive. Feel your heart. Imagine it as a ball of fire. Vibrant fire. Now feel that fireball grow in every direction. Let it shine outside your chest. Good."

Everyone took a deep breath, then exhaled.

Ruxton and Sydney looked around the meditation shop. On the walls, there were big, vibrant paintings. They displayed exotic animals—elephants, jaguars, bears—all of them sleeping with one eye open. There were also paintings of trees, huge, thick trees, all of them caught in brutal, thrashing storms. Each tree was just a few roots away from getting ripped out of the earth altogether.

A dozen people sat in the meditation shop, some on pillows, some on chairs. Sasha walked barefoot through the candlelit shop. He wore linen slacks, a white t-shirt, and rose-gold sunglasses.

"Let's stop on Five today. Let yourself rest. Take a deep breath, but very, very slowly. Imagine a feather in front of your nose. Breathe through it, but don't move it. Gentle air in. Gentle air out. Good. Now relax. And smile. And open your eyes."

The session was over and, one by one, people took turns thanking Sasha and shaking his hand. When the last person left, Ruxton stepped forward.

"Ruxton!" Sasha bellowed. "I'm so glad you came."

"Do you always wear those shades?"

"Almost always." He turned to Sydney. "You must be Sydney."

"Hi, nice to meet you. You must be Hugo's brother."

"Please, call me Sasha."

"Well, Sasha, there is something I really want to ask, so I'm just going to ask it: What was Hugo like as a kid? Was he good? Was he bad? Was he weird?"

Sasha chuckled. "Hugo and I got into trouble, that much is certain."

"What kind of trouble?" Sydney asked.

"We pulled pranks, mainly on Glowers."

"Does that mean Hugo is anti-Glow Domes?"

"Hugo despises Glow Domes."

"I knew it!" Sydney said. "He never admitted it in class, but you could always tell."

Sasha nodded. "That's Hugo for you."

"What do you mean?"

"Hugo hates picking sides, even when he has a favorite side." Sasha stepped back. "But enough about Hugo. Come, you two. Enter the space. Feel it. Be a part of it."

Ruxton and Sydney slowly stepped forward. They looked at the paintings, the candles, the rugs on the floor.

"Are we going to do what those people did?" Ruxton asked.

"What do you mean?"

"Are you going to talk to us about fireballs in our chests?"

Sasha laughed. "Goodness, no. That's intro stuff. Very basic. Those folks pay a monthly membership. They come here a few times a week to clear their heads."

"Did you say membership?" Ruxton asked. Then he added, "I thought you said we didn't have to pay."

"You don't!"

"I also thought you said you had a special meditation for Sydney and me."

"I do!"

Sasha rushed to the front of the room. He grabbed two short stools and placed them next to each other.

"Come! Both of you. Sit."

Ruxton and Sydney sat on the stools. Sasha crouched in front of them.

"Tell me. What are your intentions? Why did you come here today?"

"Well, Sydney and I would like to … connect more. We love each other very much, but I have some stuff that I'm dealing with, and she has some stuff that she's dealing with, and lately, we're just not seeing eye-to-eye."

Sydney added, "He ate glass in public. He spat glass in a stranger's face."

"Which is bad," Ruxton said. "Very bad. But I want to get better. And I want to do it with Sydney."

"Is that what you want, Sydney?"

Sydney nodded.

"Do you want to *understand* Ruxton, so that you can heal him and heal each other?"

"If I can, yes."

Sasha grinned. "I have an ancient meditation. It's called Solosis."

"Solosis?"

"Yes, Solosis."

"What is it?"

"You know that saying: When you die, your whole life flashes before your eyes."

"Yeah."

"Solosis is like that, except someone *else's* life flashes before your *own* eyes."

"Like when *they* are about to die?"

"No. Anytime. Solosis can be done between two people, any two people."

"And one life flashes before another life?"

"Yes."

"Do you see everything? Every little thing that person has done, good or bad?"

"Yes, but more importantly, you *feel* their lifetime's worth of emotions. You *feel* the thoughts they've carried through their years."

"Huh," Ruxton said. "How old is this Solosis meditation?"

"Very, very, very old. It goes all the way back to the first bell tower."

"What do you mean?"

"Well, the first bell tower didn't tell time."

"It didn't?"

"No. The first bell tower reminded people to look at each other. When the bells would ring, you would find a stranger, a friend, an enemy. You would look them in the eyes and say a sacred phrase. Then your souls would connect. You would see a problem and forge a solution. You would grow in the healthiest way." Sasha paused. "Does that sound like something you two want to try today?"

Sydney and Ruxton looked at each other. Then they nodded in sync.

"Very good," Sasha said. "Now, I must be clear. Solosis only works one way at a time. Today, only one of you will feel the other person's life."

"Who is going to feel who?" asked Ruxton.

"I don't know. That's for Solosis to decide." Sasha smiled. "Okay, for this to work, you two must face each other."

Ruxton and Sydney turned on their stools and faced each other.

"Now, look deep into each other's eyes. See and be seen."

Ruxton looked into Sydney's frosty blues. She looked back into his ivy greens.

"Now," Sasha said, "the sacred phase: *When eyes meet eyes, we find the prize—a reason to live, a reason to thrive.*"

A quiet moment passed. Sasha repeated the phrase: "When eyes meet eyes, we find the prize—a reason to live, a reason to thrive."

Ruxton nodded. "I think I got it." He took a deep breath. He looked at Sydney. Very slowly, he said: "When eyes meet eyes, we find the prize—a reason to live, a reason to thrive."

Their irises swirled around their pupils, like molten rings of blue and green.

Sydney felt Ruxton's life rush into her. She felt his habits as an addict and his crave to just break. She trembled in his shakes, every finger, every ache. The weight of his days pressed on her mind. She buckled from his hate, his self-directed lies. She widened and widened her unbelieving eyes.

Thousands of nights ended in defeat—a choice to break free or give in to relief. She spun in his cycle, and his addictions got faster. Everything swelled, like a beautiful disaster. His entire sick life rushed through her, rushed at her—one big, lonely wave capped with mad-hatter laughter.

The entire thing took nine seconds. As soon as it was over, Ruxton grabbed Sydney's wrist.

"Sydney, are you okay?"

Sydney was breathing heavily. She gave Ruxton a big hug and burst into tears.

"I'm so sorry," she cried.

"Sorry for what?"

She didn't answer. She stood up and rushed out of the shop.

"Sydney!"

Sasha put his hand on Ruxton's shoulder.

"Let her be. She's in a bit of shock."

Ruxton looked dumbfounded. "What the hell was that?"

"That was Solosis."

"Did you see her eyes? They *moved*. The color—it moved, like liquid paint."

"So did yours."

Ruxton looked out the door. "Is she gonna be okay?"

Sasha nodded. "Just give her some time."

"She's not gonna leave me forever, is she?"

"I doubt it. She just needs to process."

"This isn't a trick or a game show, is it?"

"I assure you it is not."

"How can I believe you?"

"Ruxton, look at me. Tell me: How do you feel?"

Ruxton looked at his hands. He wiggled his fingers.

"Honestly, I feel … lighter."

"Do you think you'll drink tonight?"

Ruxton lowered his head. "Probably. But something does feel different. I don't know how to explain it." He rubbed his eyes. He was worried the green would spill right out of them.

"Don't worry," said Sasha. "The eyes only do that for nine seconds. Then they go back to normal."

"I thought you said Solosis would make us bond. But how can we bond if she ran away?"

"Like I said, just give her some time. She lifted a heavy weight today. She carried your pain that you've carried for years."

Ruxton felt guilty. "What happens next?"

"When she's ready, she'll talk to you."

"What if she doesn't? What if this whole thing just freaked her out?"

"It didn't. And it won't."

"Sasha, man, I really need this to work."

"It will."

"Sydney is the best thing I have going for me. Without her, I'm just a poor LowLight who makes really good eggs."

Sasha smiled. "I like you, Ruxton. I think there's more to you than scrambled eggs."

"Like what?"

"Strength. I sense great strength in you."

"I'm not strong enough to quit drinking."

"You will be."

"When?"

"Very soon."

Ruxton let out a sigh that was half hope, half disbelief. "Listen, Sasha. If this gets me sober—and I mean good sober, like happy-to-be-alive sober—I will personally endorse this meditation shop."

"I don't need endorsements. But I might ask a favor one day."
"Like I said, if Solosis works, I'm your guy, for whatever you need."
Sasha reached out his hand.
Ruxton and he shook.

8
Infinity Lake

The next day, Ruxton visited the flower shop. He walked up to the counter, where Sydney stood, working on an arrangement, a summery mix of daisies and daffodils.

"Hey."

"Hey."

"Yesterday was pretty crazy."

"It was."

"Did you see my eyes move?"

Sydney nodded. "Did mine do the same?"

"Yeah. Your frosty blues melted. They whirled around your pupils."

Sydney sniffled. She put her hands on the counter and started to cry.

"Hey, what's wrong?"

"I felt your whole life, Ruxton! I felt it! All of it! In nine seconds! It was unbearable!"

"I'm sorry you had to feel that."

"I can't believe the pain, all the pain you've been in."

"Maybe Solosis was a bad idea."

"No, I'm glad we did it."

"You're glad?"

"I don't know. I understand you better."

"Did you see my nightmares?"

"Not really. But I felt them. I felt their effect on you."

"And?"

"And I think you should talk about them."

"Right now?"

"Right now."

Ruxton took a deep breath. "Okay. In this dream, this nightmare, I'm underground. I'm in this cave or something. It's dimly lit. And there are two metal doors, spaced apart, built right into the rock. I stand there for a while. Then the cave starts shaking. Huge rocks fall from above. I have to choose a door. If I don't choose a door, the rocks will crush me.

"On some nights, I open the door to the right. When I step through, there's an old man. He hands me a pillowcase. It's heavy, like there's meat inside. Then the old man shoves me onto an escalator. It goes up and up and up. When it gets to the top, I step off the moving stairs. I look around. There's nothing. Nothing but a bed. In the dream, I feel tired, exhausted. So I get in the bed. I lay my head on the pillow, the pillow filled with meat. I try to fall asleep. But then I hear whispers, little kid whispers. They're chanting. Over and over, they say: '*Adults lose their way—and children will pay. Adults lose their way—and children will pay.*'

"Suddenly, I realize—the meat in the pillowcase, it's lips. It's hundreds and hundreds of human lips. And they're moving, they're chanting: '*Adults lose their way—and children will pay. Adults lose their way—and children* will *pay.*'

"I try to twist out of bed, to bolt as fast as I can. But the bed sheet, it wraps around me, secures me tight. I thrash my head left and right, but I still hear the lips: '*Adults lose their way—and children will pay. Adults lose their way—and children will pay.*'

"And then ..." Ruxton paused. He swallowed hard. "And then these kids approach the bed. They approach it from all sides. The kids are missing their lips, like someone ripped them right off their faces. You can see their teeth, their gums. The kids stand around the bed and stare at me. They look hungry, angry and hungry. Then the lights go out. My pillow whispers: '*Adults lose their way—and children will pay. Adults lose their way—and children will pay.*'

"Someone bites my bottom lip. They begin to tear it off. Then I wake up."

Sydney reached out. She touched Ruxton's cheek.

"What's behind the other door?"

Ruxton rubbed his face. "The other door. Okay. On other nights, when the cave is crumbling, I go to the door on the left. There's a thin slit at the bottom of the door. The slit has a sound, like a strong wind or a powerful vacuum. When I grab the doorknob, it's cold, ice-cold. I turn it, and the door snaps open, faster than a bullet, and I'm yanked through the doorframe just as fast.

"Extreme cold shocks my body. Everything stings. I realize I'm floating. And everywhere is black. I can't even see my own hands. I look around and spot, in the distance, a small rectangle of dim light—the door. Within a minute it shrinks to a dot, and then it's completely gone.

"There's no light or stars anywhere. Just me floating through cold, dark space. Don't ask how I can breathe. I don't know. But I'm so cold in this place, this place with no stars, no fire, no warmth. I have to create my own star.

"So I push my hands together, and to my surprise, I actually spark up this little ball of light, this baby star. But it only shines for a second. Then it dies out. I try again. I try hundreds of times, but it never works. The light never lasts. I'm always starting over. Eventually, I cuss at the void. I cuss at myself.

"Then, I reach in my pocket and find a razor. I slit my wrists. And the vacuum of space pulls the blood from my veins. I can't see it, but I imagine the blood branching outward, flowing and floating in all directions, like a river delta or a scraggy tree. Some of the blood hits my face. Some of it gets in my mouth. I taste pennies. I wake up."

Sydney batted her eyelashes. "How often do you have these nightmares?"

"Almost every night."

"Since when?"

"Since I was a kid."

"Did you ever tell your parents?"

"Ha! My parents were part of the problem."

"What do you mean?"

"You know how my parents are pharmacists?"

"Yeah."

"Turns out, they used to be crooked pharmacists."

"What?"

"They used to run two pharmacies in town. And they would use each other to 'cross-reference' bogus names and fake prescriptions. Then they'd each get a little treat for the week." Ruxton paused. "And sometimes, they would share their treats with me."

•

Five-year-old Ruxton cried and cried. His mother picked him up and bounced him on her hip. "What's wrong, Rux? Why are you so fussy all the time?"

"I don't want to be alone!"

"Well, Daddy and I have to work today, so you're going to be alone, okay?"

"I don't want to."

Ruxton's mother rolled her eyes. She set Ruxton down and grabbed something off the counter. It was an orange bottle. She reached inside and pulled out a pill.

"Open your mouth."

Ruxton opened his mouth.

She placed the pill on his tongue.

"Now, close."

Ruxton closed his mouth.

"Let it dissolve on your tongue."

"What's that taste?" Ruxton asked.

"That's the taste of happy. I think you'll like being happy."

Ruxton's mom hurried out the door. Then his father came in.

"Did your mother leave already?"

Ruxton nodded. His father sighed.

"I can't take care of you today, little buddy. Here, have one of these." Ruxton's father grabbed the same orange bottle. He didn't know that Ruxton's mother had already given him a dose. "Open your mouth." His dad put the pill on his tongue. "Now let it dissolve."

Ruxton swished his tongue around. "This is the taste of happy."

"Hey, kid! You're starting to get a hang of life."

After Ruxton's dad left, Ruxton quickly fell into a daze. He stumbled around the living room until he passed out on the couch. Several hours later, he awoke to yelling and screaming. His parents had come home from work.

"I have it under control!" his mom yelled.

"No, you don't! You're mixing too many things."
"Are you saying you're better at this than me?"
"I'm saying people are noticing. Someone at work called you 'flighty.'"
"I'm not flighty. I'm cheerful."
"Oh yeah," his father said sarcastically. "You're a real ray of sunshine."
"Maybe you should shove some sunshine up your ass. Then your eyes wouldn't be so sunken and dead."
As Ruxton's parents yelled and slung insults, Ruxton became sad. He slid off the couch and went into the kitchen. On the counter, he could see the orange bottle. He reached and reached but he couldn't touch it.

•

Ruxton smiled tiredly. Purple-black bags gleamed under his eyes.
"What do you think came first? The addictions or the nightmares?"
"Hard to say," he answered.
"When was the last time you got a good night's rest?"
"Don't know."
"When was the last time you fell asleep naturally, no booze, no pills?"
"Can't remember."
Sydney closed her eyes and paced behind the counter.
"What are you doing?"
"I'm remembering Solosis with you."
"Why?"
"I don't know. Something is clicking. Things are falling into place. I felt your whole life. I heard about your nightmares. I

learned about your parents. And now I'm ... I'm seeing everything. It's all connected. There's a solution, a cure. Yes ... Yes! ... That's it!" She opened her eyes and beamed at Ruxton. "I know what we have to do."

"What are you saying?"

"Solosis—it showed me how to heal you!"

"Okay. What do we have to do?"

Sydney grabbed her keys. "I'll close the shop early. Then we'll stop by your place."

"For what?"

"Swim trunks."

"Why?"

"We're going to Infinity Lake."

"That's an hour-long drive."

"I know. But I think it'll be the perfect spot."

"For swimming lessons?"

"No." Sydney grinned. "Sleeping lessons."

•

Infinity Lake was a small lake. Two circles of water were joined by a thin liquid bridge. From above, it looked like the mathematical symbol for infinity.

Sydney stood at the shore, staring intently across the blue-green surface of water that widened, thinned, and widened again.

"Isn't it beautiful?" Sydney said.

"Delightful," Ruxton answered.

Sydney took off her shirt and pulled down her shorts. She revealed a white bikini, a moon-dust white that complimented her starry, silver hair.

Ruxton gawked at her body from the side, oddly fascinated, as if struck not by challenge or chase, but by art.

She stepped into the water.

"Come on," she invited. "We have to go out where it's deep."

Together, they swam. They swam until their feet couldn't touch the bottom. Then Sydney slowed to a doggie paddle.

"Do as I do."

She closed her eyes. Her legs rose to the surface. She floated on her back.

Ruxton did the same. He coughed on water a few times, but eventually he got it. He floated on his back.

"Can you hear me?" Sydney asked.

"Yes, I can hear you."

"Are you relaxed?"

"I think so."

"Good. We're going to play a game."

"What's it called?"

"Seven Billion Heaven."

"How do you play?"

"You think of something that only takes a second to do, something like catching a baseball or flipping a pancake or locking a door—just a random, fleeting human experience."

"Okay."

"And then you just say whatever it is, *but* there has to be a high probability that someone, somewhere in the world, is doing the exact thing you say *as* you say it. For instance, if it's my turn, I'll say, 'Right now, someone in the world is flipping a pancake.' If we both agree, it's your turn. You might say, 'Right now, someone in the world is locking a door.' If I think there's a low probability of that, I'll challenge your answer, and you get to make your case before it's my turn again. Get it?"

"I think so."

"Okay, I'll go first ... Right now, someone in the world is spilling a drink."

"Huh ... okay ... uh ... Right now, someone in the world is tearing duct tape."

"Tearing duct tape," Sydney repeated. "I like it, but I might have to challenge it."

"Are you kidding? Everyone uses duct tape. Even astronauts use duct tape to repair satellites."

"Hmmm ... alright, I'll take it ... Let's see. Right now, someone in the world is blowing out a candle."

"Now *that* I'm going to challenge."

"Ever been to a temple? Temples love their candles. Religion might be on the down slope, but there are still millions of temples out there, and even more candles."

"You really think so?"

"I think candles are just as widespread as duct tape."

"Fair enough." Ruxton thought for a moment. "Right now, someone in the world is belly-flopping into a pool."

"Right now, someone in the world is flipping a coin."

Ruxton took a moment to really hear the coin.

Ping!

Ruxton revisited the other sounds: the tear of tape, the puff of an extinguished candle, the splash of water—distant, fleeting, yet mesmerizing sounds.

"Right now," he said, "someone in the world is biting on licorice."

"Right now," she said, "someone in the world is snapping their fingers."

The *snap* really struck him. He thought about the snap, the sound, and he realized that the present moment really is infinite, as people say. With enough people on the planet, particular moments—like flipping a coin or snapping fingers—are always happening somewhere at some time.

"Right now, someone in the world is cracking an egg," Sydney said.

"Right now, someone in the world is tightening a knot."

They paused longer and longer between each turn.

Ruxton felt more and more relaxed. The water on his back felt cool while the sun on his front felt warm, creating a dreamy, ambivalent temperature at his core.

"Right now, someone in the world is starting a car."

A soft breeze brushed the surface of the lake. They could hardly feel it, but the breeze nudged their bodies towards the narrow straight that connected the two pools of water.

"Right now, someone in the world is sipping tea."

"Right now," Sydney said, "someone in the world is jumping out of a plane."

"Yeah," Ruxton said. And he imagined himself jumping out of a plane, opening up his parachute, and falling, gracefully falling towards the ground, gracefully falling towards sleep.

There was a long silence.

"Ruxton?"

Sydney heard nothing in return.

"Ruxton?"

Nothing. His body went on drifting—drifting across the blue-green, drifting through the narrow straight, drifting through the liquid crosshairs of infinity.

For the first time in years, Ruxton felt at peace. He was half-asleep, if only for a few minutes, while floating across the lake.

9
It Works!

Two days later, Sydney and Ruxton burst into Hugo's classroom.

"Hugo! It works!"

Hugo put his finger to his lips. "Shhh. One moment."

Sydney and Ruxton froze. They watched Hugo as his eyes scanned lines of text on his laptop. He read quietly for a moment, then shook his head.

"Have you read this article?" he asked. "Thanks to Glow Domes, the national attention span is down to three seconds."

"Fuck Glow Domes. Look at this!"

Ruxton held out his hand.

"What am I looking at?"

"My hand! No tremors. No shakes. I've been sober two days!"

"That's fantastic!"

"I know!"

"What unlocked your sobriety?"

"Your brother, Sasha!"

Hugo frowned. He suddenly felt uneasy.

"Sasha led us through a meditation, an ancient meditation. It's called Solosis."

"Solosis?"

"Yeah!" Ruxton spoke excitedly. "Sydney and I faced each other. We looked into each other's eyes. And then I said a phrase."

"A phrase?"

"A sacred one. One that unlocks Solosis."

"What's the phrase?"

Ruxton shivered. "I'm almost scared to say it out loud." He closed his eyes. He spoke with cadence: "When eyes meet eyes, we find the prize—a reason to live, a reason to thrive."

"What happened when you said it?"

"As soon as I said it, our eyes began to *move*."

"Move?"

"Yeah, like the color, the color in our eyes—it swirled around our pupils, like little hurricanes."

"Huh," Hugo said skeptically. "And then what?"

"And then I *felt* it," Sydney said. "I felt Ruxton's life, his entire life. The ups, the downs, the pain, the exhaustion. His entire life rushed through me, all of it, in nine seconds."

"Like, his memories?"

"Not just his memories, but the weight of his troubles, the shape of his demons."

"Yeah," Ruxton added. "It's like ... empathy. But like, a super, cosmic empathy. A *next-level* empathy."

Hugo looked around his room. The great horned owls watched from the walls.

"What happened after nine seconds?"

"After nine seconds, I *understood* Ruxton, fully and completely, for the very first time."

Ruxton added, "I was able to open up to Sydney. I was able to talk about my nightmares and my parents."

"When did the sobriety start?"

"That's the craziest part!"

"What do you mean?"

"After Ruxton opened up, something clicked in my brain. All these pieces fell into place. I suddenly *knew* what Ruxton needed. He needed to fall asleep, all on his own, no booze or pills." Sydney smiled. "I took him to this lake. We played this game. And it worked! Ruxton relaxed! He fell asleep on the water, no booze or pills."

"How did you come up with the game?" Hugo asked.

"I don't know," Sydney said. "It was Solosis. It showed me what to do. It showed me the exact combination of words and actions to *help heal Ruxton*."

"So the goal of Solosis is to heal?"

Sydney and Ruxton looked at each other and nodded in unison. "YES."

Sydney added, "You feel it right away—this urge to heal."

Hugo turned to Ruxton, "You have no desire to drink? To relapse?"

"Hell no! Now that I know peace and sleep, I'm never going back."

Sydney stood on her toes. "Hugo, this Solosis meditation is incredible! Imagine if more people knew about it. Imagine if anyone could *heal* anyone else."

Hugo took a deep breath. Then he walked to the window. In the distance, he saw a slender yet rigid tower. It was the tallest bell tower in Albuquerque.

"Did Sasha ..." He hesitated. "Did Sasha say anything about a bell tower?"

"Yeah. He did."

"What did he say?"

"Sasha said that the first bell tower didn't tell time."

"Then what did it do?"

"It reminded people to look at each other, to feel each other, to solve each other's problems."

Hugo turned around. He looked at Sydney and Ruxton. There was something different about them, the way they looked at each other. It was like they had fallen in love all over again.

"So," he said, "Solosis works?"

"Yes!" Sydney exclaimed. "Think of what it could do for other people! Not just addictions or nightmares, but any pain. Any pain could be cured!"

Hugo sighed. He looked sad.

"Hugo, how are you not more excited about this?"

"It sounds wonderful, maybe even magical. But it will never reach that many people."

"What do you mean?"

"It took you five minutes to explain Solosis. And the national attention span is down to three seconds. How are you going to convince a Glower to do Solosis?"

"I don't know..."

Hugo chuckled bitterly. "This is just our luck, isn't it?"

"What do you mean?"

"Glow Domes, Ruxton. The state of the world. People's minds are fried. Their focus is shot. And you two have this beautiful meditation, this healing superpower. But it takes focus. It takes stillness. And that's not something people have these days." Hugo paused. "I get it. I see it now. Sasha wants to use Solosis to save the world, but the world can't focus enough to use Solosis."

Outside the classroom, there was a loud crash, then a scream. Hugo rushed to the hallway. Ruxton and Sydney followed.

At one end of the hallway, a young student had fallen down a set of stairs. She had twisted her ankle and busted her lip.

Hugo rushed to the girl and knelt down. "Hey, are you okay?"

"It hurts!"

"What hurts?"

"My ankle!"

Hugo looked down. Her ankle was rapidly swelling.

"Ice! Can someone get some ice?"

Students had gathered around the girl. They had glowing white rings in their eyes. They stared and recorded her cries.

"Hey! Stop that! Stop recording her!"

The girl wailed. Blood gushed from her lip and ran down her chin. She had hit her face on the stairs.

The students pushed closer. They aimed their eyes at her blood, her agony.

Hugo looked at the girl's ankle. The swelling was getting worse.

"I think she needs an ambulance! Will someone call an ambulance?" The students didn't move. They just kept recording. "For god's sake! Will one of you help?"

Ruxton pulled out his phone. "I got it, Hugo!" He stepped back and made the call for an ambulance.

The girl began to hyperventilate.

The Glower students had formed a tight circle. Hugo stood up and spun around and shouted: "What is the matter with you? This girl is in *pain*. Stop recording her and have some decency!"

Nothing. The students didn't budge. They recorded the girl and her sobbing cries.

"I said *enough!*"

Hugo lifted his arm. As hard as he could, he slapped one of the students across the face.

All the students jumped back. They turned their attention to Hugo.

One of them whined, "You can't do that! You can't hurt a student!"

Hugo lowered his voice to a growl. "I told you to *stop*."

"But you can't hurt a student! It's against the law!"

"The law! Do you even know what laws are for? They're for keeping society civil and decent! When you record this girl's pain and share it online for a few fucking likes, are you acting civil and decent?"

None of the students answered.

"Get out! All of you!"

The students backed away.

Hugo knelt next to the girl. He used her backpack to elevate her ankle.

A minute later, medics rushed into the hallway. They hurried to the girl. One of them used gauze to put pressure on her bleeding lip. The other took her pulse.

"We've got it from here, sir," one of them told Hugo.

Hugo walked away. He went back to his classroom. Sydney and Ruxton followed. The classroom was silent for several minutes.

Then Ruxton said, "I've never seen that side of you."

"Yeah," Sydney added. "You like, *hit a kid*."

"I'm sorry you had to see that."

"I mean, it's okay."

"No. It's not okay. I don't like acting that way."

"What way?"

"A violent way. I don't like violence. I don't believe in it. I mean, I do, but only as a last resort when everything else has failed."

Ruxton shrugged. "You tried talking to them."

Hugo sighed. "I hate this."

"Hate what?"

"I hate how communication is breaking down. Empathy is all but gone. These damn Glow Domes—they're bringing out the worst of humanity."

Sydney said, "Maybe Solosis can help?"

"What do you mean?"

"Solosis—it's empathy. It helps people heal each other. Maybe if we spread it to enough people, there would be more empathy—and less of those shitty kids back there."

"Yeah!" Ruxton said. "What if more people went to Sasha's meditation shop!"

Hugo looked at Ruxton intensely, gravely.

"Listen, I want you two to be very careful around Sasha."

"Why?"

"He's dangerous."

"Dangerous? He's a meditation teacher. He's super calm."

"He wasn't always that way."

"What do you mean?"

Just then, Sasha strolled into the classroom. He wore his sunglasses and he grinned like a devil.

"My ears are burning!" he said. "Sydney, Ruxton—how are you both?"

Sydney smiled. "We're like, really great actually."

"So Solosis worked?"

"Yes! Ruxton is healed!"

"Tell me more."

"It's like: Every person has a lock, and Solosis is the key. It opens your mind. And, together, you pull out the pain."

"I'm very happy for you both."

Hugo slammed his fists on his desk.

"Damn it, Sasha!"

"What's the matter, little brother?"

"You're stealing my students! And you're using them for your plan!"

"What plan?" Ruxton asked.

"Sasha is plotting to destroy Axiom."

"Ha. That's a joke right?"

"It's not a joke. Hugo is right. I'm going to destroy Axiom. I'm putting an end to Glow Domes."

Sydney started to laugh. "That's the craziest thing I've ever heard."

"Want to hear something even crazier?" Sasha said. "Hugo's last name is not Smith. No, Hugo comes from royalty. His last name is *Sumzer*."

Sydney gasped. "Hugo, is that true? Are you a Sumzer?"

"Yes," Sasha answered. "Our father is Bill Sumzer."

"If you're a Sumzer, why are you teaching at a community college?"

"We ran away from home."

"Wait a second." Sydney turned to Hugo. "You're not one of those boys, are you? I thought the *Sumzer Brothers* were a myth, a freaky, made-up story."

"It's not a myth. The story is real. We're the Sumzer brothers."

10
The Sumzer Brothers

"Are you sure you wanna do this?"
"I'm sure."
"Isn't Dad still pissed at you for visiting the wanderers?"
"All I did was give them burgers."
"Still, Dad was pissed."
"I don't care about Dad. All I care about is fucking with these dumbass Glowers."

Twelve-year-old Hugo looked worried.

Sixteen-year-old Sasha squatted low, behind a bush.

They both heard a whistle. It was lunchbreak at a Scrolling Center. Glowers poured out of the building and into a courtyard. They filled the seats of picnic tables.

"Look at that. White circles on every pair of eyes. They scroll through stupid shit at work. They scroll through stupid shit at lunch. And they'll scroll through stupid shit at home. When is anyone *not* scrolling through so much stupid shit? I mean look! Hugo, look!"

"I'm looking."

"They're not even talking to each other!"

Hugo glanced at the box next to Sasha.

"Is it time?"

"Hell yeah, it's time."

Sasha grabbed the box. He and Hugo walked to the nearest picnic table where Sasha bellowed like a salesman: "Good Glowers! Good friends! May I interest you in some spiders? Free of charge!"

Nothing. The Glowers shoveled food into their faces. And their faces glowed with milky-white circles.

"Can anyone hear me? Anyone at all?"

The Glowers had earpieces set to full volume.

"No one is listening! And no one can see!"

"Idiots." Hugo snickered.

"I will extend my offer one more time! A full box of spiders! Free of charge! All you have to do is say nothing and do nothing!"

The Glowers chewed their food in unison.

"Going once! Going twice! Sold!"

Sasha opened the box. He held it over the middle of the table. Then he turned it upside down. Dozens of tarantulas fell on the table. They scattered and crawled in every direction.

Sasha and Hugo stepped back. The Glowers were oblivious.

"Oh shit!" Hugo said. "Look at that one!"

A big, furry tarantula crawled onto a woman's salad, right on top of her fork. The woman blinked her right eye often, skipping through photos in her Glow Dome feed.

"No way," Sasha said. "*No way.*"

The woman grabbed her fork. She lifted the tarantula toward her face.

As her mouth widened, she shoved the spider inside. A second later, she screamed. Her scream was so loud, the other Glowers heard through their earpieces. They turned off their

Domes. That's when they saw it—tarantulas all over their table, their food, their laps.

Hugo laughed. Sasha cackled.

The Glowers jumped up and screamed. They ran around and flailed.

"Dance, motherfuckers, dance!" Sasha slapped his brother on the back. "Look, Hugo! Glowers using their bodies for the first time in their lives!"

The woman stuck out her tongue. It had two huge bumps right in the middle.

"Sasha, are these tarantulas venomous?"

"I don't know. I picked the cheapest ones."

"Should we get out of here?"

The courtyard had erupted into chaos.

"Let's get out of here."

Hugo and Sasha got on their bikes and rode away from the Scrolling Center.

"What's Mom making for dinner tonight?"

"Meatloaf, I think."

As they rode home, Hugo felt bad about the woman who got bit, but he liked hanging out with his older brother. He felt cool and adventurous whenever Sasha was around.

•

Later that evening, the boys sat at the dinner table of the Sumzer family mansion. They ate hurriedly and unapologetically.

Bill Sumzer did not touch his food. He watched his two boys.

"Did you hear about the incident at the Scrolling Center today?"

"Nope," Sasha lied. "No idea."

"Apparently, someone let a bunch of tarantulas loose."

"Huh. That's weird."

"A woman got bit on her tongue."

"Her tongue? How did that happen?"

"She wasn't paying attention. The tarantula was on her fork."

"I guess it was her fault. Maybe she should have been more mindful of her surroundings."

Bill grabbed his plate and threw it at the wall. It exploded into shards.

"God damn it, Sasha. I *know* it was you."

"What was me?"

"The spiders today! Don't act stupid!"

"Dad, *I'm* not stupid. *Glowers* are stupid."

"Those people work for us, Sasha! You can't harass them!"

"Whatever." Sasha stood up to leave.

"Sit. Down."

Sasha slowly slipped back into his seat.

Bill stared at him. "You know, Sasha. I think it's time."

"Time for what?"

"It's time for you to get Glow Domes."

"What? No way. I'm not getting Glow Domes. I'm not ending up like those idiots in the Scrolling Center."

"You don't have to work in a Scrolling Center."

"I don't care. I'm *never* getting Glow Domes."

"Oh yes. Yes, you are."

Hugo put down his fork. "I feel woozy."

Sasha turned to his little brother. "You alright?"

"I feel tired. Like, super tired."

Their mother walked in with a glass of wine. She had trails of tears on her cheeks.

"Mom?"

"Oh boys. Why can't you stay out of trouble?"

Hugo's eyes rolled back into his head as he slouched in his chair.

Sasha suddenly felt tired, and his vision began to blur. He turned his head. The last thing he saw was his father's face, a face with beady, gray eyes and a big, lethal grin.

Sasha slumped forward. His face crashed into his meatloaf.

•

The next morning, Sasha woke up with a horrible headache. His eyelids felt puffy and raw. He sat up in bed and blinked several times. When he looked around his room, something followed his gaze.

"What is that? What the fuck is *that*?"

Sasha saw, in the bottom right corner of his vision, a digital clock. It read: 9:02 a.m.

"No. No, no, no, no, no!"

He sprung out of bed. He looked left, right, up, and down. He even clamped his eyes shut. But no matter what he did, he saw that digital clock in the corner of his eye. It now read: 9:04 a.m.

Sasha rushed to the door, but it had been locked from the outside.

"Dad! Did you put Glow Domes on me?"

His father spoke through the door: "Yes, I certainly did."

Sasha pounded on the door as hard as he could.

"You put fucking Glow Domes on me?!"

"Yes, Sasha. This is what it's like to grow up, to become an adult."

"Let me out of this room, Dad. Let me out now!"

"Just give the Glow Domes a try, Sasha."

Sasha kicked the door so hard that it cracked.

"Now, now. No need for violence. Just hang out in your room and try out your Domes. There's lots of engaging stuff on them—games, news, all kinds of apps."

"I *hate* apps."

"Well, too bad. You're going to try them."

Bill pushed a button on his tablet.

Dozens of apps clouded Sasha's vision.

"I can't see!"

"You'll adjust. Everyone does."

"How do I turn it off?"

"You can't."

"What do you mean?"

"I have parental controls."

Sasha picked up a chair and threw it across the room. It punctured a hole in the drywall.

Bill rolled his eyes. "So dramatic."

"Dad! Turn them off!"

"You haven't even tried them."

"I don't want to try them."

"What's that phrase? Don't knock it before you try it."

"That applies to broccoli and baseball. Not *this*, you sick fuck."

A headline ran across the top of Sasha's vision, followed by another one, and another one, and another one.

"Go away. Get off my eyes!"

"Enjoy your new Domes, Sasha. I'll be back in a bit."

Bill turned away from the door and started down the stairs. Halfway down, Sasha's mother stopped him.

"Bill, I don't know if this is right."

"Sasha is a wildcard. He needs to be broken."

"What if he doesn't break?"

"He will."

Sasha angrily paced in his room. Stock prices rose and fell on the left side of his vision. Social media alerts popped on the right side of his vision. And every time he glanced at an app, it opened up to another app, which opened up to another app. He couldn't look anywhere without activating something in his Glow Domes.

Sasha went mad. He kicked things. He threw things. He completely trashed his room.

As he panted with anger, he caught sight of himself in a mirror. It was hard to see with all the apps and headlines in his vision, but in the mirror, he saw his face, he saw his eyes. They glowed as two white circles.

"I'm a Glower ... I don't want to be a Glower ... I don't want to be a Glower."

Sasha punched the mirror and fractured his reflection. Then he went to his bed and reached under the mattress. He pulled out the meditation papers.

"Where is it? The Maxis meditation ... Where is it ..."

He could barely see through the clutter in his Domes.

"There! Maxis ... The sacred phrase ..."

Sasha took a deep breath.

"I *will* myself with all my might. I *squeeze* the dark and out comes light."

He felt nothing.

"I *will* myself with all my might. I *squeeze* the dark and out comes light."

Still nothing.

"I *will* myself with all my might. I *squeeze* the dark and out comes light."

Nothing.

"Fuck! I can't focus with all this meaningless shit on my eyes!"

Suddenly, Sasha heard something, a whimpering. He went to the wall, to the hole where he had thrown the chair. Through the hole, he could hear his little brother Hugo. Hugo cried softly.

Sasha spoke into the hole: "Hugo, is that you?"

"Yeah."

"Are you locked in your room?"

"Yeah."

"Did Dad put Domes on you?"

"Yeah."

"Jesus. You're only twelve."

"Sasha, it hurts. The apps, the headlines—they're everywhere. I can't look away from them."

"Same here."

"My head hurts. How do people live like this?"

"I don't know, little buddy. I don't know."

"Are we stuck like this forever?"

"Not if I can help it."

Sasha squeezed the meditation papers in his hand.

"I'm scared, Sasha."

"Me too."

"Dad's controlling our Domes."

"I know."

"How do we stop him?"

"I'll figure something out."

"Are you going to hurt Dad?"

"Maybe."

"What if that pisses him off even more?"

"I don't care. We need to get to those parental controls. We need to turn off the Domes and have them removed. As soon as they're out of our eyes, we get the fuck out of here. Got it?"

"Got it."

Sasha added, "Listen, Hugo. Things might get dicey. But no matter what happens, if I say run, we run, okay?"

"Okay."

"I mean it: When I say run …"

"We *run*."

11
Bumblebee Pets

Hugo thought back to that day. He remembered the Glow Domes and headaches and how scared he was. More than anything, he remembered Sasha and Bill, his older brother and his dad, the two most important male role models in his life—at odds, hell-bent on destroying each other. At twelve years old, Hugo had to pick between two titans, and at the time, he picked Sasha.

"I have class in five minutes," Hugo said.

"What?" Ruxton exclaimed. "When do we hear the rest of the story?"

"Come back tomorrow, I suppose."

"Yes," Sasha added. "I'll come back as well. It's a story worth finishing."

"Fine," Ruxton said. Sydney and Ruxton left the classroom. They walked down a stairwell, through a hallway, and out the front doors of the community college.

"I can't believe this."

"Me neither," Sydney said.

"Hugo's dad is the richest man in America."

"And he's a lunatic."

There was a silence.
Ruxton turned to Sydney. "Hey, I've been thinking ..."
"What's up?"
"What if we did Solosis again?"
"What do you mean?"
"What if we did it again, but this time, I healed you."
"Hmm?"
"I don't know. Maybe, if we did it again, your life would flow through mine. And I would understand how to heal you."
"You think that would work?"
"Only one way to find out."
"You want to do it here? At the community college?"
Students rushed through the entrance doors in hoards.
"Maybe not here. How about somewhere more intimate?"
"Like where?"
"The flower shop!"
"You want to do Solosis in the flower shop?"
"Maybe not *in* the shop. But what about the back lot? That's a nice romantic area."
"Yeah," Sydney nodded slowly. "You wanna go right now?"
Ruxton smiled. "Let's do it."

●

Ruxton and Sydney sat in the back lot as they faced the two flowerbeds.
"Everything is in full bloom."
"The seasons are changing."
"A lot is changing."
It was silent for a few moments.
Then Ruxton said: "I know bumblebees are important to you. I know the *bumblebee pet* is your Zen, your special moment,

the thing that gets you by in life." He paused. "But I also know that you haven't pet one in a long time, because your mom is gone. And I know Solosis won't bring her back, but maybe, just maybe, it can give you a reason to pet bumblebees again."

"You think so?"

Ruxton held Sydney's hand. "I do."

"Okay." She paused. "Let's try it."

"Do you remember the words?"

"I think so. Let me practice."

Sydney closed her eyes and lowered her head.

With cadence, she whispered: "When eyes meet eyes, we find the prize—a reason to live, a reason to thrive."

She looked up at Ruxton and stared into his green, green eyes.

"I think I'm ready."

Ruxton nodded.

Sydney said: "When eyes meet eyes, we find the prize—a reason to live, a reason to thrive."

In both their eyes, their irises swirled.

Sydney's entire life flowed into Ruxton.

He felt her whole childhood, her long afternoons with her mom in the shop. He felt all the flowers that blossomed and popped. He breathed in their fragrance, their heavenly scent. Beauty was the means, the means and the end. Sydney pet bees, she made little friends.

The flower shop was home, home to her—a safe little haven hidden on earth. But then came the storm, the death of her mom. The flowers still bloomed, but something felt wrong. The bumblebee pet—it was gone with her mom. He felt the loss like he lost it himself. He mourned and he mourned but the loss was still there. He felt Sydney's heartbreak, her lonely despair. Her life rushed right through him, all broken and bare.

Nine seconds had passed.
Their irises stilled.
"Wow."
"Right?"
"Still as crazy as the first time."
"What did you feel?" Sydney asked.
"Your life. Mainly the flower shop. Bumblebees. And your mom."
Ruxton gave Sydney a big hug. She cried into his shoulder.
"Oh my gosh," she said. "It felt so good to have everything just, I don't know, pour out of me like that."
"You loved your mom, didn't you?"
"She taught me everything. Everything about flowers. Everything I know."
"I didn't realize how much you missed her."
"I wish I could stop mourning, but I can't."
"What was she like?"
"My mom?"
"When you were younger—what was she like?"
Sydney smiled. "Mom was pretty kooky. She had weird habits, weird ways of thinking. She liked time-tested things: redwoods, flowers, converse shoes. She always said the world was in too damn of a hurry, even though it had nowhere to go or nowhere to be." Sydney chuckled. "When I was eight, I asked my mom what I should be when I grow up. She said: 'immersed.'"
Ruxton smiled.
Sydney continued: "My mom was always making up jingles. We had a song for putting on socks. We had a song for washing dishes. We even had a song for flossing our teeth. And the songs, they never rhymed right. They were always out of tune.

But she put so much gusto into them that they simply worked. She was good at that. She was good at tricking you into the present moment."

"Sounds like a lovely lady."

"She was lovely, and she loved love, you know? If someone came to the shop and asked for a romantic arrangement, she went above and beyond. She picked the best flowers with the best colors. She made the most beautiful arrangement she could, even if she sold it at a loss—because she truly believed in flowers and their power to bring people together."

Sydney looked at the flowers. A bee circled around her head, then landed in front of her.

"I think I have an idea," said Ruxton

"What?"

He closed his eyes and rocked back and forth.

"I think I have something. Solosis—it's showing me something."

"What is it?"

"Wait for it... Wait for it... Boom! That's it!" Ruxton opened his eyes. "I'll be right back."

"Where are you going?"

"Just inside. Real quick. Don't go anywhere."

Ruxton rushed into the flower shop. He headed for the coolers and went inside. At the back of the cooler, there were several storage bins. He dug through each one.

"Come on. It's gotta be in here."

He rummaged through pots, ribbons, and twine.

"Come on. I felt it in her memory. Where is it?"

At the bottom of a bin, he found a blue plant pod, bulbous on one end, pointed at the other.

"Yes!"

Ruxton grabbed the blue plant pod. Then he filled up a glass of water and went back outside to meet Sydney.

"What is that?" she asked.

"You don't remember? Your mom gave this to you on your eighteenth birthday."

Sydney gasped. "That's a Rhodatantium! I forgot all about that!"

"When your mom gave it to you, what did she say?"

"She said to save it for a rainy day."

"I think today is that day."

Ruxton sat down. He put the plant pod between him and Sydney. The pod stood upright, perfectly straight.

Ruxton raised the glass. "Just add water, right?"

"I don't know. It's so old. It might not work."

"Let's try."

He poured water over the blue plant pod. The pod split at the tip and peeled itself downward, blossoming as a star with rich, red insides.

Ruxton and Sydney leaned forward and sniffed.

"To us," she said, "the smell of a Rhodatantium is very faint. To bumblebees, however, it is incredibly potent. They can detect it for miles."

Ruxton looked up. Dozens of bees flew into the back lot.

"That was quick."

More and more bees showed up every second. They coated the fence. They peppered the flowers. They landed in waves—thrumming, humming waves.

"Oh my gosh," Sydney said. "I've never seen this many."

They created a cloud, a circular swarm. It went round and round, above Sydney's head.

"The Rhodatantium—they love it."

The hum of the bees was incredibly loud. Sydney felt the vibration in her chest.

"What would your mom do right now, if she were here?"

"She would pet one. She would pet all of them if she could."

"If you pet one, your mom can live on — through you."

"It's hard."

"I know. But try. Just try."

Sydney reached out her finger towards the Rhodatantium, but suddenly the Rhodatantium wilted. Its juicy, red insides dried up and died. The flower rotted and repelled the bees. They began to take off, buzzing away as quickly as they came.

"Try, Sydney. Before they're all gone."

A stubborn bee crawled over the Rhodatantium. It paused to flex its wings.

Sydney reached out. She thought of her mom, her beauty and her weirdness, her little quirks that gave life worth. Sydney breathed. She reached out her finger. She pet the fuzz on the bumblebee's back. One stroke. Two strokes. Three strokes.

"I did it," she whispered.

The bee flew away. The back lot went quiet.

Sydney threw her arms around Ruxton. She squeezed him tight.

12
Vicarium

The next day, Sydney and Ruxton went back to Hugo's classroom at the community college. When they walked up to his desk, where Hugo and Sasha were sitting, Sasha smiled and said, "You two look refreshed."

"We did Solosis again."

"And?"

"I felt Sydney's pain. Then I knew how to heal her."

"And how did you heal her?"

"With a *lot* of bumblebees."

"You should have seen it," Sydney added. "It was magic."

Hugo cleared his throat. "Unfortunately, no amount of magic can compete with *this*." Hugo pointed to the television mounted on the far wall.

An Axiom spokesman appeared on the screen. He held out his hand where a blue pill floated above his palm.

"*This* is Vicarium. Vicarium is a new drug—created, tested, and sanctioned—by Axiom. Vicarium works on the nervous system. Anytime you're on your Glow Domes, Vicarium will stimulate your tactile senses. It will make you *feel* whatever you *see*. For instance, if you're scrolling through your Domes and you *see* a skydive, you'll *feel* the wind on your face. If you *see* a tropical beach, you'll *feel* the sand on your toes. If you *see* a warm meadow, you'll *feel* the sun's rays on your skin."

The spokesman smiled. He raised the blue pill.

"With Vicarium, we can take Glow Domes to a whole new level. We can feel the things we scroll through. We can sit on the couch and never leave. Isn't that the goal in life? Go nowhere but feel everything." The spokesman smirked. "Not all of us can climb the tallest mountain. Not all of us can dive in the deepest sea. But with Vicarium, we can *feel* what it's like for the people that do. That's why we call it Vicarium—so you can live vicariously through all the *best* lives that the world has to offer."

The blue pill floated upward. It spun through empty space. "Take it! Take Vicarium! Feel the things you see in your Domes. Feel a better life like it's your own!"

"The commercial dropped this morning," Hugo said. "It's been playing non-stop on every channel."

"Who cares?" Ruxton said. "It's just more gimmicky bullshit coming out of Axiom."

"I wish that were the case," said Sasha.

"What do you mean?"

"This isn't another fad. Axiom has been working on this drug for years."

"Okay, but still, how does that affect us? We're LowLights. No Glow Domes, no Vicarium."

Sasha stood up and walked to the window. For a long moment, he stared at the bell tower in the distance.

"Ruxton," he said, "I want to spread Solosis to as many people as possible. I want to revive empathy in this country. But that is very difficult with Glow Domes in the way. And it will be near impossible once Vicarium comes out."

"So? Screw Glowers. We'll just spread Solosis to other LowLights."

Sasha whipped around. "No. That won't work."

"Why not?"

"Don't you get it, Ruxton? LowLights are shrinking. They have been for decades. In a few short years, everyone ten and older will have Glow Domes. Everyone will work in Scrolling Centers. They'll use their Domes for work. They'll use their Domes for leisure. And with Vicarium, they'll be more distracted than ever. Every minute of every hour of every day will just be a quick fix, another scroll, another swipe, another blink left or blink right. *That* is the future that Axiom is planning. That is the future that my father wants."

"Sounds bleak," said Sydney.

"It is very bleak. And if we don't stop Vicarium, that's what's going to happen."

Ruxton chuckled. "Let me get this straight." He pointed at Sasha, then Hugo, then Sydney, then himself. "We have a meditation teacher, an anthropology professor, a florist, and a recovering alcoholic. How in the hell are *we* going stop this new drug, Vicarium?"

"I have two more meditations, ancient ones, powerful ones."

Sydney pointed to the television.

"This just in! Axiom has announced that there will be a Vicarium release party next weekend! To be accurate, there will be three parties! One in Los Angeles, one in New York, and one in Denver—all coordinated to be at the same time. Who gets to go to the parties, you ask? Only the country's most famous people are invited. They will be the first to try Vicarium and testify to its wonders. After the Vicarium parties, the drug will be available in all public stores. So don't forget!

Tune in next weekend to see what famous people have to say about Vicarium!"

The television went black.

"This is how we attack Axiom—through the Vicarium parties."

Someone knocked on the doorframe. A suited woman entered.

Hugo stood up from his desk. "Ms. Williams!"

Ruxton whispered to Sasha, "That's Hugo's boss."

Ms. Williams stood across the desk from Hugo.

"Hugo, may I speak with you in private?"

"It's okay, they can listen."

"I don't think you want students to hear this."

"They're former students. They're not enrolled anymore."

Ms. Williams sighed. "Hugo, I'm here to tell you that your position is being terminated."

"Did I do something wrong?"

"Not at all."

"Then what's the issue?"

"The community college is closing its doors."

"What?"

"We're shutting down for good."

"But this is the only college left in Albuquerque. Where will people go for higher education?"

"Higher education is dying."

"But people need to *learn*. They need to think. If we close the college, how will people *think*?"

"You'll get a severance package."

"I don't want a severance package. I want people to use their brains and *think*!"

"Hugo, calm down."

"What are they going to do with the college?"

"They're turning it into a Scrolling Center."

"Are you fucking kidding me?"

"Hugo, that's not appropriate."

"A Scrolling Center?" He threw up his arms. "This is a place of learning! A place to strengthen and grow your mind! And now people will come here to rot their minds into mush?"

Ms. Williams reached inside her jacket pocket. She pulled out a folded form and placed it on Hugo's desk.

"What's this?"

"I'm required to give it to you. It's an application."

"For what?"

"To work at the Scrolling Center once they build it."

Hugo chuckled bitterly. "Salt in the wound."

"Have a good day, Hugo."

Ms. Williams turned and left. There was a weird tension in the room.

"You okay, Hugo?"

He hung his head low. "I just wanted to teach. I wanted people to learn. I wanted them to question things, to look at things, carefully and curiously. I wanted them to use their imagination, to get bored and dream big. I wanted them to *produce* thoughts, not just consume them." He paused. "I thought we could strike a balance."

"A balance?"

"Yes. I thought we could live *with* Glow Domes. I thought we could use them in moderation. But clearly, we can't. They've taken over. We, as a people, have lost ourselves—and the human spirit is dying."

Sasha spoke: "Tell me brother, if you were the human spirit, and this was your final moment, your dying breath, what would you do?"

Hugo squeezed his fists. "I would rage. I would rage against the void. I would rage against the emptiness that's coming for us all."

"Then *do* that brother. Join me. And together, we'll rage. We'll fight for what's right in this lost, broken world."

Hugo stood tall. Sasha stood too. They looked at each other for a long moment. Then they clasped hands and hugged.

"It's been too long, little brother."

"Ten years is a long time."

"We have a lot of work to do, a lot of Glowers to fuck with."

Ruxton raised his hand. "I'm sorry, what's happening right now?"

"Listen," Sasha said. "I have a plan."

"What kind of plan?"

"With the other meditations, we're going to infiltrate the Vicarium parties. We're going to botch the release of Vicarium. And we're going to do it in a way that makes Axiom look really, really bad."

"That's a pretty vague plan."

"I can't explain everything now. But I will say this: We're going to do some very dark things. We're going to experience some very dark things. And it will be scary. It will be challenging. But if we do it, and we stick to the plan, we can put an end to Glow Domes. We can make the world a better place." He paused. "But I need to know, right here, right now, if you guys are in this."

Sydney and Ruxton looked at each other. Their love had never been brighter, and it was thanks to Solosis, it was thanks to Sasha.

They nodded in sync.

"I'm in," Ruxton said.

"Me too," Sydney added.

Sasha turned to his brother. "Hugo?"

Hugo took a calming breath. Then he nodded. "I'm in."

Ruxton said, "Wait a second. Hold on. Before we save the world or whatever, I want to see something."

"Yes?" Sasha said curiously.

"I want to see you take off your shades."

"Of course."

Sasha pulled off his sunglasses. His rust-red irises startled them all.

13

A Warm Meadow

Sasha was still locked in his room. His Glow Domes fed him pics and clips, hundreds of them, maybe thousands. Sasha felt nauseous and edgy. It had been like this for two full days.

Hugo whispered through the hole in the wall. "When will this stop?"

"I don't know. I think Dad is trying to break us."

"But why?"

"He wants us to submit to Glow Domes. He wants us to submit to all this stroboscopic bullshit."

"Sasha..."

"Yeah?"

"I feel gross."

"Me too."

There was a knock at Sasha's door. Bill entered holding a tablet. He tapped a button on the screen. Then, suddenly, all the apps and alerts in Sasha's vision had vanished. Even the digital clock was gone.

"Just wanted to give you a little break, and see how you are doing."

Sasha looked at his hands. He could see them clearly.

"Would you like to come downstairs? Have some lunch?"

Bill stepped back to the upstairs hallway. Sasha slowly followed.

"Are you hungry, Sasha?"

"Not for food."

"What are you hungry for?"

"Revenge."

Sasha shoved his father down the stairs. Bill tumbled, cracked, and rolled.

Sasha hurried down the stairs and snatched the tablet. He pressed buttons at random.

"Where are the parental controls? Where the hell are they?"

He swiped left and right. He opened different apps.

"Fuck! I can't find them."

"Sasha!" Hugo yelled.

Sasha ran back up the stairs. He unlocked Hugo's door.

Hugo beamed, "The Domes are off! I can see!"

"We gotta get out of here, Hugo."

"Sasha, look out!"

Bill grabbed the back of Sasha's collar. He dragged him down the stairs.

"Let go of me!" Sasha cried. Bill continued to drag him. He pulled him through the kitchen, right up to the basement door.

"I've *had* it with you, Sasha. You're wild. You're disobedient."

Bill curled his lip in disgust. Then he shoved Sasha down the basement stairs.

"Dad!" Hugo cried. "What are you doing?"

Bill looked at Hugo. "Might as well teach you the same lesson."

He grabbed Hugo by the hair, then hurled him down the stairs as well.

Hugo crashed into Sasha. They both yawned in pain.

Bill walked down the wooden stairs. When he got to the bottom, he tore off Sasha's shirt, then pointed to a dingy corner of the basement. "Get over there. Now!"

"I don't want to."

"I said *now*!"

Bill kicked Sasha in the ribs.

"Ow! Fine!"

Sasha hobbled across the cement floor. He reached the corner and turned back to his dad.

"What are you doing, old man?"

"You will learn to love Glow Domes, Sasha. You will indulge in all the apps, all the news, all the headlines. You will do what everyone else is doing. You will share your information, your opinions, all of it. Then you will drop this individualism. You will become a data point like everyone else."

Bill turned a dial on the wall. Then he picked up a hose.

"Dad, what the fuck are you doing?"

"Glow Domes can save you, Sasha. They can save you from pain."

Bill pointed the nozzle at his son. Then he blasted Sasha with ice-cold water.

"Dad! Stop! It's freezing!"

Hugo tugged on his father's arm. "You're hurting him!"

Bill sprayed Sasha for a solid minute. Then he stopped. Sasha shivered in the corner of the basement, dripping wet. Bill pulled out his tablet. He opened the parental controls.

"Please, Dad. No more Domes!"

Bill tapped a button. Sasha's eyes lit up as white circles.

"What do you see, Sasha?"

Sasha blinked several times.

"What do you see?"

"I see ... a meadow ... a warm meadow."

Bill stepped forward. He held up a blue pill, then placed it in Sasha's hand.

"See this pill, Sasha? It's a new drug. Well, it's a prototype. The final version won't be ready for years, but still, this is the next greatest thing to come out of Axiom."

"Why do I care?"

"If you take this pill, you can *feel* the warm meadow. Isn't that incredible?"

"Not really."

"You don't want to feel the warm meadow?"

"No. I don't."

Bill stepped back. He blasted Sasha with more cold water.

"Look into your Domes, Sasha! See the warm meadow! It's so sunny, so comforting, so warm. You can feel it, Sasha. You can. You just have to swallow the pill. As soon as you do, you won't feel the cold water. You'll only feel the warm meadow."

Sasha squeezed the pill in his hand.

"It's non-addictive," Bill said. "No side effects."

"I don't care!"

"Oh, come on, son. Take the pill!"

"I don't want to!"

"Just take it!"

"No!"

Sasha saw the warm meadow through his Domes. But he felt ice-cold water on his skin. The pain was disorienting. His eyes saw one thing, but his body felt another. He craved oneness, alignment between mind and body.

That's when it hit him—the Maxis meditation. He remembered the words, the sacred phrase. Sasha took a breath, a deep shaky breath.

He whispered, "I *will* myself with all my might. I *squeeze* the dark and out comes light."

Bill sprayed the water even harder.

"I *will* myself with all my might. I *squeeze* the dark and out comes light."

Sasha shook from head to toe.

"I *will* myself with all my might. I *squeeze* the dark and out comes light."

The cold reached his core.

"I *will* myself with all my might. I *squeeze* the dark and out comes light!"

Sasha's entire body blinked out of existence.

Bill stopped the water. Hugo stared in disbelief.

"What the ... Where did he go? He was just there. Where the hell did he go?"

•

Sasha rubbed his eyes. The Domes were gone. The meadow was gone. He looked around. He saw black waterfalls in every direction. The waterfalls were massive, hundreds of stories tall.

"Whoa. What is this place?"

He stood on solid bedrock. It was a mile in diameter.

Sasha took a few steps. When he stared at the black waterfalls, he noticed something strange. Half of them fell downward. Half of them fell upward. The water fell this far, this deep, only to reverse flow, and go back up, up to some hazy light above.

"Is this like a well?"

He turned around and saw a little girl.

"Jesus! You scared me. Sorry. My name is Sasha."

"Hi, Sasha. I'm Lucy."

Lucy had double-ringed irises that gleamed green and gold. Even though she was young, her stare was piercing.

"What is this place?"

"It's the bottom of your soul. It's the bottom of everyone's soul."

"Okay..."

"You got here through the Maxis meditation, yes?"

"Yeah. I did."

"Do you want to maximize your true self?"

"I mean, yes. Of course. Absolutely."

Lucy looked at Sasha. She drilled him with her eyes.

"What do you *want*, Sasha? More than anything?"

"I want to heal."

"Heal who?"

"Everyone. I want to fix the numbness in the world, the void between us all."

Lucy bent down and put her hand on the bedrock. It shook for a moment. Lucy stood back up and looked at Sasha. "You're not ready."

"What? Why not?"

She shook her head.

"You're not ready."

"I am. I am ready. I'm ready now."

"No. You're not."

Sasha looked around. The waterfalls let out a deep growl.

"Lucy, please. Help me maximize my potential. I need to stop my father."

"You're not ready. Not yet."

"Lucy, please! I need to stop him!"

One of the waterfalls reached out to Sasha. Its water flowed upward.

"You're not ready. But keep trying."

"How long do I have to try?"

"For as long as it takes."

"But Lucy, I need help. I need help now!"

The black water pulled at Sasha's body. His feet floated off the ground.

"Keep trying," she said.

"Lucy!"

Sasha rushed upward. The black water took him to the hazy light above.

•

Sasha blinked back into existence.

Bill stared at him, in awe.

"What was that? Where did you go?"

Sasha rushed at his father and shoved him to the ground. The back of Bill's skull smacked the cement. Sasha looked around the basement. He spotted an aluminum bat and grabbed it.

"Sasha, wait. You don't have to do this."

"Dad ..."

"Son ..."

"Fuck your warm meadow."

Sasha raised the bat, then whacked it across his father's shin. Bill cried in agony.

Hugo cried in confusion.

Sasha dropped the bat. Then he walked to a tool shelf and grabbed a box cutter. He held the box cutter in front of Bill's face. As water dripped from Sasha's hair, he slowly slid out the blade.

"Here's what's going to happen, Dad. We're going to go upstairs to your medical office. You're going to remove the

Glow Domes from Hugo's eyes. And then you're going to remove the Glow Domes from my eyes. And then Hugo and I are leaving forever. Got it?"

Bill swallowed. "Got it."

"No funny business, okay?"

Bill nodded.

"Hugo, take the tablet. Make sure Dad can't access the parental controls."

Hugo grabbed the tablet.

Sasha looked down at his father.

"Stand up."

"Sasha, my leg..."

Sasha reached around and pressed the blade into Bill's kidney.

"I said *stand up*."

Bill slowly rose to his feet.

The three of them stepped through a puddle of cold water. Then they made their way upstairs to the medical office where Hugo laid back in an operation chair.

"How long will this take?" he asked.

"About fifteen or twenty minutes."

"Hurry up," Sasha snapped.

Bill squirted saline into Hugo's eyes. Then he typed into a laptop.

"Ouch!" Hugo flinched. "What was that?"

"Your Glow Domes—they have tiny roots that grow into your irises."

"That felt weird."

"I just retracted the roots."

Hugo blinked several times.

"Okay," Bill said, "I need you to stay still, very, very still."

A mechanical arm reached out to Hugo's face. The end of the arm had a small circle of metallic teeth. They homed in on Hugo's eye.

"Be still."

The metal teeth pressed against Hugo's eyeball.

"Be still."

They latched onto a Dome and pulled it off of Hugo's eye.

"Yes!" Hugo exclaimed.

Sasha pressed the box cutter into Bill's back.

"Now do the other one. But faster."

Bill lined up the mechanical arm with Hugo's other eye. The teeth latched again. The Dome began to pull away.

"I said faster!"

Bill jerked the controls. The Dome pulled away, but it pulled away sideways. The roots tore through a part of Hugo's iris. His deep blue ring now had a freckle of red.

Sasha leaned over his little brother.

"You okay? Can you see?"

"I can see."

"Good. My turn."

Sasha turned.

Bill had pulled a phone out of his pocket. He had opened up the parental controls.

"Don't you dare!"

Bill tapped a button.

Sasha's eyes lit up with glowing whiteness. Apps and alerts bombarded his vision.

"Fuck!"

He swung the box cutter at random. The blade sliced through Bill's hip. Bill stumbled and fell. Sasha seethed with anger. He grabbed the mechanical arm and broke off the end piece.

"Hugo. Pull my eyelids back."

"That's dangerous."

"Pull my eyelids back!"

Hugo stood behind his brother. He reached around and pulled his eyelids back.

Sasha lifted the metal teeth to his eyeball.

"Hold steady, Hugo."

Hugo braced.

Sasha squeezed a lever. The teeth latched onto his Glow Dome.

"You got me?"

"I got you."

Sasha pulled on the Dome.

"Come on, you fucker."

He felt the roots. They began to rip.

"Come on ..."

He squeezed and shook.

"Come on!"

Sasha *ripped* the Glow Dome out of his eye.

Tears of blood ran down his face.

"Are you okay? Sasha, are you okay?"

Sasha rocked back and forth.

"Wipe your hands, Hugo."

"What?"

"I said: Wipe your hands."

"Why?"

"We have to do it again ... for my other eye."

Bill stared from the floor. He stared in shock and horror. There were seven billion people on the planet. Most of them had Glow Domes. Most of them subscribed to Glower culture, Glower life. Not a single person, in the history of modern time, had ever thought, had ever dared, to rip the Glow Domes out of their eyes, out of their life.

Sasha stood tall, blood dripping from his eyes.

"You can't stop me, Dad. I am me. I am free."

Hugo tugged on Sasha's arm.

"We gotta get out of here!"

"You lead the way."

"Can you see?"

"Everything is blurry."

Hugo led Sasha out of the medical office. They hurried down the hallway to their father's business office. Hugo grabbed a bunch of jewels their father kept on his desk.

"Did you get car keys?"

"Fuck."

Hugo rushed back to the office and grabbed a set of keys.

"Okay, let's go!"

Sasha walked slowly.

"I think I'm in shock."

"It's okay. Let's walk. We'll walk to the front door."

Hugo put his arm around Sasha's waist and guided him.

"Boys!"

They froze.

"My boys!"

They heard a lonesome wail.

"My boys!"

"Fuck. It's Mom. She's drunk."

"What do we do?"

"Run!"

Hugo hurried. He hauled Sasha through the Sumzer mansion.

"Boys! Come back!"

They got to the front door. Hugo jiggled the knob.

"It's locked. Sasha, it's locked!"

"It's the home security system. Dad must have it on lockdown."

"How do we get out?"

"The scanner. The Glow Dome scanner."

"We just took out our Domes!"

"Not ours. Mom's. Use her Domes."

Their mother rushed up to them. She tried to hug them, but Hugo batted away her arms.

"Mom, let us out!"

"I'm so sorry."

"Let us out!"

"It wasn't my idea. It was your father's."

Sasha growled, "You should have stopped him."

"I'm sorry, boys. Please stay!"

"No. We're leaving."

Hugo grabbed his mother's head.

"Mom, look at the scanner."

She clamped her eyes shut.

"Come on, Mom. Let us out!"

"No!" She wailed. "You can't leave me!"

Hugo pressed her head against the scanner. Her body wobbled in place like an upright fish.

"Mom! The scanner!"

"I'm so sorry. I love you boys."

"If you love us, then let us go!"

Hugo slammed her head into the scanner. She let out a moan and loosened her eyelids.

Sasha heard footsteps.

"It's Dad. He's coming. Quick, Hugo, scan her eye!"

Hugo pushed his mother's head up to the scanner. He pulled back her eyelids. The scanner recognized her Domes. It beeped. The door unlocked. Sasha and Hugo went outside. They escaped the Sumzer mansion.

14
The Vastus Meditation

Late in the afternoon, Sydney and Ruxton entered the meditation shop. They stopped to notice the blue walls with gold trim. They also noticed how dark it was; big, thick curtains covered the front window. The only light was soft yellow light from a few dozen candles.

"Sasha?" Ruxton called.

Sasha stepped out of the back room. He wasn't wearing his shades.

"Are you two ready for the Vastus meditation?"

"Let me guess: It's vast."

"It is a vast, eternal silence—one that goes inside you."

"And this is how we'll stop Vicarium?"

Sasha nodded.

"We'll be safe, right?" Sydney asked.

"Maybe. Maybe not."

"What's that supposed to mean?"

"Of all the meditations, the Vastus is the most dangerous one."

"Dangerous?"

"It's painful at first, incredibly painful. But the reward—the reward is well worth it."

Ruxton and Sydney looked at each other nervously.

"Who's going first?" Sasha asked.

"I'll go," Ruxton answered.

"Very well. Wait here."

Sasha went to the back room.

Sydney turned to Ruxton. "Are you sure this is a good idea?"

"What do you mean?"

"Sasha said the meditation was painful."

"So?"

"Ruxton, you just got sober. Should you really be pushing your mind like this?"

"It's a silence meditation. How bad could it be?"

Sasha returned with a power drill and a set of shackles.

"Uh, what are those for?"

"To protect you."

"From what?"

"Yourself."

Sasha knelt down. He drilled two holes. Then he bolted the shackles to the floor.

"Whoa," said Ruxton.

Sasha tugged on the chains. They felt secure. He grabbed a stool and set it between the shackles.

"Have a seat, Ruxton."

Ruxton stepped forward.

Sydney stopped him. "No!"

"No, what?"

"We didn't agree to chains!"

Sasha sighed. "We had a deal, Ruxton."

"What deal?" Sydney snapped. "What is Sasha talking about?"

"I, um, I kind of made a deal with Sasha."

"When were you gonna tell me about this?"

"Now?"

"What is the deal?"

"When I first met Sasha, I told him we were having issues. He said he could help us, but only if I helped him in return."

"Helped him with what?"

"Anything. I gave him a blank check to cash."

"Damn it, Ruxton."

Sasha shook the shackles. "It's time."

Ruxton kissed Sydney on the cheek. Then he stepped forward and sat on the stool. Sasha locked the shackles to Ruxton's wrists.

"Little tight, don't you think?"

"It's safer that way."

Sasha stood behind Ruxton. He tied a blindfold over his eyes.

"A blindfold? Is that necessary?"

"It's not necessary. But it certainly helps."

Sasha picked up a bronze bell and hit it with a mallet. It rang inside the meditation shop.

"Are you ready, Ruxton?"

Ruxton lifted his hands to feel the weight of the chains.

"I guess."

Sasha leaned down. He rubbed his lips together. Then he whispered, very slowly: "Smile at your chances. / Chuckle at your tomb. / Laugh at your chances. / Cackle at your doom."

Ruxton opened his eyes. He wasn't blindfolded anymore. He wasn't in the meditation shop. He was standing in the middle of a graveyard, a vast, ancient graveyard. There were tombstones of every size, kind, and culture—Roman, Persian, Chinese—all of them cracked, weathered, and forgotten.

Ruxton heard a laugh. He turned. He saw an aboveground tomb. At the top of the entrance, inscribed in stone, it read: RUXTON RIGGINS.

A voice called from inside the tomb. It said, "Come, Ruxton. Come to the silence."

"Yeah, I don't know about that."

Ruxton stepped back. He bumped into an egg, a large white egg. He turned. There were dozens of eggs before him. They started to shake and crack.

"What the hell?"

One by one, the eggs split open. Each egg gave birth to a severed human hand. The hands ran around. They formed little gangs. Each gang singled out a loner hand. They flipped it on its back, pinned it atop a stone, and, one by one, bent back each finger until it snapped.

Ruxton's tomb called him. "Come, Ruxton. Come to the silence."

One of the hands grabbed his ankle, squeezed it tight. Ruxton shook his leg, but the hand squeezed tighter. Ruxton grabbed a rock. He bashed the hand several times; he broke two of its knuckles. The hand loosened its grip, then fell off.

"Come, Ruxton. Come to the silence."

More hands crawled in Ruxton's direction.

Ruxton looked at the tomb, then the hands, then the tomb.

"Fine! I'll go with the silence."

He ran into his tomb. The door slid shut. It was pitch-black.

A huge pair of lips appeared before Ruxton. They were ghostly and white, and they smiled in mid-air.

"Who are you?" Ruxton asked.

The white lips bellowed. They bellowed like a god: "Ruxton Riggins. What is the greatest thing you have ever done?"

"Wow, that's an intense line of questioning."

"Answer!"

"Okay! Jesus. I don't know. I recently got sober, which has been good for my relationship with—"

"Pathetic!"

"Ouch."

"Ruxton Riggins. What is the worst thing you have ever done?"

"Well, I don't actually remember doing it, but one time, I was on a school field trip, and I got blackout drunk, and—"

"Pathetic!"

"Is everything pathetic to you?"

"Humans are pathetic."

"I can't disagree."

"You humans. You fill the silence with noise. You think noise will save you. But nothing can save you from the silence. The silence always gets the last laugh."

"Um, come again?"

"Every star will die. Every planet will perish. The universe will end in silence. You might as well get used to it."

The lips pursed together and blew cold air in Ruxton's direction.

Ruxton saw something float towards him. It was a thin, sharp shard of purple ice.

"What is that?"

"That is the purple ice. The purple ice is silence. It is vast, eternal silence."

The purple ice floated up to Ruxton's lips. It hovered for a moment. Then it shot up his nostril and pierced his brain.

"Ow, fuck!"

"The silence is in you. The silence is in you."

Ruxton grabbed his head. He screamed in agony.

The purple ice penetrated his brain. It froze his memories, shattered them one by one. Ruxton forgot what day it was, what month it was, what year it was. He forgot what kind of car he drove. He forgot the diner where he worked. He forgot all his recipes, all his fluffy-egg recipes.

He pounded on the walls of the tomb.

"Let me out!"

The white lips bellowed with laughter.

The purple ice pierced deeper into Ruxton's brain.

He forgot every movie he had ever watched, every television show he had ever seen. He forgot every book he read. He forgot every piece of advice he either accepted or rejected. He forgot all his favorite songs. He forgot music altogether, what it sounded like, what it felt like.

"Stop it!"

The purple ice pierced the deepest part of Ruxton's brain. He forgot the community college. He forgot Hugo's class. He forgot the notes that he left under Sydney's desk.

"No. Don't take Sydney. Not Sydney!"

He saw Sydney in his mind's eye—her frosty blue eyes, her silvery-white hair. She smiled serenely. Then she evaporated, completely disappeared.

Ruxton cried.

He felt a sharp, searing pain, a final stab. The purple ice erased his name from his brain.

The white lips bellowed: "The silence is in you. Now go."

The door of the tomb slid open.

The white lips bellowed: "Go!"

Ruxton left the tomb. But it didn't lead to a graveyard. It led to a theater stage, a broad, wooden theater stage. In the middle of the stage, he saw a circle of light, warm yellow light. It looked welcoming, so he sat in it. The light filled him with warmth.

Ruxton looked out at five hundred theater seats, all of them empty. The whole place was empty. No director, no actors, no drama, no music. No cues, no props. No one to impress. No one to disappoint. Nothing to plan. Nothing to analyze. No ratings. No reviews. No song and dance. No pomp and circumstance. Nothing. Absolutely nothing. Just a beautiful, quiet, empty space.

Ruxton took a deep breath and exhaled. His entire identity had been wiped out by the silence. He didn't know his story. He didn't know his name. He was just an awareness, an awareness of silence.

"Ruxton!"

He heard a voice.

"Ruxton!"

He turned around. It was coming from the tomb. He looked at the letters inscribed above the entrance: RUXTON RIGGINS.

"What the hell is a Ruxton? What a funny word ..."

The voice called again. "Ruxton! Come back!"

He squinted. "I know that voice."

"Come back!"

"I know that voice. That's ... that's Sydney."

His mind was shattered, but the pieces were rebuilding.

"That's Sydney. That's the girl I love."

His entire identity rushed back to him.

"I'm Ruxton. I'm Ruxton Riggins. I can't die. Not now. Not yet!"

The tomb called: "Come back!"

He sprung up and ran back into the tomb. As soon as he hit the darkness, the blindfold slid off his head. He opened his eyes. He was back in the meditation shop.

Sydney threw her arms around him.

"Rux? Are you okay?"

"I think so."

Sasha knelt down and removed the shackles. Ruxton looked at his wrists. They were red and raw.

"What happened?"

"You thrashed around," Sydney answered. "You looked like you were in a lot of pain."

"How long was I gone?"

"Nine minutes."

"That's it?"

"Yes, why?"

"The silence—it felt like eternity."

"Can I try something?" Sasha asked.

"Sure."

Sasha went to the back room for a minute, then he returned with a set of chimes.

"These are very old, very cheap. Many are broken and out of tune."

Sasha shook the chimes. He shook them violently for a long minute. Sydney put her hands up to her ears. Ruxton simply sat there. He stared at the chimes, curiously.

Sasha stopped. "The noise—does it bother you?"

"It's annoying. But it only goes down to a certain point."

"What's beyond that point?"

"A theater stage, an empty one."

"Is there anything special about this theater stage?"

"I don't know. It just feels like … a sacred space."

"That's the silence. It is in you now. You can tap into it whenever you need."

"But what about the scary stuff? The graveyard, the tomb, the white lips?"

"That's the hard part of the silence. You only have to do the hard part one time. The good part—that stays in you forever."

Ruxton inhaled. "Whoa."

"What is it?"

"When I take a deep breath, it's like a dose of silence, a shot of it." Ruxton stood up and started to pace. "I have an idea. I need a hotplate. Yeah, I definitely need a hot plate. And eggs. And mushrooms. And parsley. Sasha, I need everything in your fridge."

Sasha retrieved everything Ruxton asked for.

"What are you doing?" Sydney asked.

"I haven't tried a new egg recipe in a while. And I suddenly have an idea for one."

In the middle of the meditation shop, Ruxton worked over a hotplate. He threw together ingredients like a madman. He folded and fluffed yellows and whites. He created a frittata.

Sydney tried a bite. "Ruxton, this is so good. You've never done anything like this."

"It just sort of came to me."

"That's the silence," Sasha answered. "Silence gives birth to new ideas."

Sydney pointed to Ruxton's face. "You're bleeding."

Ruxton wiped his nose and looked at the blood. It was purple. "Sasha?"

"That's the purple ice. You're a keeper now."

"A keeper?"

"A keeper of silence, which means you can spread the silence to others."

"How do I do that?"

"Just whisper the words that I whispered to you."

"Huh. If I say those words to, I don't know, a Glower..."

"For a Glower, the silence will be particularly painful."

"Yeah?"

"The silence cleanses your mind. If you've spent your whole life filling your mind with noise, the silence will not be kind to you."

Ruxton smirked with satisfaction. Sydney elbowed him in the ribs.

"Ow! What was that for?"

"I saw that look on your face."

"What look?"

"Like you were ready to dish out some silence to a Glower—put them through hell, put them through pain."

"Can you blame me?"

Sydney rolled her eyes.

Ruxton slouched into a cushion and yawned. "Man, I need to rest." He looked around the meditation shop. He stared at the paintings on the wall—exotic beasts sleeping with one eye open.

"Hey Sasha, did you build this place yourself?"

"Hugo and I built it together."

"After you escaped from your dad?"

"Yes. After we escaped."

"Where was your dad's mansion again?"

"Philadelphia."

"What did you and Hugo do when you first got out?"

"We got on a train. Headed west. Ended up here in Albuquerque."

"Then you built the shop?"

"Not at first. We spent a few years right across the street, at the university. It was still open back then, but barely. Security was low. We crashed on couches. Stole food. Read a lot of books."

"Were you and Hugo tight back then?"

"That's a great question."
"Well?"
"Yes and no."
"How so?"
"I suppose you could say: the trauma that brought us together … also drove us apart."

15

Black Waterfalls

Sasha and Hugo walked through the entrance of the university. Sasha wore his first in a long line of sunglasses.

"Look at this place! The University of New Mexico! We can pretend we're students. Sleep on couches. Shower in dorms. Raid the cafeteria."

Hugo frowned. "How long do we have to stay here?"

"Until I figure something else out."

Hugo stared at the ground.

Sasha nudged him. "Hey, little brother."

"What?"

"We have to move forward."

"But ..."

"But what?"

"I hurt Mom. I hit her head against that scanner."

"You did what you had to do."

"Sasha?"

"Yeah?"

"I don't want to hurt any more people."

"What do you mean?"

"We hurt that lady with the tarantula. Then you hurt Dad with the box cutter. Then I hurt Mom's head." Hugo paused. "I feel like ..."

"Like what?"

"Whenever I'm around you, people get hurt."

"Hugo, I'm not the bad guy. Dad is the bad guy. He did something terrible to us. But we were lucky enough to get away. We are *free* Hugo. No parents. No Glow Domes. No one to tell us what to do. We make our own choices now."

"What if Dad tracks us down?"

"He won't."

"How do you know?"

"Because I nearly broke his shin with a baseball bat. I don't think he wants us in his house anymore."

"Can we tell someone what happened?"

"Why would we tell anyone?"

"I don't know. We could report Dad to the police."

"Ha!"

"Why is that funny?"

"You want to go to the police?"

"It's just an idea."

"You wanna tell the police how you bashed your mom's head against a scanner?"

"No."

"You wanna tell them how we stole Dad's jewels?"

"No."

"Then don't."

"So we can't talk about it? Ever? To anyone?"

"Hugo, if we draw attention to ourselves, Dad might do something rash. If we don't draw attention to ourselves, Dad can't find us. If he can't find us, he can't hurt us."

Hugo squinted. He clearly wasn't satisfied.

"Listen, little brother. Something bad happened to us. But the police aren't going to help us. A corporation isn't going to help us. And a dumbass government isn't going to help us. It's just you and me. We work through this together. Okay?"

Hugo looked at the university, all the redbrick buildings and long, curvy sidewalks.

He sighed. "Okay."

•

One year later

Hugo walked with a book in his hands and his eyes on a page. He was on the southern tip of campus completing one of his reading routes. On the campus, he had mapped out nine total routes. Four of them were reading routes. Five of them were thinking routes. On the reading routes, he read books. On the thinking routes, he reflected on what he had read on the reading routes.

During today's reading route, Hugo passed the theater department. He noticed an open door emitting soft yellow light. He decided to slip inside. Three sections of tiered seats faced a square stage.

In the middle of the stage sat Sasha, alone, on a chair, his linen pants and white t-shirt glowing in the yellow light. His eyes were closed and his hands were clasped. He sat perfectly still.

"Sasha?"

Sasha smiled. "The acoustics in here are amazing."

"What are you doing?"

"Meditating."

"Don't you have to cross your legs for that?"

"Crossing your legs is not the point of meditation."
"What's the point?"
"Focus."
"On what?"
"Anything, really."
"Well, what about you? What are you focusing on right now?"
"Temperature."
"Hot or cold?"
"Cold. Ice-cold."
Hugo backed away, wide-eyed and worried.

•

Another year later

Sasha and Hugo sat on a low brick wall that winded through the northern half of campus. The summer sun had gilded their bronze-brown hair. Sasha wiped his forearm across his lips. They had just finished lunch.

"Have you noticed a lot more Glowers wandering around campus?"

"Yeah," answered Hugo.

"How would you describe them, categorize them?"

"I don't know. Semi-loners. Introspectives."

"Say more."

"They live that Glower life but secretly they crave something more."

"Exactly!" Sasha exclaimed. "But why do you say that, little brother? What gives it away?"

Hugo shrugged. He pointed to a Glower crossing the street. "Look, they walk towards the campus with white rings in their eyes. As soon as they cross the threshold, they turn off their Domes. Then they slowly walk around campus for an hour, usually sad, but also relieved. It's not the prettiest campus. But it's quiet. The sidewalks have weeds but they don't have ads. Nothing here is busy or clicky or baiting. That's why Glowers come here. Something is missing in their lives."

Sasha grinned. "And I think I know what it is."

•

Another year later

A wooden sign stood in the grass. It read: *Meditation Lessons. 30 Minutes. $30.*

Hugo waited ten yards behind the sign. A Glower nervously approached.

"Hi there! First-timer or returnee?"

"Uh, first time. First-timer."

"Great! Well, as advertised, sessions are thirty minutes. As of now, there are nine people in today's session. You'll just head through that door, walk down the aisle, and have a seat on any of the chairs or cushions on stage. Sasha will lead you and the rest of the group through a meditation. He might ask you to close your eyes. He might gently touch your arm or shoulder. And he might conduct some breathing exercises."

"Okay."

"As long as you have an open mind, you will leave here feeling better about yourself and the immediate world around you."

"Do I need to blink for a waiver?" the Glower asked.

Hugo chuckled. "Most certainly not. We don't believe in litigious America here. Plus, nothing harmful could ever happen from thirty minutes of mindfulness."

Hugo held up a phone with a white ring in the center of the screen. "Now if you could look here and blink twice for a thirty-dollar transfer."

The Glower stooped his head. He zapped thirty dollars out of his bank account with two blinks of an eye.

"Great!" Hugo opened the door to the theater. "Oh, and uh, don't mind Sasha's sunglasses. He has a rare ... eye condition."

•

Another year later

Sasha and Hugo were on the west side of campus. They walked on a sidewalk that ran parallel to a road. Up ahead was a stoplight. Sasha was about to say something, but suddenly, there was a screech, followed by a loud crunch of metal. A car had rear-ended another car. The driver at fault was a Glower. He got out of his car with white rings in his eyes. He didn't apologize. He didn't offer any insurance information. He simply recorded the other driver, and the other driver was angry. She shouted and cursed at the man who rear-ended her. It was obvious that she was pregnant.

"Look," Sasha said. "Someone is getting skezzed."

"It's the new craze," Hugo said.

"Or people are just crazy."

"They're crazy for likes, for the quickest way to EmLight status. Gotta get that money and fame."

Hugo went back to reading the book he was reading.

Sasha grumbled about Glow Domes; he muttered about the decay of humanity for half a mile.

Then Hugo looked up and said, "Dude! Can you chill?"

"Chill?"

"All you think about is Glow Domes. I mean, yeah, they suck, but there's so much more in the world to think about."

"Like what?"

"Like this." Hugo raised his book. It was a book about North American birds. "Did you know crows and owls are natural-born enemies? In fact, the moment a baby crow is born, it instinctually *knows* that it hates all owls, without ever having seen an actual owl." Hugo skipped a few lines, then continued. "Granted, owls are nocturnal and crows are diurnal, so their paths seldom cross. But when they do, the outcome is never good." He skipped a few more lines. "If owls find crows roosting near their home, they will sometimes kill the crows. On a few occasions, crows have been found dead, their bodies in perfect condition, but the tops of their skulls removed, and their brains eaten."

"So owls are they bad guys?"

"Not necessarily. If a large enough murder of crows ever discovers a roosting owl during the daytime, they will angrily harass, peck, and mob the owl, sometimes to the death."

"Who pissed off who first?"

"That's just it!" Hugo exclaimed. "No one knows. Their feud is older than time itself."

"Whose side are *you* on?"

"That's tough. They're both very intelligent birds. But when crows are together in a group, they're quite loud, loud and annoying." He paused. "I like how owls are quiet, but they're solitary creatures. I wish ..."

"You wish what?"

"I wish owls would gather in a group. It would be nice to witness a group being quiet."

•

Another year later

Sasha walked around the theater stage as he led a meditation. Today, he had nine attendees. All of them sat upright with their eyes closed.

"Exhale ... and be still."

As Sasha walked by one of his attendees, he noticed that she was not still. In her lap, her fingers repeatedly flicked and tugged on one another.

Sasha leaned down and whispered: "See me after today's session."

After everyone left, the Glower sat before Sasha. Next to Sasha were two lit candles.

"Why do you do that with your fingers?"

"Nerves, I guess."

"Would you like to calm your nerves?"

The Glower nodded.

Sasha lifted a candle. "Hold out your hands."

The Glower obeyed.

Sasha dripped hot wax across the Glower's fingers. She instinctively pulled away, but Sasha grabbed her wrist and held it still.

"Feel the wax. Feel it solidify. Feel your fingers. Feel them solidify." As much as it hurt, the Glower felt comfort in Sasha's charm, in his mesmerizing voice. A minute later, he peeled the wax from her fingers and said, "Don't you feel better?"

She nodded, then left.

When she walked out the door, Hugo said, "Thank you! Come again!"

Sasha stood next to Hugo. "How much did we make this month?"

"Seven hundred and forty dollars."

"Not bad."

"I guess."

"You guess?"

"I don't know. How much longer are we going to sell your meditation lessons?"

"Do you not enjoy selling them?"

Hugo shrugged.

"We're helping people, Hugo. We're healing their scattered, tattered minds." He paused. "But you're right. The boredom is setting in here. There's only so much I can do with that theater space. I want to try new meditations on people. I want to involve more props. I've been experimenting."

"I know. I don't like it."

"Why not?"

"I don't want you to disappear again, like you did in Dad's basement."

Sasha smirked. "Follow me. I want to show you something."

Sasha led them to the library where they ascended a stairwell, climbed a ladder, and opened a hatch that led to the roof. Once on the roof, Sasha led them to the ledge.

"I think it's time for us to get our own place. A true home." He pointed to a building across the street, a modest three-story structure with a dull, blue complexion. "The first floor used to be a recording studio. We could refurbish it while keeping its acoustics."

"What are you getting at?" asked Hugo.

Sasha pinched an inch of air between his thumb and forefinger; he ran it across the front of the building while eyeing through the space: "*Meditation Shop.*"

Hugo rolled his eyes.

"Come on, hear me out. People really need this stuff—now, more than ever."

"I don't know, man."

"It won't have any religious affiliations. No spiritual stuff. No crystals. No chakras. Just the art of focus, a kind of brain-training. You know, strengthen the mind as if it were a muscle."

"I think, initially, you'll get interest. But no one is going to pay for meditation long-term."

"That's because people have such a limited view of meditation! I can make it more interactive, more profound." He started pacing. "I think personalization is key."

"Sasha—"

"We can use the front room for generic meditation classes, intro stuff. But then we can have a backroom for customized sessions with one-on-one clients."

"Sasha—"

"It'll be a process. I'll talk with them intimately. Get to know them, their deepest wants, most cherished desires. I'll figure out what they respond to—smells, colors, textures. I'll create an experience, a guided journey. I'll meld their mind to their body and their body to, I don't know, to something, anything, whatever they care about most. It'll be a complete psycho-physical experience. It'll be something totally new!"

"Sasha!"

"What?" Sasha whipped around so fast that his shades flew off his head. He stared at Hugo with his rust-red eyes.

"I don't know if I want to do this whole *meditation shop* thing."

Sasha picked up his shades and slid them back on.

Hugo continued: "Look, man. I'm happy that you're into this stuff. I'm glad you have a thing. But it's not really my thing." Hugo paused. "And ... and I kind of want to be on my own for a while."

"What do you mean?"

"I think we should split up."

"What are you going to do?"

"I don't know. I've read half the library here. Maybe I can become a teacher or something."

Sasha swallowed hard. "So no more *Sumzer Brothers*, huh?"

"You're my brother, Sasha. I look up to you. I've always looked up to you. But when I go to sleep at night, all I see in my head is Dad spraying you in the basement, spraying you with ice-cold water. I see you beating the shit out of him. I see you ripping out your Domes. I see blood dripping from your eyes." He paused. "I see that shit every night, Sasha. Every fucking night."

"So you're gonna leave? Because of me?"

"That's not what I'm saying."

"What are you saying?"

"Sasha, you make all the decisions all the time. I'm almost eighteen. I need to make a decision for me for once."

Sasha hung his head for a long moment.

Finally, he said, "Tell you what. If you help me renovate this shop, get it up to code, and have it ready as a fully functioning business within—let's say, a year—I'll give you half of the jewels we stole from Dad. I'll dig them up myself. And then you can go on your way."

Hugo sighed. "Thank you, brother."

Later that night, Hugo wandered about the campus. He held up a phone light, looking through dorms and dusty departments. It was nearing midnight and he couldn't find Sasha.

In the mess hall, Hugo saw light from the back of the kitchen. He headed in that direction. He passed boilers, vats, and industrial-sized fryers. Then he turned a corner and saw a line of ovens. All the ovens were open. Coils of glowing orange fed on the emptiness of open air.

Sasha was on the floor, next to the last oven. There were fresh burns on his right arm, and the smell of seared flesh lingered in the air.

"Sasha!" Hugo rushed to him. "Did you stick yourself inside there?"

Sasha started laughing. He grabbed a bottle of liquor. "I'm so close, Hugo. I'm so damn close."

"What are you talking about?"

"The black waterfalls."

"What?"

"The black waterfalls! When Dad sprayed me and I disappeared, that's where I went. I went to the black waterfalls. I met the girl. Lucy. She knows things. She can help us. I just have to get back to her."

"God, Sasha, you must be super fucking drunk."

"I thought it was cold. I kept focusing on cold. But maybe it's heat. That's why I came here. I turned on all the ovens. I focused on the heat."

"Sasha, you need help."

"I *need* to get to those waterfalls."

Sasha climbed to his feet. He spun a dial on the stove. The stove ignited with a ring of blue flames.

"What are you doing?"

Sasha held his hand over the flames.

"Sasha, stop!"

Sasha's hand trembled. His skin blistered.

"This is the way ... the way to the black waterfalls."

His hand burned over the flames. His skin began to melt.

"I *will* myself with all my might. I *squeeze* the dark and out comes light."

"Sasha, stop it!"

"I *will* myself with all my might. I *squeeze* the dark and out comes light."

"Sasha! Stop!"

"I *will* myself with all my might. I *squeeze* the dark and out comes light!"

Hugo grabbed Sasha by the waist and jerked back. Sasha tripped. They both fell backwards and crashed to the floor.

Hugo widened his haunted eyes. "Why are you doing this to yourself?"

Sasha breathed heavily and angrily. "You don't understand, little brother. You didn't go down there. You didn't meet the girl. She knows things. She can help us. She can help *me*." Sasha slammed the back of his head into the kitchen tiles. "I can fix everything. I know I can. I just have to get back to her. I have to get back to her, Hugo."

They remained on the kitchen floor for a long time. It was late and quiet. The only sound was the faint hiss of burning blue flames.

16
The Vastus, Part II

Sasha stared at a candle in the meditation shop. He watched the shape of the flame as it wavered side to side, like a little belly dancer.

Sydney said, "Can I see your hand?"

Sasha extended his palm. The skin was melted and scarred.

"I thought it would complete the Maxis meditation. But I was wrong. Wrong, drunk, and foolish."

Sydney's phone binged. "Sorry," she said. "I keep getting all these alerts for Vicarium. It's blowing up on the internet right now."

"Vicarium," Ruxton said. "What a lame drug."

"Lame?"

"Yeah, if you're gonna do drugs, go for the hard stuff. Don't take a pill that makes you *more* addicted to screens."

Sydney rolled her eyes. "I have a question," she said. "The Vastus meditation—how did it come to be?"

"A long time ago, there was a group of monks—men, women, and children. They lived in a monastery. They lived there in peace and harmony for a thousand years. And the key to their success was: silence.

"They still laughed and played games and had raucous fun. But in between the games and fun, they practiced silence. They *knew* that the human brain needed regular bouts of silence and vastness—in order to reflect and grow."

"Did they have to make the meditation so scary?" Ruxton asked.

"It wasn't always that scary."

"What happened?"

"The world got louder. It got noisier. The human brain collected more junk. So the Vastus, the cleansing of the mind—it became a more painful process."

"So ... am I a monk now?" Ruxton asked. "A modern-day monk?"

Sasha nodded. "You're a monk, one of the toughest."

Ruxton beamed. "Sydney, I'm a monk! You should be a monk too!"

Sydney swallowed. "I have to do the Vastus meditation, don't I?"

"If you want to stop Vicarium, then yes."

She looked at the shackles bolted to the floor.

"I have to put those on?"

"For your own safety, yes."

Sydney turned to Ruxton. "I'm scared."

"You're a mindful soul. You'll do well."

She hugged him. Then she sat on the stool.

Sasha locked the shackles to her wrists.

He tied a blindfold over her eyes.

"You're sure you're ready?"

"I think so."

"Your mind is calm?"

"As calm as can be."

"Here we go."

Sasha took a deep breath. He leaned towards Sydney's ear. He whispered, very slowly: "Smile at your chances. / Chuckle at your tomb. / Laugh at your chances. / Cackle at your doom."

Sydney opened her eyes. She wasn't in the meditation shop. She was in a graveyard. Above her, the sky was gray and heavy. Ahead of her, she saw a tomb. At the top of the entrance, engraved in stone, it read: SYDNEY SALAZAR.

A voice called from inside the tomb. "Come Sydney. Come to the silence."

Sydney shivered as she stepped back, but as she stepped back, her foot sank into the ground.

"What the ..."

She turned around.

An elephant stood before her, shaking its head in distress. The elephant stood in a pit of tar, slowly sinking. Sydney wanted to help but didn't know how. The elephant looked at her as tears came out of its eyes. It lifted its trunk and jolted the night with a trumpety wail. Sydney cried back. The elephant sank deeper and deeper. The tar was up to its ears.

As the elephant sank to its death, hateful rats emerged from the edges of the tar pit. They ran away freely. Sydney dropped to her knees. The sight was unbearable—majesty swallowed, vermin birthed in every direction.

"Why?" she cried. "Why?"

The oil-slicken rats headed for Sydney. They clicked their teeth and squeaked.

The tomb called for her.

"Come, Sydney. Come to the silence."

She ran from the rats. She entered the tomb. The door slid shut behind her.

"I can't see."

Then, in the middle of the tomb, in the middle of the darkness, she saw a huge pair of lips—white, ghostly lips. They bellowed like a god:

"Sydney Salazar. What is the most profound thought you have ever had?"

"Um, I don't know."

"Answer!"

"Okay, okay! Um, I guess one time, I was staring at a tulip and—"

"Pathetic!"

Sydney winced.

The lips spoke again: "Sydney Salazar. What is your deepest fear?"

"I don't know. Getting lost and never—"

"Pathetic!"

"You're mean."

"I am not mean. I am a fact."

"What fact?"

"Every star will die. Every planet will perish. The universe will end in silence. Every thought and every emotion will return to silence. You might as well get used to it."

The lips pursed together. They blew chilled air in Sydney's direction. She saw something—a thin, sharp shard of purple ice. It floated up to her lips.

"What is that?"

"The purple ice—it is silence. Vast, eternal silence."

Sydney stood still and stared at the purple ice.

The white lips began to laugh.

"What's so funny?" she asked.

The purple ice shot up her nostril and pierced her brain.

Sydney cried out as she grabbed her head.

"The silence is in you. The silence is in you."

Sydney forgot what day it was, what month it was, what year it was. She forgot her morning commute. She forgot the shape of the flower shop. She forgot every type of flower arrangement—birthday flowers, romance flowers, funeral flowers—she forgot them all, she forgot how to mix and match colors.

"Stop it!" she screamed. "Stop!"

The white lips bellowed with laughter.

The purple ice pierced deeper into her brain.

Sydney forgot her mom—her lively spirit, her quirky jingles, her oddball gusto for life. She forgot her mom's face, her mom's hair, her mom's eyes.

"Stop it! Don't take any more!"

The purple ice pushed deeper.

Sydney forgot the community college. She forgot the notes that Ruxton left under her desk. She forgot Ruxton—his messy, black hair, his restless green eyes, his thick full lips. All of it disappeared.

"No!" she cried.

Sydney felt a sharp, searing pain.

The purple ice—it erased her name.

"The silence is in you. The silence is in you. Now, go!"

The door of the tomb slid open.

Sydney was empty and confused.

"Go!"

Sydney walked out of the tomb. She stepped onto lush, green grass. She was in a tiny, ancient forest, hidden at the bottom of a sinkhole. There were only a dozen trees, a few bushes, and a mound of moss.

She looked up. There was a hole high above. It offered a few rays of sunshine, just enough to keep the tiny forest alive.

Sydney sat on the mound of moss. She admired the trees and their leaves. It was quiet at the bottom of the sinkhole, very quiet. She had never experienced anything like it. Everything was still—still on the inside, still on the outside. No stress, no deadlines, no orders, no to-do list. No laughs, no cries. No highs, no lows. No anxiety, no tragedy. No one to blame. No one to shame. Nothing. Absolutely nothing. Just this tiny ancient forest hiding at the bottom of a sinkhole—a sacred, untouchable place.

"Sydney!"

She looked at the tomb. She read the inscription above the entrance: SYDNEY SALAZAR.

She chuckled. "What a funky phrase."

"Sydney!" the tomb called.

"That voice..." she said. "I know that voice."

"Sydney!"

"It sounds so familiar."

"Sydney! Come back!"

She looked at her hands. She looked at the forest.

"Sydney!"

"Wait a second..."

Her entire identity rushed back to her.

"Oh my gosh. I'm Sydney. I'm Sydney Salazar! And that voice is Ruxton. Ruxton Riggins! I can't die. Not yet. Not now!"

She sprung to her feet and ran towards the tomb. She dove into the darkness. The blindfold slid off her eyes. She was back in the meditation shop.

Ruxton grabbed her shoulders.

"Sydney! Are you okay?"

"I think so."

"You kicked yourself off the stool."

Sasha unlocked the shackles.

Sydney rubbed her wrists; they were red and raw.

"How long was I gone?"

"Nine minutes."

She rubbed the side of her head.

"That purple ice is *so* painful."

Sasha nodded. "That's the silence. It breaks down everything, shatters it completely. But then, your mind, it heals, and it becomes stronger than it's ever been."

Sydney took several deep breaths.

"Wow," she said. "I feel so refreshed. So recharged."

She headed for the door.

"Where are you going?"

"I want to try something."

She went out the door and turned into the side alley. She found a patch of grass. All it had was a few daisies. She plucked the daisies and a handful of grass, then walked back into the shop.

"What are you doing?" Ruxton asked.

"Shhh."

She pinched the blades of grass, bent them like ribbon, tied them around the daisies. Then she adjusted the daises, fluffed their petals, and staggered their heights. Within a minute she was done. She held out a tiny bouquet.

"Whoa," said Ruxton. "Simple yet beautiful." He admired the curves of green and pops of white. "You've never made anything like that."

"It just sort of came to me."

"That's the silence." Sasha nodded.

"Everything feels so new." Sydney looked at Ruxton. She cupped his cheek and kissed his lips. "Mm. It's like feeling their fullness for the very first time."

Sasha chuckled. "The silence between the notes."

"Huh?"

"It's an old saying ... about music, about life."

"What's it mean?"

"It means we need silence between the notes. If all we hear is notes, then the notes mean nothing."

Sydney took a deep breath.

"You feel it, don't you?" Ruxton said.

"Yeah. It's a stillness, deep inside—a sacred space."

"Is your sacred space a theater stage?"

"No. Mine's a tiny forest, hidden at the bottom of a sinkhole."

"Huh." Ruxton turned to Sasha. "Does everyone have a different sacred space?"

"Yes."

"But everyone experiences the purple ice?"

"That's the hard part. The tomb, the white lips, the purple ice—everyone goes through that. But the sacred space at the end—that's different for every individual."

There was a knock at the door. Ruxton answered.

"Hugo!"

"How's it going?"

"Oh, it's going. Sydney and I experienced vast, eternal silence, and now it's in us, forever and always."

"Hmm." Hugo walked inside. "Anything else?"

"Sasha told us how you guys escaped from your dad, how you landed in Albuquerque, how you crashed at the university for a few years."

Hugo squinted. "How specific did Sasha get?"

"He told us the part where he burnt his hand on the stove."

"Remember that night, little brother?"

"I try to forget ... all the time."

"What happened after that?" Sydney asked.

"Yeah!" said Ruxton. "Tell us the end of the Sumzer Brothers story!"

"Should I tell them?" Sasha asked Hugo.

"No. I'll tell them."

Ruxton and Sydney sat upright with perked ears.

Hugo continued the story: "After Sasha burnt his hand, he refocused. He bought this building and we worked really hard on fixing it up, on creating the first ever *Meditation Shop*."

17

The Maxis Meditation

The meditation shop had been in full swing for months. Sasha and Hugo labored every day. They installed new wiring, fixed faulty plumbing, tore up floors, laid down new ones.

Hugo worked hard but mostly kept quiet. Ever since Sasha's drunken episode, Sasha began acting differently. He sobered up the next day and hadn't touched a drop of alcohol since. In fact, he didn't let any toxins touch his body. He ate hearty, healthy meals. He worked out vigorously every day. He strived for strength, speed, and agility. Fitness and health became paramount to his meditations. And his meditations had gotten longer, more intense. It seemed like Sasha was ramping up towards something.

One day, Hugo entered the shop. He walked to the back room where he found Sasha. Sasha wore nothing but his briefs.

"What are you doing?"

"Hugo, I need you to do me a favor."

"What favor?"

Sasha held out a hose. "I tampered with the water regulators in the basement. This water is cold, ice-cold."

"I don't understand."

Sasha pointed. "I'm going to stand over there with my hands above my head. I'm going to hold on to the pull-up bar. I need you to spray my entire body for exactly five minutes."

Hugo's stomach dropped. "No. Uh-uh. No way." He dashed for the front door. Sasha quickly caught up. He seized Hugo's arms and pinned him against the wall.

"I don't want to!"

"You have to."

"No!"

Sasha growled at his brother. "Hugo, listen! It's the Maxis meditation. I think I have it figured out. But I need you to spray me with cold water, just like Dad did."

"Why do you want to relive that?"

"Because it worked! If I want to go to the black waterfalls, you *have* to spray me with cold water."

"No, Sasha. I'm not doing it."

"Goddamn it, Hugo. Please. Just do this one thing! Just squeeze a trigger for five minutes. It's not hard."

"But it's messed up!"

"Who cares? You're leaving soon anyway."

"What does that matter?"

"Come on, Hugo. I've practically raised you and protected you your entire life. The least you could do before you leave is point and squirt a hose for five minutes."

Hugo curled his upper lip. "You're turning into your father."

"What?"

"Yeah. A fucking psycho!"

Sasha pushed away from Hugo. "You have no idea. You hardly know anything." Sasha pointed. "Now pick up that hose—or I won't give you your half of the jewels."

"What?"

"Yeah. I dug them up and buried them somewhere else."

"God damn you, Sasha. God damn you to hell." Hugo stormed to the rear room. He snatched up the hose and pointed at the brick wall. "Let's get this over with."

Sasha smiled. He set up a timer for five minutes. Then he stood under the pull-up bar. He reached up and squeezed the cold metal.

"Okay, I'm ready."

Hugo hit the timer. He lifted the nozzle. Then he blasted Sasha with dangerously cold water. Sasha tensed his whole body. He locked his bones in place.

One minute passed. Sasha pushed through the initial shock. He focused on his breathing. He whispered, "I *will* myself with all my might. I *squeeze* the dark and out comes light."

Two minutes passed. Hugo squeezed the nozzle. He sprayed his brother out of anger, out of violence, out of fear.

Three minutes passed. Sasha put his mind in every square inch of his body. He embraced the cold; he embraced the pain. He whispered, "I *will* myself with all my might. I *squeeze* the dark and out comes light."

Four minutes passed. The temperature of the entire room began to drop. Hugo stared through the white cone of water. He saw Sasha's face, his closed eyes. Sasha whispered, "I *will* myself with all my might. I *squeeze* the dark and out comes light."

Hugo remembered that day in the basement, the day his father sprayed Sasha, the day Sasha disappeared. Hugo couldn't do it. He couldn't relive that day. He dropped the hose. The water stopped spraying.

Sasha opened his eyes. "Why did you stop?"

"I can't do this." Hugo rushed towards the door. He threw it open and left the shop. He ran down the street, away from his brother.

Sasha stepped outside. He stood on the sidewalk, barefoot and mostly naked. He was dripping wet and trembling from the cold. He screamed after his brother, "I was so close, Hugo! That was the closest I've ever been! But you stopped! Why did you fucking stop?"

Nearby pedestrians glared in shock.

Above Sasha's head, gold letters read: *Meditation Shop.*

•

Two weeks later

Hugo came back to the shop. He called for his brother: "Sasha? ... Sasha?"

Hugo found Sasha in the back. Sasha sat on the floor, working intently, surrounded by pipes, fittings, and clamps.

"What are you building?"

"Nothing."

A long moment passed.

"Look," said Hugo. "I don't need the jewels."

"Yes, you do."

Sasha reached in his pocket, pulled out a piece of paper, and tossed it at Hugo's feet. "Those are coordinates. That's where I buried the jewels. You can dig them up yourself. Take your half."

Hugo picked up the paper. "Are you sure?"

"I said you could have half—as long as you helped build the shop. The shop is almost ready, so you're entitled to your half."

Hugo slid the paper into his pocket. "Thank you."

"Can you hand me that wrench?"

Hugo handed Sasha the wrench.

"I'm staying at the campus across the street. I've been looking at apartments on the east side of town, next to the community college."

"K," replied Sasha.

Hugo sighed. He walked away.

●

One week later

Hugo had his bags packed. He was about to move into a new apartment, his own place. He even had an interview lined up, a position as a professor's assistant. He felt good about it. After all, Hugo had read scores of books on history. He was fascinated by the past. In his mind, civilizations swelled and shrank with tide and time. Maybe he should use that line in his interview, he thought.

Hugo left the university. He was ready to start a new chapter in his life, and he was happy about it. But first, he wanted to say goodbye to Sasha, so he went to the meditation shop one final time.

"Sasha! You here? Yo, big brother! Where are you?"

Hugo reached the door to the backroom, but it was shut and locked.

"Huh."

He peered through the window in the door.

Across the room, Sasha stood under the pull-up bar, gripping it with all his might. He had constructed a system of pipes and nozzles. They blasted his body with ice-cold water.

"No!"

Hugo jerked the door handle.

"Sasha!"

He kicked the door.

"This is dangerous!"

Sasha breathed slowly and said: "I *will* myself with all my might. I *squeeze* the dark and out comes light."

"Sasha! Stop it!"

"I *will* myself with all my might. I *squeeze* the dark and out comes light."

"Sasha!"

"I *will* myself with all my might. I *squeeze* the dark and out comes light!"

Sasha's entire body blinked out of existence. He disappeared for several seconds. Then he blinked right back into existence, except he wasn't standing. He was on his knees.

Sasha looked up at Hugo through the glass in the door. His smile looked absolute—unquestionable. He looked like he had just become the most powerful man in the world.

Hugo backed away in disbelief.

He turned around and ran. He ran away from Sasha Sumzer, he ran away from his family, he ran away from the source of his pain.

•

When Sasha disappeared, he went to the black waterfalls. They surrounded him on all sides, half of them falling downward, half of them falling upward.

"I did it," Sasha said. "I did it!" He held out his arms in triumph. "I finally fucking did it!"

He turned around and saw the little girl, Lucy.

Lucy giggled. "Why are you always wet?"

"That's how I got here."

"With a bath?"

"No ... with pain."

"What happened to your eyes?"

"I ripped out my Glow Domes."

"Follow me," she said. "We don't have much time."

Sasha followed Lucy.

"What is this place?"

"I told you. It's the bottom of your soul."

"But what does that mean?"

"It means you got here through the Maxis meditation."

"Yeah, but ... how does it work?"

"When you're here, you grab the fabric of space-time. You twist it like a towel. Ring out every star and planet. Empty all but one celestial drop. Then enter that drop. Embody the godliness of any truth you want. What do you want, Sasha? What do you *want* more than anything?"

"To heal."

"Yourself?"

"Everyone." He paused. "I want to be a healer for all people. I really do. I want health and happiness for all humankind. As much as they drive me crazy, they're my people. They're my species. It's our planet. I want us to truly enjoy our bodies and our minds while we have them. But first, we have to heal. We have to focus."

"Are we not focused?"

"Not at all! Our minds are scattered and shot. And it hurts. It hurts to never be immersed."

"Immersed in what?"

"A person. A skill. Anything with lasting value."

Sasha and Lucy walked up to a large circular opening in the bedrock. It looked thirty yards across in diameter.

"That wasn't here last time," Sasha said nervously.

"It didn't think you were ready back then. It does now."

They neared the edge and peered into the hole. The bedrock reached downward for ten feet before curling back under itself. From there, it was another thirty feet before one would splash into a subterranean pool of black water.

"Lucy, what is this?"

"This is your full potential."

"What's gonna happen?"

"You are going to feel pain."

"What? Why?"

"So you can learn how to heal."

Sasha looked down. The black water rippled.

"What are those?" Sasha pointed. He saw movements in the water, long, curvy creatures. They were vague in shape but vivid in color—a lively, exotic green.

"Lucy, what are those?"

"Those are your full potential."

"Do I have to go in there?"

Lucy nodded. "It will be the absolute worst and the absolute best at the same time."

Sasha shook his head. "I'm scared."

"There's no time."

"Lucy, I don't know."

"Do you want to heal your world?"

"Yes."

"You're certain?"

"Yes."

Lucy smiled. She shoved Sasha into the hole. The fall felt long. His back smacked the water. He tried to swim, but green snakes quickly wrapped around him. They pulled him under. They pulled him deeper and deeper into the liquid abyss.

Fangs sank into his forearm, his chest, his neck. Sasha felt pain. Every bone in his body broke. Every strip of skin split. Sasha reached the highest cosmic expression of pain. He felt pain the way a god would feel pain. He grew to the size of a galaxy, a galaxy that had clawed at its own belly and tore out its nasty, lacerated innards—sickly, rotted galactic swirls.

Then, Sasha began to heal. His bones reset. His skin sealed up. His mind came together, calmer and stronger than ever before. A great vitality rushed through him.

Freshness flowed through every fiber of his being. He felt a powerful, profound sense of newness. Black water had filled his lungs only to transform into the richest, cleanest air he had ever breathed.

And Sasha did breathe. He took the biggest breath of his life. He opened his eyes. He was back in the meditation shop. He had a new understanding of the brokenness in the world, the toxicity. He knew it was fixable. He didn't have all the pieces yet. But he knew there was a way—and he was either going to find it or forge it.

Sasha smiled. He looked through the glass in the door. He saw his brother all wide-eyed and backing away. He saw Hugo for the last time for many years.

18
The Vastus, Part III

Ruxton, Sydney, Hugo, and Sasha sat around the meditation shop.

"That was the last time you guys saw each other?" Ruxton asked.

"Yup," said Hugo. "Ten years ago. Right here in the shop."

Hugo wondered if he made the right decision by teaming up with Sasha. The shop reminded him of how manipulative and dangerous Sasha could be. But, Hugo thought, ten years is a long time. Maybe Sasha had changed. Maybe he truly wanted to make the world a better place. After all, Sasha was good at taking action. He had a confidence that Hugo never had.

"Enough story time. We need to get back to work."

"Work?" Hugo said.

"Yes. The Vicarium parties are this weekend. There are three of them—one in Los Angeles, one in Denver, and one in New York. In order to stop Vicarium, we need three keepers, three keepers of silence. We have two: Ruxton and Sydney. We need a third. That's you, little brother."

"What do I have to do?"

Sasha pointed to the shackles.

"Is it gonna hurt?"

"Badly."

Hugo turned to Ruxton and Sydney. "What's the worst part?"

"It wipes out your identity. You forget who you are."

"Honestly, there are some things I'd like to forget."

"Have a seat, Hugo."

Hugo rolled up his sleeves. He sat on the stool in the middle of the shop. Sasha rang a bronze bell. The ring lingered for a long time.

Then, Sasha locked the shackles around Hugo's wrists. He tied a blindfold over his eyes.

"Ready, little brother?"

"Why the hell not?"

Sasha leaned down. He licked his lips. He whispered very slowly: "Smile at your chances. / Chuckle at your tomb. / Laugh at your chances. / Cackle at your doom."

Hugo opened his eyes. He wasn't in the meditation shop. He was in a vast graveyard. There were thousands of tombstones in every direction, as far as the eye could see.

Hugo turned. He saw a large tomb. Above the entrance, inscribed in stone, it read: HUGO SUMZER.

A voice called to him. "Come, Hugo. Come to the silence."

Hugo swallowed.

Behind him, he heard a noise, a soft cooing.

He turned around and jumped.

"What the hell?"

Thick trees had appeared in the graveyard. On the trees were doves, white doves, all of them crucified. Their wings were outstretched, pierced to the wood with nails. Bright red blood slowly dripped down their feathers.

Hugo shuddered.

The doves sang together. They sang a song of sadness.

Hugo slowly backed away. Something was wrong with the doves. Their coos turned into coughs. Their coughs turned into gurgles. A black sludge poured out of their beaks. They vomited volumes larger than themselves.

The tomb called: "Come, Hugo. Come to the silence."

Hugo looked at the doves, then at the tomb, then at the doves.

"I'll take silence."

He rushed into the tomb.

The door slid shut.

The big white lips appeared before him.

"Hugo Sumzer. What is your greatest achievement?"

"Teaching kids, showing them how to think for them—"

"Pathetic!"

"Well, it's more noble than making money or—"

"Hugo Sumzer. What is your biggest regret?"

His face saddened. "Hurting my mom. I didn't want to, but—"

"Pathetic!"

"How in the hell is that pathetic?"

"You humans. You cling to your greatness. You cling to your mistakes. But it all ends the same. It all ends in silence."

"What then? Nothing matters? Rape, kill, steal? Because it all ends the same?"

"That is not the point."

"Then what's the point?"

"You must practice silence while you are alive."

"Why?"

"It will hurt less when you actually die."

The white lips pursed together. They blew chilled air in Hugo's direction.

Hugo saw something—a thin, sharp shard of purple ice. It floated up to his face.

The white lips began to laugh.

The purple ice hovered under Hugo's nose. Then it shot up his nostril and pierced his brain.

"The silence is in you. The silence is in you."

Hugo forgot what day it was, what month it was, what year it was. He forgot his classroom. He forgot the chairs, the desks, the owls on the walls. He forgot his favorite students. He forgot how to teach.

The purple ice froze his memories, shattered them one by one.

Hugo screamed. His knees buckled and he dropped to the floor.

He forgot his dad. He forgot that day in the basement. He forgot the cold water. He forgot Sasha ripping out his Glow Domes. He forgot the blood in his brother's eyes. He forgot his mom.

The white lips laughed.

"Make it stop!"

The purple ice stabbed deeper into his brain.

He forgot Sydney and Ruxton. He forgot their bright young faces. He forgot everything, everything except his name. That was the last thing left in his brain. He thought losing his name would hurt the most, but that's when he began to laugh. He laughed and cackled bitterly.

"Take it," he said. "Take the name Sumzer. Take it away!"

The purple ice pierced the center of his brain.

"The silence is in you."

The door to the tomb slid open.

"Now go!"

Hugo hobbled out of the tomb.

He stepped onto white dust. He looked around and saw craters. He realized he was on the moon. Ahead of him, he saw the earth, blue and green, in all its glory.

Hugo sat down. He stared at the earth for a long time. As he stared, he felt a stillness inside him, a great relief.

Then he noticed something. The earth, it started to shrink. And as it shrunk, Hugo saw the whole of human history. Every war, every battle, every empire, every government, every billionaire, every peasant, every romance, every break-up, every success, every failure, every pleasure, every pain—all of humanity, everything we've ever done, everything we've ever felt, all of it happened on this little blue dot.

Hugo watched the dot. He watched it as it continued to shrink, smaller and smaller, until, finally, it popped out of existence.

Hugo sat on the moon. He was no longer tied to earth, no longer tethered to the hype of it all. He and the moon were free. They careened through space, quietly, silently. It was bliss, pure, celestial bliss.

"Hugo!"

He looked at the tomb. Above the entrance, he saw the letters inscribed in stone: HUGO SUMZER.

A voice called from inside the tomb. "Hugo! Come back!"

"Hugo ..." he said. "What is a Hugo? Must be something round."

"Come back! We need you!"

Something stirred inside him. His memories, his shattered pieces—they began to reform.

"Wait a second ... I'm Hugo. I'm Hugo Sumzer. I'm an anthropology professor."

"Come back!"

"I teach. That's what I do. I teach about history and culture and humans."

"Hugo!"

His entire identity rushed back to him.

"Sydney! Ruxton!"

He sprang to his feet and ran into the tomb. The blindfold slid off his eyes. He was back in the meditation shop.

Ruxton grabbed his shoulder.

"Are you okay?"

"Holy hell. That was nuts. That was wacko. That was ... peaceful, so peaceful."

Sasha smacked Hugo on the back.

"Well done, little brother. Well done."

Sasha unlocked the shackles. Hugo rubbed his wrists.

"How long was I gone?"

"Nine minutes."

"What was my body doing?"

"You kept trying to run. You yanked on the chains pretty hard."

"What was your sacred space?"

"Huh?"

"After the purple ice, after the tomb, what was your sacred space?"

"It was the moon, but with no earth, no human history."

Hugo began to laugh.

"What's so funny?"

"Silence—I've never thought about it from an anthropological perspective, but now I see it. Now I understand it."

"What do you mean?"

Hugo spoke excitedly. "Before we had a global society, humans lived in small groups. For *two million years*, we lived in small, local communities. We sometimes played music. We sometimes talked long into the night. But otherwise, our days were filled with silence. Hours and hours of silence. It made sounds more special. It made thoughts more meaningful."

"Whereas today," Sasha said, "nothing means anything. It's all one big blur."

Hugo stood up and paced in the shop.

"It's like food!" he said.

"Food?"

"Yes. For two million years, famine was one of the leading causes of death. For two million years, many died from a lack of food. And then bam! The Agricultural Revolution happened. In the blink of an eye, we reversed our fate. With farming techniques and mass production, we created an abundance of food. And today, obesity is rampant. More people die from over-eating than under-eating."

"What does that have to do with silence?" Sydney asked.

"It's the same phenomenon. It's the same problem. For two million years, humans suffered from a lack of knowledge. Then, boom! Overnight—the internet, smartphones, Glow Domes—an abundance of knowledge. Too much knowledge. For the first time in history, humans suffer from knowing too much instead of knowing too little."

"Hugo ..." Sydney pointed. "Your nose."

Hugo wiped his nose and looked at his finger. There was blood. And it was purple.

"Wow," he said. "That feeling I felt on the moon, that stillness—I can still feel it."

Ruxton looked at Sasha. "I have a question."

"Yes?"

"If we actually stop Vicarium ..."

"*When* we stop Vicarium ..."

"Okay, *when* we stop Vicarium, are you going to make everybody go back to spears and stones and shit?"

"Why would I do that?"

"I don't know. You seem anti-technology."

"I love technology. I love science. Bullet trains, rocket ships, nuclear fusion—these are marvels of the human mind. Even the internet started out as something great. But with Glow Domes, it has morphed into something sick. We, as a species, have taken a wrong turn."

"And you're going to correct our course?"

"Yes. But before we move forward, I want to try something."

"What's that?"

"The three of you, have a seat, in a row, right here."

The three of them sat cross-legged, in front of Sasha, Sydney to the left, Hugo in the middle, Ruxton to the right.

"Very good. Now please, close your eyes."

All three of them closed their eyes.

"Take a deep breath."

They inhaled and exhaled in unison.

"Good. Now go to your sacred space, your silence inside of you."

Ruxton tapped into his empty theater stage.

Hugo sat next to his tomb on the moon.

Sydney slipped into her little ancient forest, hidden at the bottom of a sinkhole.

"Very good," Sasha said. "Now, all three of you, at the same time, say the words of the Vastus meditation."

Ruxton opened one eye. "You're sure the bad stuff won't happen again?"

"No. The bad part is over. It can't touch you, ever again."

"Then why do we have to say it?"

"Say it for me, pretty please."

Ruxton closed his eye.

"Ready. All three of you, at once, say the words."

The three of them spoke. They paced their words carefully. In unison, they whispered: "Smile at your chances. / Chuckle at your tomb. / Laugh at your chances. / Cackle at your doom."

Sasha grinned with sinful delight. The pieces were coming together. His grand plan just might work.

19
The Skezz

Sasha crossed his arms. "Alright everyone. The Vicarium parties are in a few days. There are three parties: one in Los Angeles, one in Denver, and one in New York."

"Aren't the parties for famous people? Like really, really famous people?" Sydney asked.

"Yes."

"Are we going to the parties?" Ruxton asked.

"Yes."

"But we're not famous. And we don't know anyone who is famous."

"Correct."

"Plus," Hugo added. "Most famous people are famous for the wrong reasons."

"Also correct."

"So what are we gonna do?"

"We have to create three famous people."

"You mean, like ... us? Are you gonna make us famous?"

Sasha laughed. "No, no. That won't work."

"Why not?"

"We need three people with showy talents. And no offense," he looked at Ruxton, then Sydney, then Hugo, "but cooking eggs and making flowers and teaching anthropology are *not* showy talents."

"But the only other way to become famous is to," Sydney hesitated, "is to skezz someone. We're not gonna skezz anyone, are we?"

"Absolutely not. The skezz is evil. And we will take no part in it."

Hugo threw up his hands. "Well, if we don't have any showy talents, and if we're not going to skezz anyone, how do we create three famous people?"

Sasha smiled. "We're going to do it the old-fashioned way. We're going to make three people really, really good at something."

"Who's the first?" Ruxton asked.

"His name is Eli Soto. He's a drummer. He does shows at a nightclub here in Albuquerque. I've seen him play. This guy can drum, I mean really drum."

"So he's good, but not famous?"

"Correct."

"What's your plan?"

"I'm going to unlock his full potential. I'm going to make him the best drummer in the world."

"Have you met him? Have you talked to him?"

"No," Sasha said. "I want Sydney to talk to him."

Sydney raised her eyebrows. "Me? Why me?"

"You and Eli have something in common."

"What's that?"

"Your mother, Sydney. She committed suicide, yes?"

"Yeah…"

"Why did she commit suicide?"

"She got skezzed by Glowers."

"Eli's wife—she also committed suicide, because she got skezzed by Glowers."

Sydney frowned.

Sasha continued: "I think you should go to the nightclub tonight. Talk to Eli. Share your mom's story with him. Share your pain. It might resonate. If it does, tell him there's something he can do about it."

"What can he do about it?"

"Simply convince him to come to the meditation shop. I'll take it from there."

Sydney looked at Ruxton. "I guess I'm going to a nightclub tonight. Do you want to join?"

"Probably not."

"How come?"

"Too much booze around."

"What are you going to do then?"

"I want to quit my job at the diner."

"Why?"

"I don't know. We're going to save the world this weekend. No need for a minimum-wage job."

Sydney rolled her eyes. "Fine. I'll go to the nightclub by myself."

Sasha leaned forward. "Be sure to get there by 9 p.m. Eli does a drum solo on Wednesdays. And it is rich—thunderous and rich."

•

Sydney entered the nightclub. A few heads turned to stare at her silvery-white hair. Sydney looked around. There was a bar, a main floor, and a stage. On the stage, there was an exotic-looking drum set. It had big steel bowls, long thin pipes, and thick wooden slats.

Sydney took a seat at a table on the main floor. A waiter approached her.

"Can I get you anything?"

"Just tea."

"You got it."

He started to walk away.

"Excuse me," Sydney called.

He stopped. "Yes?"

"Is Eli playing tonight?"

"He'll be on in a minute."

"Thank you."

Sydney sat quietly. She looked around some more. The ceiling had blue lights. They coated everything in blue. Blue tables, blue chairs, blue stage, blue drums. Everything was blue.

A man walked onto the stage. He had a big forehead and a boyish face.

The waiter returned with Sydney's tea.

"Excuse me," Sydney pointed to the man on stage. "Is that Eli? Eli Soto?"

The waiter nodded. "That's him alright."

"Thank you."

"You new here?"

"Yes. First time."

"You don't have a pacemaker, do you?"

"A pacemaker? No. Why?"

"Eli's beats are deep. They're so deep, they can disrupt pacemakers. His drum solo has sent two people to the hospital."

"Wow."

"Yeah." The waiter smirked. "Enjoy the show."

On the stage, Eli sat on a stool in the middle of the drum set. He wore a white dress shirt and a skinny black tie.

"Hello everyone. Thanks for coming out tonight."

A few people cheered.

Eli held up two wooden sticks. They were bulbous on both ends.

He took a deep breath, then he went into his drum solo.

It started slow but picked up quick. He thrummed his drums and spun his sticks. He leaned to his left and tapped to his right. The banging was loud but the melody was tight. It ripped through the club, it ripped through the night.

Eli wailed on his drums, faster and faster. He let out a thunder, a growling disaster. The nightclub shook, from glasses to plaster. The rhythm revved up to the speed of a master. Eli crashed on the cymbals and the sounds rounded out. He finished his solo, he finished his bout. Eli stood up. All sweaty, he bowed.

"Thank you, everyone! Thank you!"

People clapped. They whistled in praise.

Eli walked off the stage and headed to the bar for a drink. As he passed Sydney's table, she grabbed his arm.

"Excuse me."

"Do I know you?"

"No. My name is Sydney. Sydney Salazar."

"Hi ... Sydney."

"That was a great drum solo."

"Thanks, kid. You want an autograph or something?"

"No. I want to make you famous."

"Ha! Kid, I am famous. I'm the best drummer in Albuquerque."

"I know. But I want to make you big famous, world famous."

Eli shot her a mean look. "Why the fuck would I want that?"

Sydney frowned. "You don't want to be world famous?"

"Why? So a million petty people can dig up all my dirty laundry—every dumb thing I've ever said, every stupid mistake I've ever made?"

Sydney saddened her eyes.

"Look, kid. I'm a local artist. This is my town. I have a small following, but it pays the bills. I have no desire to go any bigger."

Eli began to walk away.

Sydney called out. "I know about your wife."

He froze.

"She got skezzed, didn't she?"

Eli turned and looked at Sydney. "Why did you say that? Why would you bring that up?"

"The same thing happened to my mom. She got skezzed. Then she ... she ended her life."

Eli let out a sigh. "I'm sorry, kid. I mean, Sydney, right?"

"Yeah. Sydney."

"What do you do for a living, Sydney?"

"I'm a florist, like my mom was."

Eli sat at Sydney's table.

"Your mom, what was her name?"

"Cynthia."

"If you don't mind me asking, how did she get skezzed?"

•

Cynthia was working in the flower shop. A young Glower wandered inside with white rings in his eyes. He recorded everything he saw. Then he picked up a rose and started plucking the petals. That was one of Cynthia's biggest pet peeves—that *pluck* sound, over and over again.

Cynthia asked the kid to stop. But that only made him do it more.

"Excuse me! You have to pay for that."

He didn't listen. He just kept plucking the petals. He picked and plucked and recorded her reaction. Eventually, Cynthia kicked him out of the shop.

But the next day, he came back with his friends. And they did it again. Each of them grabbed a rose. They picked and plucked at the petals. Cynthia pleaded with them to leave.

But the kids didn't leave. They chanted: "Is she crazy? Is she not? Is she crazy? Is she not?" They repeated this as they plucked the petals off the roses. "Is she crazy? Is she not?"

The sheer disrespect—it drove Cynthia crazy. She yelled at them, cursed at them. And they recorded it. They posted the video of her losing her cool. The whole town saw it. Everyone saw her in her worst possible moment.

Cynthia was a sensitive soul. She couldn't handle the way people looked at her after that video went viral. She avoided everyone. She stopped going to work. She stopped leaving her house altogether. She spiraled into a deep depression, a depression that ended with her in a bathtub, a bathtub filled with crimson-colored water.

•

Sydney sighed. "These Glower kids—they don't catch you on a bad day. They drive you to it."

Eli nodded. "More than a person's best work is a person at their worst—that's what people really want today."

There was a long silence.

"What happened to your wife?" Sydney asked. "How did she get skezzed?"

"My wife, Rosie, was a writer. Poems, short stories, literary trinkets. She never published anything. Never cared to. But every time she finished a story, she would make me read it. She would tell me to turn her story into a drum solo. And I would. I would read it, feel it, then drum it out. And she would sit right over there." Eli pointed to a table near the front of the stage. "She would watch me drum and she would *hear* her stories. It was a beautiful process, you know?" Eli paused. "When she was at that table and I was on that stage, when her prose became my rhythm, she was the happiest person in the world."

"I like that," Sydney smiled.

"We were in love," Eli said. "We were madly in love."

"How long were you married?"

"Just a few years. We were blissfully ready to spend the rest of our lives together."

"Then the skezzers got her?"

"Then the fucking skezzers got her."

•

Rosie finished writing a short story. She was really proud of it. It might have been her best. She printed out several copies. With the copies in hand, she walked across town to meet Eli at the nightclub.

She got to an intersection and waited for the light so she could cross. When the light turned green, she stepped off the curb and tripped. Her papers went flying. They scattered everywhere, all over the pavement. Rosie panicked. She crawled on her hands and knees, right in the middle of the intersection. She tried to grab her papers as the wind blew them around.

"My story!" she cried. "My story!"

Cars honked and flashed their lights. No one helped her. No one cared.

A kid on the corner, a young Glower, he recorded her. He stared at her obscure moment with white rings in his eyes.

Eventually, Rosie collected her papers, at least one copy of her story, but by the time she got to the nightclub, the video of her in the intersection went viral. In twenty minutes, it had twenty-thousand views. Within an hour, it had a million.

People mocked her online. Rosie got anxious easily, and this completely rattled her nerves.

•

Eli wiped his hands down his face. "Everyone thinks she killed herself. But she didn't, not on purpose."

"What happened?"

"She took pills to calm her nerves. But one night she took too many." He paused. "She overdosed."

"I'm sorry, Eli."

"That kid, that Glower that recorded her—he became famous. He's still famous, famous for catching the best angle and the best filter of someone's worst day."

"You're right," Sydney said.

"Right about what?"

"More than a person's best work is a person at their worst—that's what people really want today."

Eli shrugged. "It is what it is."

"What if we could change things?"

"What do you mean?"

"Glow Domes, skezzers—what if we could change it all?"

"Ha! That would require some kind of magic."

Sydney closed her eyes. She slipped into her sacred space, her ancient forest at the bottom of a sinkhole. She sat with her trees for a moment.

"Sydney, your nose, it's bleeding."

Sydney opened her eyes. Eli leaned forward.

"What the hell?"

"What's wrong?"

"Your blood—it's purple, like really purple. I've never seen that before."

Sydney wiped her nose with a napkin.

"Why is your blood like that?"

"It's magic."

"Huh?"

"Your wife's last story—did you ever drum it?"

"Excuse me?"

"Rosie, her last story, did you ever drum it?"

"No."

"Why not?"

"She died before I ever had a chance to."

"Have you ever tried?"

"Have I ever tried to drum her last story?"

"Yeah. Have you?"

"Not that it's any of your business, but yes, I've tried."

"And?"

"It's too hard."

"How so?"

"The story—it's rich and beautiful, dense and fast. I've tried to drum it, but I can't. I don't know how."

Sydney smiled. "I know someone who can help you."

"Who?"

"His name is Sasha. He's a meditation teacher."

20
Rhythm

Eli walked into the meditation shop, then stopped for a moment to look around. He noted the deep blue walls with gold trim. Then he noted the paintings on the walls, the exotic beasts—elephants, jaguars, bears—all of them sleeping with one eye open.

"Strange," he said. Then he noticed the other paintings, the ones of huge, ancient trees, all of them caught in brutal, thrashing storms.

Sasha walked out of the backroom. He was wearing his sunglasses.

"Eli Soto. It's very nice to meet you."

Sasha shook Eli's hand.

"You must be Sasha."

"Yes."

"Sydney, the girl, the girl with white hair, she sent me."

"Yes, I know."

Eli scratched his head. "I'm sorry, have we met before?"

"No. But I've seen you play. I'm a big fan of your work."

"Hey, thanks." Eli looked around the shop again. "Sydney tells me you're a meditation teacher?"

"That's right."

"What kind of meditations do you teach?"

"I have one for empathy, one for silence, and one for maximizing the true self." Sasha paused. "Would you like to maximize your true self, Eli?"

Eli blinked several times, curiously caught off guard.

Sasha took off his sunglasses. He revealed his rust-red irises.

"Jesus, man. What happened to your eyes?"

"I used to have Glow Domes. But I ripped them out."

"You *ripped out* your Domes?"

"I think Domes are a waste of energy. They scatter your focus, rob you of skills." Sasha smiled. "And you, Eli, you have a beautiful skill."

"You mean drumming?"

"Yes. You are the best drummer in Albuquerque. But I can make you the best in the *world*."

"And how might that work?"

"It's quite simple. I'll guide you through an ancient meditation. It's called the Maxis meditation. It will unlock your full potential."

"What if I don't want to become the world's best drummer? What if I don't care about fame?"

"Then why did you come here, Eli?"

Eli reached in his pocket. He pulled out some papers and unfolded them.

"This is my wife's story. It's the last story she ever wrote."

"Tell me more."

"My late wife, Rosie, she was a writer. She used to write stories. And I used to drum them."

"Did you drum her last story?"

"No."

"Why not?"

"I don't know. It's her best story, by far. But it's rich and dense. And the plot moves fast. To drum it would require an insane level of rhythm."

Sasha pulled a notecard out of his pocket and handed it to Eli.

"Can you memorize this phrase?"

Eli read the card aloud: "I *will* myself with all my might. I *squeeze* the dark and out comes light."

"Again."

Eli cleared his throat. "I *will* myself with all my might. I *squeeze* the dark and out comes light."

"Again. More forceful."

"I *will* myself with all my might. I *squeeze* the dark and out comes light."

"That's it." Sasha turned around. "Follow me, Eli."

They walked to the backroom of the meditation shop. In the middle of the room, Eli saw a sturdy wooden chair. In front of the chair, he saw five metronomes, spaced across a shelf.

"What's this?"

"Of all the meditations, Eli, the Maxis meditation is the hardest to achieve. It takes a great deal of focus. But it also takes customization. It's an experience that's tailored to one individual, one specific skill."

"I don't know, man. This is kind of weird."

"Do you want to drum your wife's last story?"

"I mean, yeah, of course."

"Then have a seat."

Eli thought about Rosie. He thought about her story. Then he sat in the chair.

Sasha grabbed five wires. He inserted each wire into the back of each metronome.

"Tell me about your parents, Eli."

"My parents?"

"Yes. What were they like when you were a child?"

"Well, my dad was a German engineer. My mom was a Panamanian dancer. My entire childhood was a constant clash of cold, hard math and fluid, circular expression. I guess that made me a good drummer. You need both to drum a full-bodied hit."

"I like that." Sasha smiled. "Now roll up your pant legs please."

"What?"

"Roll up your pant legs, Eli."

Sasha drilled him with his rust-red eyes.

Eli rolled up his pant legs.

Sasha attached a wire to Eli's left thigh. Then he attached a wire to his right thigh.

"Your shirt sleeves—roll those up as well."

Eli obeyed.

Sasha attached a wire to each arm.

"Now lean forward."

Sasha attached a wire to the back of Eli's neck.

Eli shifted in the chair. "Um, Sasha, why am I hooked up to five metronomes? And why are the metronomes hooked up to an electric generator?"

Sasha turned on a metronome. The head rocked side to side.

"Whoa!" said Eli. "I feel that ... in my left thigh."

"It's an electric pulse, yes?"

"Yes."

"A slow one?"

"Very slow. A slow tempo."

Sasha turned on another metronome.

"That's my right thigh," said Eli.

"But the tempo is quicker, yes?"

"A little quicker, yes."

"The two tempos, the beats in your legs—are they layered?"

"Yes, actually, they are."

Sasha turned on another metronome.

Eli felt an electric pulse in his arm, an even faster one.

"That's three tempos ... in three different parts of my body."

Sasha turned on another metronome.

"Whoa, that's a lot of electricity."

Sasha turned on the fifth and final metronome.

A rapid beat pulsed into the back of Eli's neck.

"That's five tempos, Eli. Can you feel them?"

"Yes!"

"Can you layer them?"

"Yes!"

"What do the layers feel like, Eli?"

"Rhythm! They feel like rhythm!"

"Now say it, Eli!"

"Say what?"

"The Maxis words! Say them!"

"I *will* myself with all my might. I *squeeze* the dark and out comes light."

Sasha turned a knob on the generator.

Eli's body tensed.

"Say it again."

"I *will* myself with all my might. I *squeeze* the dark and out comes light."

Sasha turned the knob even higher.

He blasted Eli's body with electric rhythm.

"Again!"

"I *will* myself with all my might! I *squeeze* the dark and out comes light!"

Eli's entire body blinked out of existence.

•

Eli looked at his arms and legs. The wires were gone. He wasn't in the meditation shop any longer. He was somewhere else.

He looked around. He saw black waterfalls. They must have been a mile tall. They encircled him, roared at him from every direction.

"What the hell did Sasha do?"

Eli stared at the black water. Some of it fell down. Some of it fell up. But nothing went deeper than where Eli stood. He stood on solid bedrock.

"Hello."

Eli turned. He saw a little girl. She had rich, piercing eyes with double-ringed irises of green and gold.

"Who are you?" he asked.

"I'm Lucy. Who are you?"

"I'm Eli."

"Welcome, Eli."

"What is this place?"

"This is the bottom of your soul. It's the bottom of everyone's soul." Lucy stared at him. Her eyes demanded the best, the absolute best. "How did you get here, Eli?"

"The Maxis meditation?"

"I know. But specifically, how did you get here?"

"Rhythm. I got here through rhythm."

Lucy smiled. "Follow me."

Eli followed the little girl.

"What exactly happens here?"

"You came here to *know* something. And now you're going to *know it*."

Lucy stopped. They both looked down. In the bedrock, there were twenty-four holes, each the size of a large coin. The holes were in a straight line. They melodically hissed with shots of white steam.

"Do you know how many vertebrae are in the human spine?"

"No."

"Twenty-four. There are twenty-four vertebrae in the human spine. Seven cervical. Twelve thoracic. And five lumbar. You can remember them by mealtimes—7 a.m. for breakfast, 12 p.m. for lunch, and 5 p.m. for dinner."

Eli watched the holes as they hissed with shots of white steam.

"What does this have to do with rhythm?"

"True rhythm—it starts at your core, then radiates outward."

"I don't understand."

Lucy smiled, then shoved him to the ground.

Eli's back covered the holes. He went to stand up, but brown vines grew out of the rock and secured him in place.

"What the hell?"

"Get ready, Eli. You're about to *know* rhythm."

Rods of steel shot out of the holes and pounded Eli's back. They punched each vertebra with a buckling crack. They did so repeatedly, shooting up and down like musical pistons.

Eli cried in agony. His back arched and his eyes bulged.

The rods shot harder and faster. They played his spine like a xylophone, and, as much as it hurt, Eli felt it—a tempo, a pattern, a timeless beat.

Suddenly, Eli *knew* rhythm, more profoundly than ever before. His body blurred. His skin turned blue. Then, to his amazement, he evaporated into a shimmer, a blue, pulsing shimmer. Eli became rhythm. He became a jazzy heartbeat that floated upward, beating and pulsing, higher and higher, until he reached the top of the black waterfalls, where his blue shimmer faded, faded and disappeared.

•

In the meditation shop, Eli's body blinked back into existence. He sprung out of the wooden chair.

"Holy shit!"

"How was it?"

"That was insane!"

Sasha turned off the electric generator. "How do you feel?"

Eli looked at his hands. "I feel ... I feel good."

"How so?"

"I don't know. I feel something inside me." He nodded his head repeatedly. "It's like a beat, a tempo, a powerful one." Eli rolled his sleeves back down. "I'm sorry, Sasha, but I have to go. I have to try something."

"Try away."

Eli rushed out of the meditation shop. He got in his car and drove to the nightclub. It was early, much earlier than his show was to start. There were a few patrons in the club. They watched Eli curiously as he rushed onto the stage and sat in his drum set.

He pulled the papers out of his pocket—his wife's last story. He read it for the thousandth time.

"Yeah ... I feel it now. I feel your story, Rosie. I feel the pulse. I feel the beat."

He picked up his sticks and went for it.

He pounded the steel and simmered the snare. He stretched out a theme and ignited a flare. He dipped into madness and felt himself melt. He touched something great. He belted it out.

The sound was so fast, he could barely hang on. But he did it, he squeezed. He drummed on and on.

He remembered his wife and her beautiful soul. Thunder erupted from big, steely bowls. Everything merged and rapidity was key. Eli let loose. He let out a spree. He drummed every note. He hit every key. And finally, finally ... Rosie's story—it was free.

Eli stopped. He was dripping with sweat. A dozen people looked at him from the main floor. Some recorded with Glow Domes. Some recorded with smartphones. Either way, his performance went viral. Within twenty minutes, millions of people knew the name: Eli Soto. He quickly became the best drummer the world had ever seen.

21
Speed

Ruxton walked into the meditation shop. He was watching a video on his phone.

"Hey Sasha! Have you seen the video of Eli?"

"I've seen it."

"Did Eli do the Maxis meditation?"

Sasha nodded.

"I can't believe it."

"Can't believe what?"

"You like, turned a mortal into a god."

"I know," Sasha said. "But we need another god."

"Another musician?"

"No. This time, we're going after a pilot. A stunt pilot."

"You think we can turn a stunt pilot into a famous person?"

Sasha sat on a stool. "Have you ever heard of the Magnet Canyons?"

"Out in the desert? Yeah."

"What do you know about them?"

"They used to be a mining operation. But then they got abandoned."

"Do you know what's special about those canyons?"

"No."

"The rock there—it has long streaks of ore, magnetic ore. Very powerful. That's why it got abandoned. The ore would pull on the mining equipment. Bend it. Sometimes break it."

"What does that have to do with stunt pilots?"

"Within those canyons, there's a popular flying challenge. It's called the chimney stunt. No one has ever completed it."

"I'm guessing you have a pilot in mind?"

"Her name is Anna Moxy. She's been doing airshows in this area for quite some time. Her stunts are wild." Sasha paused. "But they could be even wilder."

"So, what am I supposed to do?"

"I want you to retrieve her. Bring her back to the meditation shop."

"Why do I have to do it?"

"Because you and Anna are going to change the world together. You might as well get to know each other."

"Where is she?"

"Anna is doing an airshow this afternoon. West of town."

"What am I supposed to say exactly?"

"Just mention the chimney stunt. I'll do the rest."

•

Ruxton stepped into a crowd on the side of a runway. He looked up. The sky was empty, not a single cloud. Suddenly, a jet ripped through the blue with a deafening boom. The crowd cheered.

Ruxton tapped on a stranger's shoulder. "Excuse me. Do you know if Anna Moxy is flying today?"

"That's her!" the stranger pointed to the sleek, black jet in the sky. "That's Anna Moxy!"

Ruxton locked his eyes on the jet. The jet made three consecutive loops, each smaller and faster than the last.

"Damn. Looks fun."

The jet peeled off and headed away from the crowd.

An old man hollered, "She's doing the drill! She's doing the drill!"

Ruxton asked the man, "What's the drill?"

"Just watch!"

The jet blasted its engine. It flew in a straight line, low to the ground. The wings spun around the fuselage and the fuselage twisted like a drill.

The crowd braced and held their breath.

The jet aimed at a hangar, an empty hangar. It drilled through the front and blasted out the back.

The crowd went wild.

After the hangar stunt, the jet circled back. It flew by the crowd, then went straight up, full vertical.

Everyone looked. They shaded their eyes from the sun.

Someone yelled: "She's gonna do the fall!"

The jet cut its engine. It coasted upward for a few seconds. Then it stopped, hovered, and dropped. It fell backwards, tumbling, end over end, faster and faster.

Ruxton grew nervous.

The jet fell to the earth, flipping like a coin.

"Will she splat?"

"Will she crash?"

"Will she splat?"

"Will she crash?"

The crowd chanted as the jet fell closer and closer to the runway. At the very last second, the jet blasted its engines. Flames scorched the runway. The jet pushed upward. It practically bounced off the ground.

The crowd hollered and cheered.

Ruxton kept his eye on the plane as it came in for a landing. The tires screeched. Then they rolled to a stop. The pilot got out and she climbed down a ladder.

Ruxton squinted. "That's Anna. That's Anna Moxy."

Anna walked off the airfield. She went inside a building.

Ruxton followed. Inside the building, he found an airport bar. Anna was sitting at the corner of the counter. She ordered one shot and one beer.

Ruxton sat adjacent to her.

"Cool stunts," he said.

Anna shrugged. "They were okay."

She wore a wife-beater. She had hard, lean arms and short sandy hair.

"How long have you been flying?" Ruxton asked.

Anna threw back a shot of tequila. "I started stealing planes when I was eleven."

"You *stole* planes?"

"Can't get a license until you're fifteen. Didn't feel like waiting."

Ruxton nodded. He noticed a tattoo on Anna's arm, a red maple leaf.

"You're Canadian?"

"I'm a Canadian *badass*." Anna let out a harsh laugh.

Ruxton ordered a glass of lemon water.

"Lemon water?" Anna said. "You're gonna come to a high-octane airshow and drink lemon water?"

"I just got sober."

Anna didn't answer.

Ruxton thought for a moment.

"Want to play a game?"

"It better be a fast game."
"It's fast."
"What's it called?"
"Quick draw."
"How's it work?"
"You answer as quickly as possible. No hesitation. No time to think. Rapidity is key. Got it?"
Anna sipped her beer.
"Sure. Whatever, kid. Go."
"Hardwood or carpet?"
"Hardwood."
"Fight or flight?"
"Fight."
"Nickel or dime?"
"Dime."
"Abortion or abandonment?"
"Abandonment."
"Why?"
"Tough love is the best love."
"A hot shower or a cold beer?"
"Beer."
"What's underrated?"
"Risks."
"What's overrated?"
"Safety."
"Coffee or tea?"
"Tar black coffee. Through an IV. Avoid stained teeth."
"Would you rather deliver a baby or deliver a eulogy?"
"Eulogy."
"How many romantic partners have you had?"
"Nine and three quarters."

"How would you like to die?"
"By not giving any fucks."
"What advice would you give to your five-year-old self?"
"I wouldn't."
"What do you mean?"
"There's no advice to give. There's no instruction manual for life. You just gotta live it."
"What's your biggest fear?"
"Wearing a cardigan."
"What's your least favorite animal?"
"Geese. I hate geese."
"Why?"
"They look pretty but honk ugly."
"How do you like your beauty?"
"Stark."
"Brass or strings?"
"Brass. Trumpet especially."
"Moral compass?"
"South-South-West."
"All-time Pearly Gates Question?"
"Excuse me?
"Pearly Gates Question. Like, if you could know one thing about life, about the cosmos, what would it be?"
"Why meat?"
"Sorry?"
"Why meat?" she repeated. "I mean seriously, of all the ways life could have manifested itself, it chose meat—flesh, tissue, gristle." She shook her head. "We could've been crystalline structures. We could've been orbs of conscious light. But no, we're made of meat. Meat that gets sick. Meat that bruises. Meat that rots while we're still alive. It's disgusting. So why? Why meat? That's my all-time Pearly Gates Question."

Ruxton nodded.

"That the end of your game, kid?"

"Yeah."

"What's it called again?"

"Quick draw. I ask random questions. You answer as fast as possible."

Anna sipped her beer. "That's cute. You pick up girls that way?"

Ruxton blushed. "I used to …"

"You know I'm like ten years older than you. And I don't like boys."

"That's not why I'm here."

"Then why are you here? What the hell do you want with a second-rate stunt pilot?"

"You ever fly in the Magnet Canyons?"

Anna shot him a look. "The Magnet Canyons. That shit is next-level."

"There's that one stunt, the chimney stunt."

"The chimney stunt!" Anna let out a laugh. "Every pilot in the world knows about the chimney stunt."

"How would you like to do it?" Ruxton grinned. "How would you like to be the first pilot to pull it off?"

"Kid, that chimney stunt is nuts. You have to fly your plane through a cavern. Do you know how many dead pilots are in that cavern? Nine! Nine pilots flew in there and never flew out. And they were nine of the best pilots the world has ever seen."

"So you don't think you can do it?" Ruxton asked.

"I don't think anyone can do it. That stunt is impossible."

"But if it were possible, what would it take?"

"Speed. Pure speed. Mind to body. Body to plane."

Ruxton smiled. "Anna, have you ever tried … meditation?"

Anna walked into the meditation shop.

"Hello? I'm looking for Sasha."

Sasha walked out of the backroom.

"Anna Moxy. Daredevil extraordinaire."

"Something like that."

"I'm Sasha. Welcome to my meditation shop."

Anna looked around. "I don't normally do this type of stuff."

"Then why did you come here?"

"That kid sent me, the scrappy one with big lips."

"Ruxton is his name."

"Yeah. Ruxton. He said you could make me a better pilot."

"I can make you the best."

"And how might that work?"

"I would guide you through a meditation. It's called the Maxis meditation."

"It's not some gimmick, is it?"

"No. The Maxis meditation is all about focus—extreme focus. Can you handle that, Anna?"

Anna scoffed. "I can hit four Gs in three seconds. So yeah, I can handle extreme focus."

"Wonderful. Let's get to it." Sasha pulled a notecard out of his pocket. "First, I need you to memorize this phrase."

Anna took the card. She read the phrase out loud: "I *will* myself with all my might. I *squeeze* the dark and out comes light."

"Can you commit that to memory?"

"Sure."

"Very good. Follow me."

Anna followed Sasha to the backroom of the shop. She saw a sturdy, wooden chair. The chair was bolted to a platform. Behind the chair, she saw an odd contraption, a set of metal gears.

"Have a seat, Anna."

Anna hesitated.

"What's the matter? Are you scared, Miss Daredevil?"

"Ugh. Fine."

She sat in the chair.

"Tell me, Anna. What do you *want* more than anything?"

"I want speed. Pure, undiluted speed. I want it in my mind, my body, my plane."

"Perfect."

Sasha picked up a long, elastic band.

"What are you doing?" she asked.

"We need to mimic gravity. We need to mimic your cockpit."

Sasha donned the band over Anna's knees, then pulled back the ends and secured them to the metal gears behind the chair.

"This is weird."

Sasha put a band over Anna's stomach, then pulled back the ends and secured them to the metal gears.

"Hey man, I don't know if I like this."

Sasha secured another band across her chest, another across her shoulders, and another across her forehead.

Anna tried to lean forward, but she couldn't.

"Sasha, man. This is uncomfortable."

"Do you want comfort, Anna? Or do you want greatness?"

Anna swallowed. She didn't answer.

Sasha stood behind the chair. He cranked the metal gears. As they turned, the bands stretched and tightened over her body.

"Feel the bands, Anna. Feel them pulling you back."

Anna widened her eyes.

"Can you feel them, Anna?"

"Yes."

"Good. Feel them. Feel them the same way you feel gravity—a force to push past, a barrier to break through."

Anna focused her energy straight ahead.

"Say the words, Anna."

"What?"

"Say the Maxis words!"

"I *will* myself with all my might. I *squeeze* the dark and out comes light."

Sasha tightened the bands. They dug into her skin.

"I *will* myself with all my might. I *squeeze* the dark and out comes light."

"Come on, Anna! Think *speed*. Embody *speed*. Will yourself forward!"

"I'm trying!"

"Mind to body, body to plane. Come on, Anna. Full throttle!"

Anna pushed forward.

"Full throttle!"

"I *will* myself with all my might. I *squeeze* the dark and out comes light!"

The bands snapped.

Anna felt free.

Anna felt speed.

Her entire body blinked out of existence.

●

Anna looked at her hands, then touched her shoulders. The elastic bands were gone. Sasha was gone. She was no longer in the meditation shop.

She looked around. She saw black waterfalls, colossal ones. They roared at her from every direction.

"This can't be real."

"It's real."

Anna turned. She saw a little girl with piercing green eyes.

"Who are you?"

"I'm Lucy."

"What is this place?"

"It's the bottom of your soul. It's the bottom of everyone's soul."

"I don't understand."

"Think of it like a well, a special well, where you have to add water before you retrieve it."

Anna looked confused.

"What's your name?" Lucy asked.

"I'm Anna."

"How did you get down here, Anna?"

"Some nut job tied rubber bands around me."

"Did you break free?"

"I guess."

"How?"

"I thought about speed. I focused on speed."

Lucy smiled. "Follow me."

Anna followed the little girl. They walked across the bedrock for several minutes.

Then Lucy stopped. They both looked down.

There was a pit in the bedrock, a massive, cone-shaped pit. It was a hundred yards across and a hundred yards deep. Surrounding the top of the pit were five holes, each of them the size of a boulder.

"Do you want to *know* speed?"

"Yes."

"To know speed," said Lucy, "is to know the gravity slowing it down." Lucy paused. "Light is the fastest thing in the universe, but it cannot escape the gravity of a black hole."

Anna pointed. "So what's with the pit?"

"If you want to be faster than light, you must be greater than gravity."

Lucy shoved Anna into the pit.

Anna rolled and bounced to the bottom.

Then she looked up. At the top of the pit, she saw huge boulders. They pushed up from the holes surrounding the pit. Then the boulders tipped. They leaned. They rolled into the pit.

Anna panicked. She had nowhere to go, nowhere to hide. Suddenly, she noticed something strange. As the boulders rolled toward her, they shrunk in size. By the time they reached her, they were the size of marbles, but they kept their weight. They kept their mass.

The first one rolled into her arm. The next one rolled into her ankle. More and more boulders rolled into the pit. They rolled and shrunk, rolled and shrunk.

Marbles of stone pooled around Anna, covered her completely. Each marble had the weight of a mountain. And the weight crushed her. It flattened her pelvis; it flattened her skull. Second by second, the weight grew heavier. It pressed into the bottom of the pit. Her flesh turned to liquid. Her bones turned to dust. She was nothing but a puddle, a red and white puddle. When she tried to cry, the puddle simply bubbled.

A few more boulders rolled into the pit. The pit was nearly full.

Anna thought she would never escape. Then, suddenly, she reached a certain point, an understanding. The crushing weight transformed her into a yellow ball of light, raying outward in every direction.

With her newfound power, she focused all her rays into a single ray. She blasted out of the pit and shot straight up. She overcame gravity. She became an unstoppable ray of light.

In the meditation shop, Anna blinked back into existence. She sprung out of the chair.

"Holy shit!"

"How was it?"

"I became speed. I *am* speed."

"What do you want to do?"

"Huh?"

"Right now, what do you want to do? More than anything?"

"I want to fly. I want to fly my plane."

"Then go," Sasha smiled. "Go fly your plane."

Anna rushed out of the meditation shop.

On her way to the airport, she called her mechanic.

"Hey, Bobby. It's Anna. Get my plane ready. I'm going to the Magnet Canyons."

By the time Anna got to the airfield, word had spread fast: A pilot was headed to the Magnet Canyons, which meant one of two things: a wild performance or a wishful death.

Anna sat in the single-seat cockpit of her small yet powerful jet.

She fired her engines and ramped off the runway. She flew west. After twenty minutes, she could see the Magnet Canyons—curvy gashes in the rocky earth.

Her mechanic called her on the radio. "Are you doing what I think you're doing?"

"Maybe."

"Anna, you'll die."

"I think I can do it."

"Anna. Do not do the chimney stunt."

"I'm fast enough."

"It doesn't matter how fast you are! Once you go underground, you lose radar."

"I won't need it."

"What do you mean?"

"Mind to body. Body to plane."

Anna turned off her radio. She dove her plane into the canyons and slipped into a gully of rock. As soon as she did, her plane fishtailed.

"Fuck!"

The ore in the rock—it pulled on her plane.

She pushed the throttle forward. She whizzed through tight gaps.

Then she saw it—a gash in the rock.

"That's it. That's the entry point."

She aimed for the gash, the entrance to the cavern.

People watched from cliffs. They watched as her plane pierced the blackness and went underground. As soon as it did, her plane jerked sideways, repelled by magnetic rock. The change in G-force was so strong, Anna blacked out. She had a full dream. Beginning. Middle. End.

Then she woke up and flipped on her headlights.

"Here we go."

She blasted her engines and sped through the dark.

"Yikes!"

She spotted a pillar ahead. She cut left and barely missed it.

"Where is the chimney?"

She looked in every direction.

"There!"

She saw a pinhole of light at the far end of the cavern.

"Let's go!"

She pushed the throttle forward and aimed for the pinhole.

Magnetic rock jerked her plane.

"Focus. Focus. Focus."

The pinhole grew in size. It became a mouth of light.

Anna dipped the plane, then pointed it straight up. She entered the light, the chimney, the long chute of rock.

"Steady ... Steady ..."

Her plane was vertical. The chimney narrowed.

"Fast. Fast. Fast."

Anna redlined her engines.

"Pure, fucking speed!"

She shot out of the ground.

Her plane pierced the sky like a hot needle.

A nearby crowd hollered and cheered. It was the first time anyone had seen a plane fly out of that hole in the ground.

Word spread fast in the flying community. Then it spread to mainstream news. Within an hour, Anna Moxy was famous. She was the first and only pilot to execute the death-defying chimney stunt.

22

Dance

Ruxton walked into the meditation shop and looked at Sasha.

"We have two famous people. Who do we go after next?"

"No one."

"What do you mean? Don't we need a third famous person?"

"We already have her."

The front door opened. A gorgeous woman walked into the shop. She had long, black hair and a calm, earthy vibe.

Ruxton, Sydney, and Hugo all exclaimed at once: "Liv Xan!"

Liv Xan smiled. "Hello everyone. Hello Sasha."

Sydney's jaw dropped. "Sasha, you know *Liv Xan?*"

"We met a few years ago, before she became famous."

Sydney turned to Liv Xan. "Is that true? Did you know Sasha before you blew up as a world-class hip-hop dancer?"

Liv chuckled. "Yes. I've known Sasha for years."

"Miss Xan," Ruxton said.

"Liv. Call me Liv."

"Liv, can I just say: Your dance videos are incredible."

"Yeah," Sydney added. "You're a mega-star, and you actually deserve it."

"Thank you," said Liv. "But it wasn't always that way."

"What do you mean?"

"Before the fame and followers, I was a sad, anxious person. But Sasha changed that. He transformed my anxiety into a beautiful dance."

"Let me guess," Hugo said. "You did the Maxis meditation?"

"I did. It was very painful. But it worked."

"Did you find Sasha? Or did Sasha find you?"

"He found me."

"Where?"

"In a back alley, not too far from here."

•

Liv sat on her back porch. She rapidly tapped her right foot. She was gunning to go somewhere, but her anxiety squeezed her, secured her in place.

That's when she heard a playful whistling. At the end of the alley, she saw Sasha in his sunglasses. He whistled while he walked. Sometimes he stopped to touch a rusted fence or a broken window. He whispered nice things to them; he said something pleasant to every open wound.

As he passed Liv, she called out: "You lost, man?"

"Not at all."

"Why are you back here?"

"You mean the alley?"

"Yeah."

"I live in this neighborhood. And I like to explore."

"You like to explore the bad parts?"

"Especially the bad parts."

A surveillance drone hovered above the alley.

Sasha pulled a slingshot from his back pocket. He pinched a rock in the patch of leather, then he stretched and aimed. The rubber snapped forward and the rock whizzed. It blew through a motor on the drone. The drone plummeted and crashed.

"The law says you can't shoot down a drone. But it doesn't say anything about slingin' at 'em!"

"You're weird."

"Actually, I'm Sasha. What's your name?"

"Liv. Liv Xan."

Sasha pointed to her foot, the one tapping rapidly.

"You okay?"

"Just anxious."

"From the drone?"

"Na. I have anxiety."

"How long have you had it?"

"My whole life."

"Is it bad?"

"It's bad."

"Is there ever a time when it's not bad?"

"When I dance."

"Then why aren't you dancing?"

"That's anxiety, man. It grips you."

"Maybe start with a walk? Loosen the grip?"

"Walk? To where?"

"A cool place. I'll show you."

Liv stared at Sasha.

He extended the slingshot. "You can have a turn."

Liv held her breath for a long moment. Then she left her porch.

Sasha handed her the slingshot. The two of them walked down the alley.

"Tell me, Liv. When was the last time you danced?"

"My dad's funeral."

"You *danced* at your father's funeral?"

"Yeah. A year ago."

"Was it a happy dance?"

"Happy, bitter, brutal." Liv paused. "My dad migrated to America when he was young. He loved everything about America, everything except the funerals. He said American funerals were too sad, too gloomy. He wanted his funeral to be a celebration. He talked about it all the time. He probably talked about it too much. One day, he got diagnosed with lung cancer. Doctors gave him six months. When he found out, he gathered all twelve of us kids. He said we had to sing at his funeral. We had to sing happy songs, joyful songs." Liv paused. "All my brothers and sisters can sing. But I'm the youngest. I don't have pipes like them. I told my dad that. He smiled. He said I could dance instead."

"So you danced?"

Liv nodded. "They lowered his body into the ground while my brothers and sisters sang. And while they sang, I ... I danced."

"Was it hard?"

"I had to search deep within my bones. I had to find motion in a motionless place."

Sasha stepped over a flattened rat hide.

"But you haven't danced since?"

"Not really. Too much anxiety."

"About life?"

"Yeah man. I'm dirt poor. I live in a two-bedroom house with eleven brothers and sisters, plus my widowed mom. We can barely afford food." Liv shook her head. "It's just not fair."

"What's not fair?"

"Here I am, starving. And a few blocks up the street, Glower kids are laid back in a Scrolling Center, all cozy and comfy, getting paid to watch the news."

Liv stopped walking. She pointed to a drone overhead.

"Can I?"

Sasha picked up a rock and handed it to her.

Liv pinched the rock in the leather. She pulled it back and aimed. Her hand shook.

"Squeeze a little harder. And don't forget to breathe."

Liv breathed. Then she released. The rock zinged into the underside of the drone. The drone staggered sideways, then crashed into the ground.

"Decent!" Sasha beamed.

They continued to walk down the alley. Then they turned a corner.

Liv looked up and said, "Where are we? What is this place?"

"It's a meditation shop. It's my meditation shop."

Sasha unlocked the front door.

"Would you like to come in?"

Liv thought for a moment. Then she walked into the shop.

"Wow," she said. "Look at these paintings."

She walked up to one of them—a jaguar sleeping with one eye open.

"Liv, have you ever tried ... meditation?"

"Not really."

"Would you like to try?"

"Depends."

"On what?"

"On what kind of meditations you have."

"I have one for empathy, one for silence, and one for maximizing the true self."

"That last one sounds cool."

"Maximizing the true self?"

"Yeah."

"Tell me, Liv, what is the truest part of yourself, the truest part of your soul?"

"Dance, I guess."

"What kind of dance?"

"Any dance. I know there's a good dancer inside of me. I can feel it."

"But?"

"But she's crippled by worry."

Sasha pulled a notecard from his pocket and handed it to Liv.

"Can you memorize this phrase?"

Liv read the card aloud: "I *will* myself with all my might. I *squeeze* the dark and out comes light."

"Perfect," said Sasha. "I'll be right back."

Sasha went to the backroom and rummaged for a minute. He came out with two items: a small wooden cage and a jar full of nectar.

"What are those for?" Liv asked.

"They're for you, for your customized meditation."

Sasha went to the backroom again. He came out with a third and final item.

"This is a slapstick," he said. "It's a musical instrument. And it's not used often."

Liv looked at the slapstick. "It's just a piece of wood."

"It's two pieces of wood, hinged with a spring."

Sasha swung the slapstick through the air. The hinge widened and the wood split open, then it *slapped* back together.

Liv jumped. She had never heard a sound like that. It was so specific, like half the crack of lightning and half the crack of a whip.

"Why do you have that?"

"The slapstick?"

"Yeah."

"The Maxis meditation—it's all about focus." Sasha swung the slapstick again. It let out a loud *slap*. "When you hear the slapstick, Liv, I want you to put your mind into your body. Feel every square inch of yourself in one instant, in one *slap*. Can you do that?"

"I think so." She pointed to the wooden cage. "What's that for?"

Sasha opened the wooden cage. A bright red hummingbird emerged. It flew around the meditation shop, pausing periodically to hover in mid-air.

"That little guy—he's your dancing partner."

"You want me to dance ... in your shop ... with a hummingbird?"

Sasha grabbed the jar full of nectar and walked up to Liv.

"Don't worry," he said. "This will enhance the dance."

Sasha stuck his fingers into the jar. Then he rubbed nectar on Liv's arms.

"Is he gonna bite me?"

"No. He'll just be attracted to you." Sasha pointed to Liv's midriff. "May I?"

She nodded, hesitantly.

Sasha rubbed nectar on her flat, lean stomach.

The hummingbird flew around Liv in zigzags.

Sasha backed away. He sat on a stool, holding the slapstick.

"Ready to dance?"

She looked at the hummingbird, then at Sasha.

"There's no music."

"Do you need music?"

"I need something."

"What if I throw something down?"

"Fine. But don't look while I'm getting into it."

"Fair enough." Sasha leaned back. He closed his eyes. "Okay. I think I have something for you." Sasha tapped his foot to a tempo. "Alright. Here we go. You feel this mania. It's this push. It's this drive. You wanna shoot forward and split from your skin. You wanna feel everything, surges and sins. Then reality kicks, it acutely sets in. Hiccups and notices and bills creep in. They reach in your engines and grind up your gears. You choke and you fear and you sputter and crash. You crack, but you bounce. You head back to the winds. You infiltrate clouds and it all happens again.

"You fly and you fall. You're hard and you're fast. You're tight-roping wisdom. You're jazzed and you're splat. You wanna find meaning but can't find where it's at. You scream and you scream but nothing comes out. You wonder, when it thunders, what it's all about.

"Christ, grab some keys and unlock the door. Spit in this wound and heal up my sores. I just wanna die and break free from this time. But I can't cause I'm here, locked into this life. I'm doomed and I'm glued to this ridiculous strife.

"Might as well tune my wounds to a riff, channel my crypt and my pain to a rhyme. Only singing and dancing will make this dirty ... time ... shine."

Sasha opened his eyes. Liv danced beautifully. She cut and scooped through empty space. The hummingbird zipped around her. It scored her moves, accented her style.

"Say the words, Liv!"

"Right now?"

"Right now!"

Liv did a series of spins.

"I *will* myself with all my might. I *squeeze* the dark and out comes light!"

Liv jumped. She split her legs for a split-second. Sasha swung the slapstick. It *slapped*. Liv felt it. She felt a sharp, splitting sound as she split her legs apart. Then she blinked out of existence at the peak of her leap.

•

Liv landed on solid bedrock. She wasn't in the meditation shop. She was somewhere else. She saw tall black waterfalls in every direction. Some of them fell down. Some of them fell up. All of them rumbled like rolling thunder.

"Who are you?"

Liv jumped. She turned and saw a little girl with piercing green eyes.

"Hi ... I'm Liv."

"How did you get down here, Liv?"

"I did the Maxis meditation?"

"I know," said Lucy. "But what exactly were you doing? Just a second ago?"

"I was dancing."

Lucy smiled. "Follow me."

"What's your name?"

"I'm Lucy."

"What is this place?"

"It's the bottom of your soul. It's the bottom of everyone's soul."

"I don't get it."

"When you're down here, you get to *know* something. You get to *become* something. What do you want to become, Liv?"

"A dancer. I want to become a dancer."

"What kind of dancer?"

"Any kind. I don't care. I just want to channel my anxiety, transform it into dance."

They stopped walking. In front of them, Liv saw four columns of stone, spaced apart in a big square. Each column had a thick, golden rope that hung from the top.

"What is this?"

Lucy pointed to the middle. "Go. Stand there."

Liv stood in the middle of the stone columns.

Lucy smiled. "I'm no dancer, but I do know this: Sometimes, you have to shake out the bad moves ... before you get to the good ones."

The golden ropes reached out to Liv. They attached to her wrists and ankles. Then, the ropes yanked on her body like a mean puppeteer. Liv stumbled sideways; she fell forward and back. Her shoulders rolled over and her kneecap cracked. Liv cried to the ropes and their jerky command. She wept for her bones that rattled like cans.

Suddenly, there were black beetles, hundreds of them, crawling down the golden ropes. They hurried towards her, ran up her legs, up her neck. They crawled into her mouth and down her throat. They collected in her stomach as a jittery ball. The jitter morphed into an ancient energy, a powerful drive.

The ropes continued to yank on Liv, but Liv began to yank back.

She ripped a rope from its stone column. Then she ripped another, and another, and another. All the ropes were down, but they were still attached to her body.

Liv danced. She danced an exotic dance. She swung the golden ropes around her, whipping them and snapping them with soulful poise.

Her final move was a tall, thin spin. She spun faster and faster every second. The golden ropes swung around her, like spokes on a wheel. They unbraided and frayed, thinly fanning outward. Liv spun even faster. The gold strings blurred into rich, rich rings—like those of Saturn.

Liv spun, standing tall on a single toe. Then she pulled her tall, eloquent spin into a tight, small ball, and then *pop* ... she disappeared. The gold strings busted from their rings, gusting in every direction. A moment later, they settled on the bedrock, all soft, gold, and still.

23

EmLights

Liv smiled humbly. "After that, I rushed out of the meditation shop and went to a park where I danced. I danced in public in broad daylight. People recorded with their phones. They recorded with their Domes. Within twenty minutes, a clip of my dance went viral. By the end of the day, a million people had seen me move."

"What's the best part about being an EmLight?" Ruxton asked.

"I never have to worry about money."

"The worst part?"

"The other EmLights..."

Someone started banging on the front door.

Sasha looked at Ruxton. "Will you answer it?"

Ruxton crossed the room and opened the door.

Eli Soto and Anna Moxy tripped into the shop.

A hoard of reporters hounded them.

"Mr. Soto! Mr. Soto! What inspired your drum solo?"

"Miss Moxy! Miss Moxy! Where did you learn to fly like that?"

Ruxton shut the door on the reporters.

Anna and Eli glared at Sasha.

"What did you do to us?"

"I made you masters of your craft."

"You made us EmLights!" Eli growled.

"Do you not want to be an EmLight?"

"No! I'm a real artist. EmLights are not. They're spoiled brats who ruin people's lives." Eli turned and saw Liv Xan. "Why is Liv Xan here?"

Anna Moxy crossed her arms. "Yeah, Sasha. What is this place? Some sort of celebrity cult?"

"No. This is a meditation shop. Everyone take a deep breath, and I will explain everything."

Anna squinted. Eli crinkled his nose.

"Come on. Deep breath in ..."

Ruxton, Sydney, Hugo, Liv, Anna, Eli—they all looked at each other.

"Deep breath in ..."

Everyone inhaled.

"Deep breath out ..."

Everyone exhaled.

"All of you are here for a reason."

"What reason?"

"I am planning an attack on Axiom."

"What? Why?"

"Because Axiom has plagued the world with Glow Domes. And Glow Domes have made people sick. Everywhere you go, you see glowing white circles on people's eyes. Every minute of every day, people are addicted. They're addicted or they're hurting each other." Sasha lowered his voice. "We, as a species, have lost the most important things about ourselves." He frowned. "Empathy is dead. Silence is dead. And focus, the sheer focus to accomplish anything worthwhile, is dead."

"Isn't that just life in 2072?" Anna said.

"It doesn't have to be that way."

"But how can you get rid of Glow Domes?" Eli asked. "They're deeply rooted in our culture. They're literally rooted in our eyes."

"Have you heard of Vicarium?"

"That new drug? Who hasn't heard of it?"

"The Vicarium parties are tomorrow night. Only the ultra-famous are invited."

"So *that's* why you turned us into EmLights. You want us to infiltrate those parties."

"Yes. There are three Vicarium parties. One in Los Angeles. One in Denver. One in New York. I want Eli to take Sydney to the party in Los Angeles. I want Liv to take Hugo to the party in Denver. And I want Anna to take Ruxton to the party in New York."

Hugo waved to Eli and Anna. "Hi, I'm Hugo. I'm Sasha's younger brother. I teach anthropology."

Eli stepped towards Hugo. "So you're related to this mysterious meditation teacher?"

"I am."

"And you're on board with this terrorist plot?"

"I suppose so."

"Why?"

Hugo sighed. "Do you know what happened five hundred years ago?"

"No idea."

"The Scientific Revolution happened. And when it happened, scientists were ecstatic. They saw the power of the scientific method. They *knew* that science could solve any problem. They *knew* that science could overcome any challenge *as long as* the public stayed educated—educated and empathetic." Hugo paused. "But something changed. We stopped educating our young. Instead of feeding them wisdom and knowledge, we fed them flashy screens and stroboscopic bullshit. And now we're paying the price." Hugo shook his head. "The fabric of society has come undone. We, as a collective, are falling apart. Science can't save us. All the technology in the world can't save us. Only *we* can save us."

"By *we*, you mean a dancer, a drummer, a pilot, two kids, and an anthropology professor?"

"Pretty much."

"What happens once we get inside the parties?" Anna asked.

"Hugo, Sydney, and Ruxton—they are armed with the Vastus meditation. One minute into the Vicarium tastings, they will whisper the words of the Vastus meditation and inflict silence on all the EmLights trying Vicarium."

"What will that do?"

"It will make the drug not work. It will make Vicarium look like a failure."

"That's it?"

"That's it."

"So a bunch of celebrities take a pill and it doesn't work. How does that put an end to Glow Domes?"

"This will hurt Axiom badly. After Vicarium fails, Axiom stocks will plummet, Glow Dome production will slow down, and, most importantly, the public will lose trust in Axiom and all of its products."

"Logistically," said Anna, "how does this work?"

"You, Eli, and Liv will be invited to the parties because you're EmLights."

"How do the two kids and the teacher get in?"

"They will be your Donor Dogs."

"Donor Dogs?"

"It's a new fad at high-end parties," Liv answered. "A Donor Dog is a kind of human pet."

Ruxton frowned. "I have to be a pet?"

"So we're disguised as pets," Hugo said, "but really we are keepers of silence."

"Correct."

"But there's only one keeper at each party. How do we whisper the words of the Vastus meditation to dozens of EmLights at the same time?"

Liv answered: "I will have an undercover worker at each party. They'll be disguised as waiters. Right before the Vicarium tastings, the waiters will give each of you a red rose. Inside the red rose will be a microphone. The microphone will remotely cut into the earpieces of all the EmLights trying Vicarium. After they take the pill, they will hear your voices. They will hear the words of the Vastus meditation."

"Then nothing happens? The drug is a dud?"

"Well," Sasha smirked, "the EmLights might squirm a little."

"Squirm?"

"A bad reaction to the drug—people will think."

Squirm is a light word, Hugo thought worriedly, as he remembered the silence.

"Hold up," Anna said. "Why do you think we're going to agree to this plan in the first place?"

"Because you owe me."

"We owe you?"

"I gave you your powers." Sasha nodded towards Liv. "I gave her ... her powers."

Liv split her long, flowy skirt.

Everyone stared at her leg.

Down near her ankle, shiny black beetles broke out of her skin. They crawled up and around her leg, like a spiral staircase. Once the beetles reached the top of her thigh, they burrowed back under her skin.

"What was that?" Anna asked.

"The Maxis meditation—it often leaves a mark."

"Do I have something like that?"

"Yes."

"How would I know?"

"You're the embodiment of speed. Just think about speed."

Anna closed her eyes. She thought about shooting forward.

From behind her ear, a streak of light went down the side of her neck. It flashed for half a second, like a temporary earring.

"Do I have a mark?" Eli asked.

"You're the embodiment of rhythm. Just think about rhythm."

Eli closed his eyes. He nodded to a rhythmic pulse.

Everyone stared at Eli's arm. It was coated with a blue shimmer. The shimmer pulsed down his arm. It pulsed across his palm. Then, with a tingling feeling, it sparkled on the tips of his fingers, and evaporated into the air.

"Well," Sasha said, "I helped you. Are you going to help me?"

Anna and Eli looked at each other nervously.

"All we have to do is take them to the party?"

"That's it."

"And then we're done with you?"

"Completely done."

Anna and Eli nodded hesitantly. "Okay, we're in."

Hugo pulled Sasha aside. "Are you sure this plan is foolproof?"

"We're going to find out."

"What about Dad?"

"What about him?"

"There's no way he'll know this was us, right?"

"Ha. Dad's expecting us."

"How do you know?"

"I saw him last year."

"What?"

"I visited the Sumzer mansion. That's how I found the plans for the Vicarium parties. That's when I ran into Dad."

24
Enlightenment Crown

Sasha wore linen slacks and a black hoodie. He snuck from room to room in the old Sumzer mansion. The night was quiet and the walls were red.

Sasha entered his father's office and rummaged through his father's desk.

"What's this?"

He found plans for the Vicarium parties—three separate parties in three separate states, all coordinated to showcase Vicarium as a huge publicity stunt.

Sasha took a picture with his phone.

"This could be big. This could be biblical."

Sasha put the plans back in the desk and made to leave the mansion. As he turned a corner, the lights came on.

Sasha stared down a long, carpeted hallway. The sides of the hallway displayed priceless artifacts and timeless art, many of them encased in glass. At the far end of the hallway, Sasha saw his father, Bill Sumzer.

"What are you doing here?" Bill asked.

Sasha unzipped his hoodie and dropped it on the floor. He reached inside the nearest display case and pulled out a long bone. It was a human femur.

"The femur," he said. "It's one of the oldest weapons in human history. Fairly lightweight, yet the strongest bone in the body." He rubbed the ball-end of the bone. "It makes for a perfect club."

Sasha walked up to a pedestal. On top of the pedestal was a Faberge egg.

"Don't you dare."

Sasha swung the femur into the egg. The egg exploded into colorful bits.

"Why did you do that?"

"Chaos, Dad. I just love chaos."

Sasha swung the femur again. He batted through a set of Egyptian embalming jars, spraying shards in every direction.

"Chaos is a gateway to change. And boy, do we need change!"

"We don't need change," Bill snapped. "The economy is stable."

"At what cost? The human mind is fucked."

"The human mind is fine."

"No one knows how to learn. No one knows how to love."

Sasha swung the femur and struck a medieval harp. He busted several strings, then raked across the rest.

Bill snarled. "For god's sake, Sasha. Why are you so hell-bent on Domes? They aligned every major network system. They created jobs and eradicated crime. They protected the economy from the student loan bubble. Don't you get it, Sasha? Glow Domes have *saved* millions of lives!"

"But is anyone really *living*?"

Sasha swung into a scepter, snapping it into halves.

"Damn it, Sasha! This is *my* house. These are *my* things."

"And these are *my* eyes. Look what you did to them."

Sasha wielded his rusty reds.

"You did that to yourself," Bill said. "You're a disgrace to the Sumzer family."

"A disgrace. Wow. You think very highly of yourself."

"I'm the world's first trillionaire. What do you have that I don't?"

"I have three meditations. Ancient ones. Powerful ones."

Bill scoffed.

"You don't think they're real?"

"Of course not."

"But Dad, don't you remember that day in the basement? I disappeared. You saw it with your own eyes."

"It was a trick of light."

"No, Dad. It was real. And it was just the beginning."

"The beginning of what?"

"The Maxis meditation. It took me a long time to figure it out, but once I did, I went to a place, an otherworldly place, a place with black waterfalls. And when I was there, I found these snakes, bright green snakes. They bit me. They sunk their fangs into my skin and filled my body with pain, all the pain in the world. It was unbearable." He paused. "But it was also enlightening. They showed me how to fix the world, how to heal the human mind."

Sasha approached his father. He raised the femur high.

"What are those?" Bill pointed at Sasha's arm, at the bright, wriggling greens inside his thick, blue veins.

"Those are my baby pain snakes. They show me how to heal!"

Sasha squeezed the femur. Bill shielded his face. Sasha swung low and deliberately missed. Bill collapsed to the floor and cowered.

"Jesus, Sasha. You're a lunatic."

"I'm a healer."

"What do you want from me?"

"I want you to watch as I rid the world of Glow Domes."

"That will never happen."

"I think it will."

"And then what? What could ever replace Glow Domes?"

"Bells."

"Bells?"

"The ringing and ringing of bells."

"Is this more of your meditation nonsense?"

Sasha chuckled. "Did you know: The very first bell tower—it didn't signify time; it signified Solosis."

"Solo-what?"

"Solosis—a soul-to-soul osmosis. A long time ago, humans discovered Solosis, this ability to funnel one life through another. A super-empathy, if you will. It was so powerful and so healing, people never wanted to forget it, so they erected a bell tower. And every so often they rang the bell. They reminded themselves to look each other in the eyes, and when they did, they would say a sacred phrase, one that unlocked a bond between two souls."

Sasha knelt down and looked at his father.

"Should we try it, Dad?"

Bill tensed with discomfort.

"Let's try it. I'll say the sacred phrase." Sasha took a deep breath. He spoke very slowly: "When eyes meet eyes, we find the prize—a reason to live, a reason to thrive."

Nothing.

Nothing happened.

Sasha stood tall and shook his head. "That's the thing with Solosis, Dad. You have to want it. You have to *want* a meaningful moment with another human being. But you don't want that, Dad. You don't want people looking at each other, finding meaning in each other. You just want people glued to their fucking Glow Domes."

Sasha stepped back. He swung the femur through a set of ancient perfume bottles; splinters of glass shot in his father's direction.

"Do you know how expensive those are?"

"All you care about is money. You don't care about people."

"That's your downfall, Sasha. You care too much about people, especially the poor ones."

"You mean LowLights?"

"Yes," Bill grunted. "You hung around LowLights as a kid. You always bee-lined to the poorest neighborhoods. I didn't know why, but I tried to stop it. I tried everything, including the dirt baths. Remember the dirt baths?"

"How could I forget..."

"Your mother and I, we bathed you in dirt for a month. We put dirt in your bed; we put it on your pillow. We thought if we gave you enough dirt, you would lose the taste for it, and you would finally stop visiting the LowLights." Bill paused. "I never understood... I never understood why you, Sasha—the heir to Axiom, the heir to the most powerful corporation on the planet—wanted nothing but LowLights and wanderers and mud."

"I guess I'm just a dirt boy, an earth boy. Don't water down my worth, boy!" Sasha raised the femur, then swung it into a mosaic; tiny tiles flew outward.

"I've had enough of this," Bill snarled. "Get out of my house."

"Your house. Your mansion—the one you paid for with money, money you got from rotting people's minds." Sasha knelt down again. "Tell me, Dad: Would you ever work in a Scrolling Center?"

Bill swallowed.

"Would you sit in a chair and watch clips of the news all day?"

Bill hesitated.

Sasha raised the femur.

"Would you?"

"No."

"Why not?"

"The studies..."

"What studies?"

"In the fifties and sixties, Axiom conducted private studies."

"Studies on what?"

"On smartphones and Glow Domes. The studies showed that Glowers had high rates of memory loss, cognitive issues." Bill coughed. "In the studies, every year was worse than the one before it. Our current projections show that in a few short years, the average Glower will have full-blown dementia by age thirty-five."

"Wow, you've robbed an entire generation." Sasha tapped the femur on the side of Bill's skull. "How would you like it if someone stole your mind?" Sasha pulled back the femur. He eyed Bill's temple on the side of his head. Just as he started to swing, he stopped. He suddenly noticed the display case above his father's head. It was a fifteenth-century enlightenment crown. The crown was made of pure gold. It gleamed with jewels of purple and red. Sasha reached for it. He pulled it out of the display case and placed it on his head.

Bill's eyes flooded with fear. "Why are you like this?"

"When I was a kid, you never supported me. You laughed at my meditations. Now I'm going to laugh when your empire crumbles."

Sasha turned and walked away from his father; shattered glass crunched under his feet. When Sasha reached the end of the hallway, he picked up his hoodie and slung it over his shoulder.

"You're a crazy person, Sasha."

"It takes a crazy person to save *this* world."

Sasha walked away with a crown on his head and a human femur in his hand.

His father remained on the floor, surrounded by broken, battered art. After a minute of silence, he heard Sasha's voice. It echoed throughout the mansion: "Soon the bells will ring! The bells will ring and stir the soul! Our minds will heal and again feel whole!"

25

Bullet Trains

Hugo suddenly realized that he barely knew his father. He only knew him through Sasha's perspective. There was the day in the basement, of course, and Bill was not a good father to Hugo then, but outside of that day, Hugo hardly had memories of his parents. Anything he knew about them was from the shadow of Sasha as the firstborn. Hugo knew that no family was perfect, but he wondered if there was any goodness in his parents, anything normal about them before Hugo came along.

Hugo said to Sasha: "Can I ask you something?"

"What?"

"When you were young, really young, before you got into your meditations, did Mom and Dad ever take you camping?"

"No."

"Out for ice cream?"

"No."

"To a toy store?"

"No."

"Did they ever congratulate you when you got a good report card?"

"No. They were never around. Remember? They were always busy at Axiom."

Hugo sighed. He knew growing up in the richest family in America was going to have its drawbacks, but, he wondered, as he looked at Sasha's rust-red eyes, did his role models have to be this ... intense?

Sasha looked at Liv, Eli, Anna, Hugo, Sydney, and Ruxton.

"Everyone get a good night's rest. Tomorrow is game day."

"Let's wreck some Vicarium parties!" Ruxton beamed.

"Tomorrow morning, Anna and Ruxton will take the bullet train to New York, and Sydney and Eli will take the train to Los Angeles."

"What about us?" Hugo asked, as he pointed to himself and Liv.

"The bullet train to Denver is delayed, so we will take Liv's private plane to Denver." Sasha paused. "Does anyone have any questions?"

Everyone looked at each other. They shook their heads.

"Ruxton, Sydney, Hugo—you remember the words of the Vastus meditation?"

The three of them nodded.

"Good." Sasha smiled. "Tomorrow, we rid the world of mindlessness."

●

The next day, Sydney and Ruxton went to the Albuquerque train station.

As they stood in the lobby, a giant screen loomed over them, playing commercials. One commercial had two LowLights sitting on a raggedy couch scrolling through their phones. One of the LowLights shoved their phone in the other's face: "Oh my gosh, you *have* to watch this."

The other reciprocated. "No, no. You *have* to watch *this*."

The camera panned to an Axiom salesman.

"Obnoxious, right? Don't be a screen-pusher. Get Glow Domes. Share all your favorite clips with the blink of an eye. Blink twice to send a clip. And blink once to receive a clip!"

The camera panned to a nicer couch with two Glowers. Their eyes glowed with milky whiteness. Each of them blinked rapidly, sharing half-second clips with each other.

The salesman's voice sounded again: "Don't be a screen-pusher! Get Glow Domes! Go Glow!"

The screen faded to black. Then the speakers blasted at twice the volume: "Tonight! Tonight! Tonight! The Vicarium parties are finally here!"

A blue dot appeared on the screen.

"See this pill? This is Vicarium. Take Vicarium and you can *feel* the things you see in your Domes!"

The blue dot enlarged to a tall spinning oval.

"Tune in tonight at 9 p.m. Central Time! Watch the Vicarium parties! See what EmLights have to say about Vicarium!"

The blue pill slowed its spin, then finally, it stopped. The pill was engraved with the letter: V.

Ruxton and Sydney looked at each other.

"Good luck in New York."

"Good luck in LA."

"Ruxton ..."

"Yeah?"

"I love you."

"I love you, Sydney. More than a bee loves flowers."

They kissed.

Then they walked in opposite directions.

Anna saw Ruxton. "Hey kid! Over here. We're at the back of the train."

"The back?"

"We have our own private car."

"Oh snap! How did we score a private car?"

"I'm an EmLight now. I get high-end luxury shit wherever I go."

"Did you even go through security?"

"Nope."

"Really?"

"Really, really."

"What happened when you got here?"

"I walked through the front door. A dozen people lost their shit. *Anna Moxy! Anna Moxy!* They started taking pictures. Then security jumped on me, escorted me through a secret hallway. Said I had a private car waiting to take me to the Vicarium parties."

"Have you been inside it yet?"

"Nah. I was waiting for you."

Anna and Ruxton walked up to the private car at the back of the bullet train.

Anna swiped a badge. The door slid open.

"Whoa!" Ruxton said. "This is nice!"

He walked the length of the car several times. The floor was carpeted, a royal red.

"Anna! Look!"

Ruxton pointed to a crystal bowl. It had a fanned-out assortment of toothpicks.

"Are these gold?" He picked one up. "These toothpicks are pure gold!"

Ruxton balanced a toothpick on his bottom lip. Then he flicked it with his tongue. The toothpick launched upward, flipping end over end. Then it fell, and Ruxton caught it between his lips.

"Cute trick."

Ruxton plopped into a big leather chair.

"So Anna, aside from that chimney stunt, what's the sickest thing you've done with a plane?"

"Hmm." Anna thought for a moment. "In my hometown, in Canada, there's a lake. It's a big lake. In the winter, it's frozen. But in the summer, when its thawed, the water is still. Real still. Like a mirror. Anyway, I took my jet out to the lake one day. I flew really close to the water. Just inches above it. Then I cut my engines, and my plane skipped across the water. Just like a pebble."

"No way. How many skips did you get?"

"Six."

"Six skips? That's awesome."

"It's okay. My aunt did it before me. She got eight skips."

"Your aunt is a stunt pilot too?"

"My family is full of stunt pilots. Pilots and drunks. We fly hard. And we drink hard."

Anna opened the mini-bar. She poured herself a whiskey.

"So," she said, "how'd you get tied up with this Sasha character?"

"He, uh ... he helped me get sober."

Anna held up her glass. "Cheers to your sobriety."

"Hey, thanks!"

She sipped her whiskey.

Ruxton looked out the window. "Huh. We're moving. I didn't even notice. These bullet trains are smooth. Smoother than a cloud."

Anna thought about clouds. She thought about piercing them with her plane.

A ray of yellow light flashed downward from behind her ear.

"Hey, Anna."

"What?"

"You did the Maxis meditation."

"Yeah."

"What was it like?"

"Brutal. Awesome."

"What happened?"

"I got crushed by boulders, by the weight of a thousand mountains."

"Then what?"

"I escaped gravity. I became faster than the speed of light."

"So cool."

"Did you do the Maxis meditation?"

"Na, I did Solosis."

"What's that?"

"It's like a super-empathy. Sydney and I did it together. I felt her whole life. And she felt mine. Then we helped each other. We healed each other."

"Young love. So cute." Anna finished her whiskey.

Ruxton leaned forward. He asked, hesitantly, "Do you have a special someone?"

"Sort of."

"On again, off again?"

"Yeah. It depends on her mood. She's bat-shit crazy."

"Do you love her?"

"I love the rush." Anna chuckled. "One time, we were making love in my bedroom. Right as things got heated, she grabbed a box of matches off the nightstand. She lit them one by one and threw them on the floor, a carpet floor. Little fires started around the bed. She wouldn't let me put them out until we both finished. So we finished. We finished loud and hard. Almost burnt the house down, but man was it worth it."

Ruxton laughed in his seat.

Anna shrugged. "I like a girl who's just like America—fucking insane."

Ruxton laughed some more. "Anna, can we be friends after this? Can Sydney and I visit you in your hometown in Canada? You could fly us around. Give us a tour of the Canadian Rockies. Doesn't that sound nice?"

"Sounds nice for you. Sounds like a chore for me."

Ruxton smiled. "Yeah. We're friends."

•

Sydney stepped into the private car at the back of the bullet train. The walls had sleek blue stripes, and the ceiling was peppered with stars, little asterisks of silver and white. They matched Sydney's hair.

Eli slouched into a big, leather chair and looked at his phone. "This EmLight status is no joke. I have three thousand emails."

"From who?"

Eli scrolled through his inbox.

"Ad companies. Ad companies. News outlets. More ad companies." He rubbed his forehead. "This is why I didn't want to become famous."

"Yeah, but ..."

"But what?"

"You nailed that drum solo. You drummed your wife's story."

"You're right." He nodded. "I wish she could've heard it." Eli opened an email. "Oh shit."

"What is it?"

"An email from Axiom. It's my formal invitation to the Vicarium parties."

"Does it say anything?"

"It has a list."

"A list of what?"

"Everyone invited to the parties."

Eli scrolled through the list. "Sydney, this is bad."

"What do you mean?"

"Every person on this list is a skezzer. Every one of them got famous by recording another person's pain."

Sydney's stomach churned. "Are you serious?"

"Yeah. These are not good EmLights. These are bad people."

Sydney groaned.

Eli put down his phone. "Have you heard about the latest skezz?"

She shook her head.

"Happened to a guy named Toby Lee. Big movie director. Made a lot of brilliant films."

•

Toby was on set, coordinating with a camera crew. The crew loved working with Toby, even though he was shy and strange. It was known that Toby had a special voice recorder. He kept his notes on there, his on-the-go movie ideas.

That day, a young intern, a Glower, snuck into Toby's trailer and found the recorder. The intern listened to it. He found something embarrassing, so he took the recorder and hooked it up to the sound system of the movie set. He played Toby's notes to the entire film crew. Everyone stopped and listened. They heard Toby's voice. At first, Toby mentioned a movie idea, but after that, he made wacky, fetish-like sounds. He crooned and babbled; he let loose with giggles. He even made sexual sounds. It was part of his process, his private, creative process, but here it was, all of it, out in the open for everyone to hear.

People stared at Toby; they looked at him like he was a freak. Toby lost it. He spiraled into a nasty fit, tipping over speakers, kicking through equipment. And the whole time, the intern watched with white rings in his eyes. He recorded Toby's worst moment ... and shared it with the world.

•

"What happened to Toby?" Sydney asked.

"Devastated. Said he'll never direct another movie."

"And the intern? The Glower?"

"He's famous, an EmLight. He'll be at the party tonight." Eli squeezed a drumstick in his hand. "Fucking skezzers. No talent. No skills. All they do is drive a good person to a bad place. And for what? Instant fame? Internet fame?"

Eli snapped the drumstick in half.

"Eli." Sydney leaned forward. "Look at me."

Eli looked at Sydney's frosty blue eyes. "I'm sorry," he said. "I just miss my wife. I miss Rosie."

"I know."

"Don't you miss your mom?"

"Every day."

"Is that why you joined Sasha? To get revenge?"

"I wouldn't call it revenge."

"What would you call it?"

"I don't know. I just want change. I want people to be better people."

Eli looked at her like she was a younger sister. "You're a good kid, Syd."

Sydney smiled shyly.

Eli fiddled with his broken drumstick.

It was quiet for a while.

Then Eli looked up. "So, what's with this Vastus meditation?"

"Ha! It's a trip."

"What does it do?"

"It cleans your mind of junk. Wipes out all the noise."

"Then what?"

"Then nothing. Nothing but silence."

"Hmm."

"What's wrong?" Sydney asked.

"It's just, back at the meditation shop, Sasha mentioned the silence. But the way he talked about it, the way he said it, he made it seem like a weapon."

"Like I said, it cleans your mind of junk. The more junk you have in your brain, the more painful the process."

"And Glowers—they've been filling their brains with junk for years ..."

26
Sad Song Singer

Ruxton left Anna's private car at the back of the train. He visited the snack car to quickly eat a sandwich. As he finished his last bite, he heard a beautiful hum, a smooth tune. He turned around. He saw a girl sitting in a booth by the windows of the train. She had blonde hair and bright red earrings.

Ruxton walked over. He slipped into the booth.
"Hi!"
"Hi …"
"I like your humming."
"Thanks."
"What do you do?"
"I'm a starving artist."
"What kind?"
"I sing."
"Nice. I'm Ruxton, by the way."
"Julie. Julie James."
"What's got you down, Julie?"
"What do you mean?"
"Your tune—it's super smooth, but very sad."
"I like to be sad."

"I used to like to be sad too."

"You're not one of those positivity freaks, are you?"

"No, no."

"Then why are you bugging me?"

"Just like to hear people's stories. What's your story, Julie? How'd you get into singing?"

"I've always sung. Ever since I was a kid."

"Whose stuff do you sing?"

"My own."

"You write your own songs?"

Julie nodded.

"Are they all sad?"

"Mostly. Yeah."

"What was your first sad song?"

Julie thought for a moment. "When I was six, I wrote a song about potatoes."

"Let's hear it!"

Julie cleared her throat. She sang softly: "I waaaant to be a po-taaaa-toe. Bury me underground. I waaaant to be a po-taaaa-toe. Safe and round and sound."

"That's good! That's not sad at all!"

Julie shrugged. "My songs got sadder as I got older."

"How 'bout your early teens. What was the best song you wrote in your early teens?"

"Mm. That's when I got into story songs."

"Story songs?"

"I like songs that tell a story."

"Let's hear one."

"I won't sing it. It's too long. But, it's a song about a scarecrow."

"A scarecrow?"

"Yeah. This scarecrow, he never sees crows, because that's his job, to keep them away. But he doesn't know that, because he's never seen a crow. He thinks he has no purpose. He thinks he's just standing in a field, wasting his life away. One day, he leaves the field. He goes on a quest. Meets all kinds of people. Tries all kinds of things. Then he passes a pumpkin field. It's full of crows. They're pecking at the pumpkins. So the scarecrow, he scares them away. And he realizes his purpose. He protects the pumpkins." Julie waved her hand. "In the song, it sounds better. It rhymes. It has more flow. But you get the idea."

Ruxton gave Julie a confused look.

"What?"

"That's not sad either. I mean, it starts sad, but it ends well."

"Thanks, I guess."

"What was your first sad song, like real sad?"

"When I was sixteen, I wrote a song about a lighthouse keeper."

Ruxton nodded. "Lighthouse keeper. I like where this is going."

Julie continued: "This lighthouse keeper—she has a twin. Together, they take care of this lighthouse, out on a pile of rocks in the middle of the ocean. One day, they realize, the ocean water is rising. They don't know what to do. So one of them takes the boat. She sets out to find answers, to see what's going on. Might take a year. Might take a few years. But every year, the water rises. It gets higher and higher. And the other twin, she's trapped at the top of the lighthouse. One day, the water reaches her. It rises above her head. It rises above the light in the lighthouse. The lighthouse and her are gone—completely underwater." Julie paused. "Eventually, the other twin comes back with the boat. But she can't find the lighthouse. She can't find her twin sister."

"Did she at least find answers? About the rising waters?"

"No. She never found any answers. And the last years of the lighthouse ... they were spent alone ... alone and scared."

"Now that," Ruxton said, "is sad."

Julie looked out the window. A tear rolled down her cheek.

"I'm sorry," Ruxton said. "I didn't mean to ..."

"No, it's not you." She wiped her cheek. "I love my songs. I love to share them. It's just ... people suck, Ruxton."

"How so?"

"I've been on tour for a year now. Small gigs. Little shows here and there. I sing my heart out. I put everything into my songs. But audiences, they're just ... they're so dead these days. They look up at me with those white rings in their eyes. They have to record everything, always. They can't just *be* in a moment."

Julie fanned out her fingernails, bright orangey reds. Then she closed them. She made a fist. "You know what's even worse?"

"What?"

"If I actually *made it*, if I became a star one day, my life as a singer would be over."

"What do you mean?"

"The major labels, the big contract deals, once you sign them, they create a synthetic copy of your voice. Then they use the copy to generate more catchy songs, more trendy tunes."

"But then, what would *you* do ... as the actual singer?"

"I would just exist for the tabloids. I would be a source of scandal—breakups, fuckups, and rehab."

Julie lowered her head. "I tell you, Ruxton, this industry is brutal. I love singing, but this shit is hard. Some days, I just wanna quit. I wanna give up. Like, what is the point? Why put *so* much out there if I'm never gonna get anything back?"

Ruxton looked at Julie intently.

"Can I try something?"

"I guess."

Ruxton put his arms on the table.

"Here, hold my hands."

She gave him a look.

"Just for a few seconds."

Slowly, she reached out. She held his hands.

"Now, look me in the eyes."

Julie looked into his green, green eyes.

"Now, listen. Listen carefully."

Julie leaned forward.

Ruxton took a deep breath. He said, very slowly: "When eyes meet eyes, we find the prize—a reason to live, a reason to thrive."

Suddenly, the color in their irises stirred. It moved like molten rings.

Julie's entire life funneled through Ruxton, every day, every year, every laugh, every tear. He felt what it was like to sing with her pipes. He stood on her stage night after night. He belted out rhymes with all of his might. He squeezed and he squeezed on a little black mic. He felt every chorus. He felt every verse. Every song was a blessing, a blessing and a curse. He felt what she needed, her spirit, her thirst. He put her soul forward, he put her life first.

Nine seconds had passed.

The color in their irises stilled.

Julie pushed back in her seat.

"What the heck was that?"

"It's called Solosis. It's like a super-empathy." He smiled. "I felt your whole life."

"You did, didn't you?"

"It showed me something, a song, one you've never sung in public."

"You felt that?"

"Yeah. And it was great! You should sing it."

"Right now?"

"Yeah!"

"Ruxton ..."

"We're in the snack car, not the quiet car."

"I don't know ..."

"Come on."

"No one wants to hear it."

"*I* want to hear it."

"Mmmmmm."

"It's a good song. It's got that WAKE UP factor."

"I still don't know."

"Come on, Julie. I felt your voice during Solosis. Now I gotta hear it, I mean *really* hear it. Please, Julie. Just sing. Sing that one song. Sing that one song, Julie!"

"Jeez! Okay, okay. Alright. Just give me a second. Hang on."

Julie closed her eyes. She took a deep breath. Then she sang softly:

"What does it mean ... to have all you need?

And crave like a critter ... all shaky and bitter?

Is it a lie? A test? A joke? A jest?

Does anyone feel at home?

In this endless row of highs and lows?

I love and I care. I strive and I cry.

I give and I share. I tremble and hide.

I just want peace—a deep sleep in my bones.

I want to feel good when I'm all alone.

I want to feel good.

I want to feel great.
I want to break free.
I want an escape!"
Ruxton stood up and started to clap. "Damn, Julie! You've got pipes!"
Julie raised her voice. She belted out lines swiftly and quickly.
"An angel heard my harm—the dark songs that I sing.
This angel had trinkets and charms and nice things.
She met me on a farm, and I asked for her wings.
But she gave me an alarm and it started to ring!"
Ruxton continued to clap. He stepped in beat, moving closer and closer to a row of Glowers. They sat in lounge chairs with white circles on their eyes.
"Sing it, Julie! Sing it!"
"I reel back from that nap and lift up my eyes!
I reel back from that nap and lift up my life!"
Ruxton hauled back his arm and slapped one of the Glowers across the face. Drool slung from the Glower's mouth and landed south.
"Reel *back* from that *nap*! And lift up your eyes!"
Ruxton slapped the next Glower in line.
"Reel *back* from that *nap*!"
Slap!
"Lift up your lives! Reel *back* from that *nap*!"
Slap!
"Lift up your eyes! Reel *back* from that *nap*!"
Slap!
"Lift up your lives! Reel *back* from that *nap*!"
Slap!
"Lift up your eyes! Reel *back* from that *nap*!"
Slap!

"Lift up your—"

"What in the hell is going on here?"

A train conductor entered the snack car. He caught the last few seconds of Julie singing and Ruxton slapping. Seven Glowers were groaning and moaning with one red cheek.

The conductor pointed at Ruxton and angrily charged. "You can't just *slap* other passengers like that!"

Ruxton giggled. "They're fine."

The conductor grabbed Ruxton by the arm. "You're coming with me!"

"No he's not." Anna Moxy entered the snack car.

The conductor let go of Ruxton. "Miss … Miss Moxy. I'm so sorry. Is he with you?"

"Yeah, he's with me. So you're gonna let this slide, cool?"

The conductor stuttered. He had never met someone as famous as Anna Moxy. "I, uh, suppose we can let it slide." He paused. "Is everything suited to your needs in your private car?"

"It is. Now scram."

The conductor left the snack car.

Julie rushed up to Ruxton and gave him a hug.

"Thank you," she said. "I needed that."

Ruxton smiled. "Just keep singing, Julie. Just keep singing."

Julie stepped back. "What's that thing called? That empathy thing?"

"Solosis. You can try it with anyone. Anyone who's open. Open to heal."

The train turned around a bend. Everyone looked out the windows. They saw the New York City skyline. In the heart of the city, there stood a 150-story building, the tallest building on the East Coast. It was called the Serdula building.

Anna pointed to the top of the building, where lights glittered and spotlights shone. "That's where the party is. The Vicarium party."

Ruxton gulped. He had never been to anything so extravagant. He had never been to anything so up high. The tallest thing he ever occupied was a tree house. But this—he stared at the Serdula building—this was next-level.

27

Times Square

The bullet train slowed to a stop. Ruxton and Anna stepped off the train. They were at the Times Square station, the busiest station in America. People rushed in every direction. Trains started and stopped with a faint, electric hum.

Anna opened her phone and read an email.

"Who's that?" Ruxton asked.

"It's Liv. She said we have to get dressed for the party. There's a tailor waiting for us across the street, on the other side of Times Square."

Anna put away her phone. They went up a set of stairs. Anna moved quickly. Ruxton tried not to lag. They pushed through a turnstile, then through a set of doors. They reached the outside. They were in Times Square.

The place was packed. It was full of Glowers. All of them had glowing white rings in their eyes. They blinked to take pictures. They blinked in every direction as screens and signs flashed all around them.

Anna and Ruxton looked up. Above Times Square, there was a huge glass dome. It was called the Fireworks Sky. Every few seconds, a firework would explode, and digital sparks would fly across the glass. The mayor had it installed a few years ago. She thought Times Square was losing its pizzazz.

Anna shook her head. "Ever since they installed those fake fireworks, this place has tripled in grossness." She started walking forward.

"Can you see the tailor's shop?"

"I think so." Anna peered over the crowd. "But we have to get through these people."

Boom. Everyone heard a loud explosion. The digital fireworks came with surround-sound speakers. Tourists looked up and went: "Ooooooo ... Aaahhhhhh."

Anna slowed down.

"What's wrong?" Ruxton asked.

"I can barely move."

Suddenly, the crowd let out a collective gasp. Everyone pointed up. Ruxton turned his head and squinted. "Are those ... people?"

The Fireworks Sky had several steel ladders. The ladders arched under the glass, almost like monkey bars. The ladders were maintenance ladders. Restricted access. But, somehow, six people were climbing them. And they were not maintenance workers. They were barefoot. They wore white leotards.

"What is happening?"

The six people reached the height of the Fireworks Sky. Then they lowered two wooden bars.

"Are those ... trapeze swings?"

One of the people unrolled a flag. It read: *TRAPEZE-SQUEEZE@2072.*

"Oh my god," said Anna. "They're trapeze artists. It's a publicity stunt."

The entire crowd looked up. Everyone had white rings in their eyes; they recorded every second. High above the crowd, one of the trapezists chalked up her hands. She lowered to a swing and grabbed the wooden bar. Her feet dangled. She rocked back and forth, back and forth. She swung wide and slipped off the bar.

The crowd gasped. She flung forward and reached. She caught the other swing. The crowd below shouted and cheered. They uploaded their videos.

The stunt immediately went viral. Thousands more people began pouring into Times Square. Every street and alley gushed with Glowers, all of them feverishly biting at a newfound nugget of hype.

"Anna!" Ruxton shouted. "I can't move!"

"Me neither!"

A stranger pushed into Anna. She felt his humid breath on her neck.

"What do we do?"

"I don't know!"

Everyone looked up. Their mouths hung open and their eyes glowed. High above, the trapezists prepared for their next move. One of them lowered onto the swing. He grabbed the wooden bar and pointed his toes downward. He swayed back and forth, back and forth. Everyone held their breath. He swung forward and slipped off the bar. He twisted through space. A digital firework exploded behind him. He grabbed the other bar. Then he hung by one hand and waved to the crowd.

Everyone cheered. They uploaded their videos. More and more people flooded into Times Square.

Anna yelled at the man in front of her. "Hey! Buddy! I need to get out of here!"

The man ignored her.

"It's an emergency!"

"Lady, this *is* the emergency."

"What do you mean?"

"We're in the splat zone. If they fall, we're the first to record guts and gore."

"You're sick."

The man shrugged. He looked up at the trapeze artists.

The trapezists prepared for their next big move. This time, it was a two-person stunt. One man lowered to the wooden bar. He hooked his knees over the bar and hung upside down. The other trapezist lowered her body to the opposite bar and hung from her hands. Each of them rocked back and forth, back and forth. They mirrored each other's swings. Then, the woman pointed her toes and let go. She spun through the escrow. The man grabbed her ankles and she hung upside down. She smiled at the crowd.

Suddenly, the man's hand slipped. He lost one of her legs. She dangled by an ankle and screamed with fright.

Below, the crowd gasped; then it began to chant.

"Fall, fall, fall ... Fall! Fall! Fall! ... Fall! Fall! Fall!"

The trapezist dangled in fear. Below her, she saw thousands of tiny white rings—hungry eyes sizing up her demise.

"Fall! Fall! Fall! ... Fall! Fall! Fall! ... Fall! Fall! Fall!"

The trapezist managed to grab his partner's leg. He hoisted her up to the wooden bar. Together, they stood. They smiled in praise at their own gallant save.

But the crowd booed. They wanted failure. They craved failure.

Ruxton yelled, "Anna!"

"What?"

"The party is starting soon! We gotta get outta here!"

Anna pushed on every person around her, but no one would budge.

"I have an idea. But it's dangerous."

"Go for it."

Anna reached in her pocket and pulled out a controller. It had a small screen, two toggles, and a few buttons.

"What are you doing?"

"Dropping a pin."

Ten minutes later, a small black jet hovered into Times Square. It carefully floated under the glass dome. The crowd forgot about the trapeze artists. Instead, they fixated on the mysterious black jet.

"Anna, is that *you*?"

She nodded.

"When did you get a remote-controlled jet?"

"Ordered it online. Right before we left Albuquerque."

"Was it expensive?"

"Very. But hey, I'm rich and famous, remember?"

Anna worked the toggles on the remote control. The jet slowly turned. It pointed its burners towards the trapeze artists. They felt the heat. It singed their hair. Terrified, they pulled up their swings and hurried down the ladder as fast as they could.

"There," Anna smiled. "The trapeze show is over. Everyone go home."

But no one moved. They stared at the jet and held their breaths.

"Anna!" Ruxton shouted. "All you did was create a new problem!"

"Shit. I guess you're right."

"Can you fly it out of here?"

"Uh, yeah." Anna thumbed the toggles, but a stranger pushed into her back. She accidentally jerked the controls. The jet's burners, its bottom burners, they fired. The jet pushed up. It rammed against the glass of the Fireworks Sky.

"Oh, fuck." Anna pushed a button, but she pushed the wrong button. The jet pushed harder. It cracked the glass.

"You're making it worse!"

"I know! The controls are stuck!"

The crowd looked up. They gaped at the jet, at the crack in the glass.

Anna tapped buttons, but the more she tried to fix the situation, the worse it got. The jet pressed upward and the glass cracked again. It fractured, like lightening.

A woman screamed, "Let me out of here!"

But the crowd didn't budge. They stared and recorded.

"Anna, fix it!"

"I'm trying!"

She pressed a button. The jet turned. A sheet of glass broke from the dome and fell to the crowd below. Right before it hit the crowd, the glass glittered with a digital firework, then it crushed several people and exploded into pieces.

The jet turned again. The entire dome shook. Another sheet of glass broke from the dome and fell. It fell edge-first. It cut through four people, like a free-falling guillotine.

Finally, the danger was real. People screamed. They ran. The crowd loosened. Ruxton and Anna were able to move. But the place was chaotic. People ran in every direction, as glass fell at random. Ruxton put his hands over his head. He ducked. He dodged. He tried to follow Anna.

A sheet of glass, the size of a bus, landed to their right. It exploded into pieces and the pieces shot sideways. They nicked Ruxton's face.

Anna reached the tailor's shop and opened the door. They rushed inside.

"Can you stop the jet?"

Anna pressed buttons on the controller as she looked out the window. The jet descended, but the glass was still cracking and pieces still fell.

"Fuck! I could get in so much trouble for this!"

"What are you gonna do?"

Anna pressed a button. The jet turned. It blasted out of Times Square.

"Where is it going?"

"The Atlantic Ocean. I set its coordinates for the water. To drown itself."

"So no one can trace it back to you?"

"That's the idea. I bought it with crypto money and a fake avatar, so hopefully I'll be safe."

They looked outside. Fake fireworks fell from a fake sky. Many were injured. Several were dead. And Times Square was littered with glass.

Ruxton swallowed. A wave of guilt washed over him. "Did we ... Did we kill those people?"

"It was an accident."

"A really big accident."

"Don't feel bad about it."

"How?"

"Those people out there, they wanted something to *fall*, and they got what they fucking wanted."

"Anna, that's dark."

"Toughen up, buttercup. It's a dark world we're livin' in." Anna turned. She walked further into the tailor's shop. "Let's get dressed. We have a party to go to."

Ruxton continued to stare out the window. He saw a group of medics. They were trying to reach an injured person, someone with a severed arm. But the medics couldn't reach the man. He was surrounded by Glowers. They stared at his stump, his bloody stump. They recorded it, uploaded it. Even the man himself, the man with no arm, he stared at his own stump. He recorded it, all of it—the blood, the bone, the squirting arteries—he shared it online. He already had a thousand likes by the time the medics got to him. The medics tied a tourniquet around the man's stump. They worked quickly to save his life. But the man told the medics to slow down. He said, "Can you explain what you're doing while you're doing it? I'm recording this for my blog."

Ruxton sighed. This was his first time outside of Albuquerque. This was the first time he really got to see the world. And he did *not* like what he saw.

Ruxton knew he had his own baggage. He knew he had only been sober for a week, but still, when he looked at the Glowers, at the white rings in their eyes, at the blood and the chaos and the constant recording, at the addiction to hype, the addiction to failure, he couldn't help but think: How did things get this way?

28

Shakers and Movers

Hugo sat on Liv's private plane. He rested his head against the window as he tried to catch some sleep. As soon as he started to drift, the sound system squeaked. The pilot cleared his throat: "We are now beginning our final descent into Denver. The current temperature in Denver is seventy-six degrees and the weather is partly cloudy. If you look out the left-side windows, you will see downtown Denver. In the center of Denver, you will see the Haines building. At 150 stories, it is the tallest building in Colorado, and tonight, the building is bright. Lots of color. Lots of lights. Tonight, the Haines building is hosting one of the Vicarium parties. And the party is starting soon. That is all." The pilot turned off the sound system.

Hugo yawned. Liv walked over and sat next to him.

"Hey," she said.

"Hey, what's up?"

"Just checking in. Making sure you're okay."

"Well, I lost my job. And now I have nothing better to do than take down a corporate empire, so sure, I guess I'm okay."

Liv tilted her head. "Are you nervous?"

"Yeah."

"About the plan?"

Hugo didn't answer. He looked back at Sasha.

"Do you trust him?"

"I do."

Liv looked at Sasha. They smiled at each other.

Hugo's eyes widened. "You don't just trust him. You love him."

Liv blushed in admission.

"Oh my god. Are you two an item?"

"We did Solosis a few years back. After that, things kind of clicked."

"Wow, I have so many questions."

"Like what?"

"I don't know. I've never met anyone who's been closer to Sasha than I have. Granted, I have a weird relationship with Sasha. We have only known each other when we've been fighting for our lives or struggling to survive." Hugo thought for a moment. "But I do have one question."

"What is it?"

"Does Sasha ever come down?"

"What do you mean?"

"Does he ever come down from his intensity?"

"He does."

"What does that look like?"

"Sometimes, I have trouble sleeping. I can't shut off my mind. When I'm tossing and turning, Sasha will lie in bed with me. He'll do this cute trick, this mini-meditation. He'll say *wiggle your toes*. And I'll wiggle my toes. He'll say *wiggle your knees*. And I'll wiggle my knees. He'll say *wiggle your hips*. And I'll wiggle my hips. He'll say *wiggle your arms*. And I'll wiggle my arms. He'll say *wiggle your head*. And I'll wiggle my head. And then, together, we'll go back to the toes. We'll do the whole thing again. We'll do it a few times. And before I know it, my mind is in my body. My body is at rest. And I quickly fall asleep." Liv paused. "Sasha can be peaceful. He wants peace. But it's an unquiet time full of unquiet minds. And he's mad about it."

"Ha! You can say that again."

"Don't you get mad, Hugo?"

"Mad at what?"

"At people, at the world."

"Sometimes."

"Do you ever get mad enough to want to change things?"

"You're implying that I have free will *to* change things."

"Do you not believe in free will?"

"I believe in shakers and movers."

"What do you mean?"

"I've studied a lot of history, and from what I can tell, most of humanity's course of action is determined by a select few—emperors and billionaires, revolutionaries and manic underdogs. The rest of us—we're just here for the ride."

Sasha walked up to Hugo and Liv. In his hand, he held a roll of black tape. He tossed it to Hugo.

"Tear off a piece. Wrap it around your neck."

"Why?"

"It denotes you as a Donor Dog."

"Oh right, I'm a human pet." He paused. "I get the *Dog* part, but what's the *Donor* part?"

"It means you need an organ transplant."

"Huh?"

"It's a whole thing at these types of parties. If you're a LowLight who needs an organ transplant, you can agree to be an EmLight's Dog for an evening. As a Donor Dog, you follow the EmLight around, you get mocked, you get ridiculed, you even get used for games, and in exchange, the EmLight pays for a brand-new synthetic organ and the operation."

"How come I've never heard of this?"

"Non-disclosure agreements. If the Dogs don't obey, they don't get the organ they need."

"But I don't need an organ ..."

"We forged your application."

"Liv, this is messed up."

"I know. I know. Twenty years ago, this would have been an outrage. But today, it's the new fad, and it's the only way to get you into that party."

Hugo sighed. "What organ do I need?"

"As my Donor Dog, you need a new heart."

Hugo put his hand over his chest.

Suddenly, the pilot threw open the door to the cockpit.

"Miss Xan! We have a problem!"

Sasha and Liv rushed up to the cockpit.

"What is it?"

"It's the front wheel."

"What about it?"

"We put down the landing gear, but the front wheel is stuck sideways. It won't rotate all the way."

"What can we do?"

"We can call a mechanic to troubleshoot, but it might take some time. Instead of landing, we'll have to circle the airport until a mechanic gives us our next steps."

There was a long pause.

Then Sasha growled: "No."

"Excuse me?" said the pilot.

"We're going to land *now*."

"But sir, we can't. The front wheel—it's stuck *sideways*."

"Bring the plane in low, long, and with the wind. We'll shred the wheel and trash the gear. The plane will slide on her belly."

"But we might have other options…"

"We don't have time for other options. We're going to land *now*."

The pilot looked at Sasha, at his red, menacing eyes.

"Now, captain."

The pilot looked ahead as the plane approached the runway. For a long time, the plane teased the ground. Everyone braced as the back wheels screeched. Then the nose dipped down. The front wheel, stuck sideways, grazed the pavement and popped. Then the landing gear snapped, and the entire plane dropped. It dropped to its belly and barreled down the runway. As the metal scraped the pavement, sparks blew out the sides.

Liv closed her eyes.

The plane ground to a stop.

Everyone breathed.

Sasha rubbed Liv's back. "You okay?"

"Let's never do that again."

Sasha shouted to the back of the plane: "Hugo! You okay?"

"My bones!"

"What about your bones?"

"They're rattled!"

"It's good to rattle your bones!"

"Why?"

"Wakes 'em up!" Sasha smirked. "Too many sleepy bones these days."

Hugo stood up from his seat. He bent his left leg, then his right. He stretched his arms, then twisted side to side.

"I think everything works."

Liv rubbed her stomach as nausea set in.

"I need earth. I need earth under my feet."

"Let's get off this plane."

Sasha opened the door. The ground was much closer with the front wheel gone. Sasha hopped down to the pavement. Then Liv sat on the edge of the doorway and slid downward into Sasha's arms. He placed her on her feet. She sighed with relief. Then Hugo hopped down.

"When does the party start?"

"Very soon. A car is waiting. It'll take you and Liv to the Haines building."

"Where are you going?"

"I'll be at a different building." Sasha grinned. "I'll be watching the show."

29
Donor Dog Games

Eli and Sydney sat in the back of a limo. Eli wore a classy, black suit. Sydney wore a short, black dress with blue lightning bolts that repeated down the sides. She also had a ring of black tape around her neck. This denoted her as a Donor Dog.

Eli looked at his phone. He reread an email from Liv, one that explained Donor Dog culture.

"Again, what's your name?"

"I don't have one. I simply answer to *Dog*."

"Donor Dog culture is layered and varied. Many types and fetishes. What kind of Donor Dog are you?"

"A peach."

"Which is?"

"Innocent. Scared. Pure."

"And what do EmLights want from of a Donor Dog?"

"To see how far they'll go ..."

"Yes. Donate yourself to the evening, and they'll donate an organ to you." Eli paused. "What organ do you need?"

"Lungs. I need new lungs."

The limo stopped and the door opened. Eli and Sydney stepped onto a red carpet. On either side of the carpet, reporters and tabloids babbled belligerently.

"Mr. Soto! Mr. Soto! What a beautiful Dog!"
Sydney looked down and walked shyly.
"Is she a peach? She looks like a peach!"
Eli wore deaf ears and a stoic face. He walked into the glittering entrance of the building. Sydney followed close behind, but before she entered the building, she looked straight up. This was the Bashoum building. At 150 stories, it was the tallest building in Los Angeles. The blue-lit edges reached upward like rails. They impossibly met at some point high above.

•

In New York City, inside the Serdula building, on the 95th floor, Ruxton stood next to Anna as Anna looked around the party. The floors were marble and the dresses sparkled. Anna felt very uncomfortable in her slim, black dress. She yearned for her wife-beater, her tattered leather jacket.

Ruxton was barefoot, like most Donor Dogs, and he had a ring of black tape around his neck. Aside from that, he wore short black shorts and a tight black vest.

An EmLight walked up to Anna. "Hey, you're that famous pilot! You did that cool trick! What was it called?"

"The chimney stunt."

"Yeah! That was so cool! So old-fashioned."

"Old-fashioned?"

"Yeah, like, getting famous for like, doing something."

"How did *you* get famous?"

"Oh my gosh, it was so funny. I skezzed this young pilot. He had just gotten his wings or however you guys say it. Anyway, we slept together one night. And the next morning, he had to fly. So I drugged his coffee. I put narcotics in it. And then I made an anonymous tip to the airline. I said he was flying under the influence. They yanked him off the plane, took away his flying license. And I recorded the whole thing." The girl laughed. "He was devastated! Flying was his whole life, his passion, his career. Oh my gosh, he threw such a nasty fit. As soon as I uploaded it, I got three billion views."

The girl giggled.

Anna clenched her fist.

"Ladies and gentlemen!" An announcer bellowed from a platform. "May I have your attention!" Everyone turned to the announcer. The announcer continued: "Soon! Soon we will advance to the rooftop. But first! We would like to indulge in some games!" The crowd murmured with delight. "Tonight's first game is a classic! Tonight's first game is: Donor Dog Tug-of-War!"

The EmLights cheered in their dazzling suits and snazzy dresses. The Dogs looked at each other nervously.

"For Tug-of-War, we need two Dogs—two scraps to be specific!" The announcer wore his hand as a visor and peered into the crowd. "You! You look like a scrap!" He pointed to a Dog, a shaggy-haired man. "Come to the front!" The man obeyed. When he got to the announcer, the announcer said, "Good little scrap. Now tell us, what organ do you need?"

"I need a kidney."

"This scrap needs a kidney!"

The crowd cheered.

The announcer scanned the room a second time. He pointed at Ruxton. "You! You're the scrappiest scrap I've ever seen! Get up here!"

Ruxton moved through the crowd and reached the front of the room.

"Tell us, what organ do you need?"

"A liver," Ruxton said. "I need a liver."

The announcer smiled at the crowd. "What is more desperate? A dying kidney or a dying liver? Let's find out!"

Security guards grabbed Ruxton. They placed him and the other man in the center of the room. "Hands behind your back." Ruxton obeyed. He felt a zip-tie tighten around his wrists.

"How do I play Tug-of-War if I can't hold the rope?"

"Open your mouth."

"Why?"

The guard smacked Ruxton on the back of the head.

"Open your mouth, Dog!"

Ruxton opened his mouth. The guard put a rope between his teeth.

"Bite down."

Ruxton bit the rope.

The rope was twelve feet long. The other end was in the other man's teeth.

"Scrap Dogs! Please step back!"

Ruxton stepped back. Him and the other man faced each other. On the ground, between them, was a thick red line.

"Scrap Dogs! This is Round One! Ready! Set! Go!"

The man jerked back and the rope slid through Ruxton's teeth; it slid so fast that it burned his tongue.

"You dropped your rope, scrap! You can't drop your rope! You lose Round One!"

Ruxton and the other man reset their stances. They squeezed the rope between their teeth. This time, Ruxton readied himself. He turned sideways and tensed his neck.

"Scrap Dogs! This is Round Two! Ready! Set! Go!"

Ruxton tugged on the rope and growled through his teeth. The crowd hollered and howled; with white rings in their eyes, they recorded the game.

Ruxton pulled back. Inch by inch, he slowly pulled back. The other man tripped and fell over the line.

"What a Round! The score is one-to-one! Winner of the next round is the winner of the game! Remember, the winner gets a brand-new organ and the loser does not!" The announcer grinned. "Which Dog has more fight? A Dog in need of a liver? Or a Dog in need of a kidney?"

The crowd split into two factions.

One chanted: "LIV-ER DOG. LI-VER DOG."

The other chanted: "KID-NEY SCRAP. KID-NEY SCRAP."

Ruxton's jaw throbbed, but he bit on the rope.

"Scrap Dogs! This is the final round! Ready! Set! Go!"

They tugged as hard as they could, and, as they tugged, veins bulged from their necks, and their gums began to bleed.

For a second, Ruxton had a moment of clarity. He thought to himself: I don't need a liver. I mean, I might. I used to drink. I used to drink a lot. But this guy. This guy is actively dying. He *needs* a kidney. Why am I playing this game? What the fuck am I doing?

The crowd screamed and something primal took over. More than anything, Ruxton felt the urge to win. He bit the rope as hard as he could, then ripped it straight back. The other man stumbled. He fell to the ground.

The crowd erupted. "LIV-ER DOG! LIV-ER DOG! LIV-ER DOG!"

Ruxton spat the rope out of his mouth. He couldn't believe what he just did. He hated himself. And he hated the EmLights even more.

•

In Los Angeles, inside the Bashoum building, on the 107th floor, Sydney stood next to Eli. The room was huge. It had granite columns and marble floors. The marble felt cold on Sydney's bare feet, and the tape around her neck itched like a leash.

Her and Eli stood still as everyone else got tipsy. The EmLights clinked their glasses and laughed in their gowns. One of the EmLights, a younger girl, turned on the white rings in her eyes. She gathered her friends for a picture.

"Ready?" she said. "Say 'EmLight life!'"

Her friends repeated, "EmLight life!"

The girl blinked twenty times; she took twenty pictures.

Suddenly, Eli tensed.

"What's wrong?" Sydney asked.

"That's the guy."

"What guy?"

"The one with spikey hair."

Sydney spotted the spikey hair. "What about him?"

"He's the one who recorded my wife. He's the one who ruined her life."

"What's his name?"

"Jonathan."

Jonathan looked at Eli and immediately walked over.

"Hey, I know you! You're that drummer guy. You did that drum solo. Man, that was awesome. So old-fashioned. I bet that was a lot of hard work."

"It was."

"Well, hey man, welcome to EmLight life. You never have to work again!"

"Tell me, how did *you* get famous?"

"Oh man. I was so lucky. One day, I was standing on this street corner, and this chick, some nerdy chick, she dropped her papers. Papers! Like who uses paper? Anyway, she dropped her papers and got all hysterical. She *crawled* through an intersection. Like, she *crawled* to pick up paper. Cars were honking, flashing their lights. It was great. I recorded the whole thing. Got two billion views."

"That women," said Eli solemnly, "that *nerdy chick*, she overdosed. She accidentally killed herself after that video went viral."

"Oh man! It's just a video! Girls can be so emotional, am I right?"

"That girl was my wife."

"No way! Small world, huh?" Jonathan let out an obnoxious laugh. Then he turned to Sydney and eyed her up and down. "Good looking Donor Dog. What does she need?"

"Lungs."

"Well, she can take *my* breath away." Jonathon smirked.

An announcer stood on a platform. She shouted to the crowd: "Ladies and gentlemen! Are you ready for another Donor Dog Game?"

The EmLights cheered. The Donor Dogs gulped.

"For tonight's next game, I will need two Dogs, specifically, two female Dogs with exceptional hair!" The announcer peered into the crowd. "You!" she pointed to a Dog. "Your hair is so red, so vibrant. And your face! An aggressive angel, a fallen goddess. You must be a rag." The announcer turned to an EmLight. "Is your Dog a rag?"

"You bet!" said a portly, young man.

"Very good! Get up here, rag!"

The rag walked to the front of the room.

The announcer scanned the room again. She caught sight of Sydney in the back. "You! You with the white! The white! The silver! My god, which is it? I've never seen hair like that! Is it natural?"

Sydney nodded meekly.

"You're a peach, aren't you?"

Sydney nodded again.

The announcer chuckled menacingly. "I don't think a peach could win this game, but I *really* want to see that hair in action!"

Moments later, Sydney sat at a small table across from the redheaded girl. Above them, there was a timer set at three minutes.

"This game is called *Blow 'Til You Glow!*"

On the table, before each girl, were twelve lines of fine, white powder. Next to the powder was a short metallic straw.

"The powder before these girls is made from Plithrithium seeds. Plithrithium is an exotic plant, and its seeds have special properties." She pointed to the lines of powder. "If you snort one line, a lock of your hair will literally glow." The crowd murmured with excitement. "However! There is a side effect. With each line you snort, your muscles will endure a brief, excruciating spasm."

The EmLights lit up their eyes and started recording.

Sydney and the redhead stared at each other.

"These Dogs will have three minutes! Three minutes to snort as much Plithrithium powder as possible. The Dog who snorts the most will win!" The announcer turned to the girls. "Are you ready?"

Both of them nodded.

"Let's play *Blow 'Til You Glow!*"

The timer blinked. It read: 2:59.

The redhead grabbed her metal straw and snorted a line. Immediately, her muscles tensed with paralyzing pain. But then, her scalp tingled, and a lock of her hair began to glow. A red current curved away from her head.

Sydney picked up the straw. She snorted a line of the Plithrithium powder. Immediately, her spine straightened and her body unbearably tensed. But then, her scalp tingled, and a streak of her hair began to glow, like a river reflecting moonlight.

Sydney and the redhead snorted several more lines. As they added more glow to their beautiful manes, they tortured themselves with muscular spasms.

The girls were line for line. Blood dripped from their noses.

The EmLights recorded. They haggled and hollered, placing bets on who would win.

Ten seconds on the clock.

The girls looked exhausted.

Each of them had two lines left.

The redhead snorted one more line.

Five seconds.

Sydney snorted a line up her right nostril, flipped the straw, then snorted a line up her left.

The timer buzzed.

The crowd went wild.

Sydney fell out of her seat. She trembled on the floor in a head-to-toe spasm.

Eli rushed to her side. He wiped the blood from her nose.

"So tired," she whispered. "I'm so tired."

The announcer stepped to the table. "I didn't think a peach could do it! But she did it! And look at that hair! That moonlit mane! Well done, Dog! Well done!"

The redhead slouched over the table and cried. A handful of assistants held her down.

"Losers lose their hair!"

The assistants pulled out buzzers and shaved the redhead's head. The girl was too tired, too fatigued to fight back. All she could do was cry. She lost her shot at a new pancreas, and she lost her luscious, red locks.

The EmLights gaped and recorded. They loved a broken spirit.

Sydney shook her head. She rarely felt hate. But when she saw those EmLights recording that girl, recording her loss of life, her loss of beauty, Sydney felt hate. As tired and exhausted and empty as she was, she felt pure hate.

•

In Denver, inside the Haines building, on the 137th floor, Hugo stood next to Liv. Liv wore an elegant blue dress that showed her back, and her back was temporarily tattooed with intricate swirls of gold.

Hugo wore short black shorts, a tight vest, and a ring of black tape around his neck.

Surrounding them at the party were EmLights who grew louder and louder as the night went on. Many of them drank champagne as they shared videos of their favorite skezzes.

Suddenly, dozens of assistants permeated the crowd. They handed each EmLight two items: a plastic poncho and a mesh mask.

"What's happening?" Hugo asked.

"I don't know."

An announcer stood on a platform. "EmLights! May I have your attention!" Everyone turned. "Before we ascend to the rooftop, we have one more event! One more Donor Dog Game!" The crowd drunkenly cheered. "For this game, I will need two Dogs. Two scruffs to be specific!" The announcer peered into the crowd. "A scruff. A scruff. I need me a scruff. A Dog with a jaw! A powerful howl!" The announcer pointed to a bearded man. "You! You look like a scruff! Get up here!" The bearded man obeyed.

The announcer peered into the crowd again. "Another scruff. Another scruff." He spotted Hugo. "You! You're a young scruff but a scruff nonetheless! Get up here!"

Hugo walked to the front of the room, where he sat at a table, across from the bearded man.

"Our final game tonight is a new game, a game we've never done before. And the game has two parts. In part one, the scruff Dogs must work together. They must *scream* together. Part one of the game is called: *Scream Team*."

Two assistants came up to Hugo. They strapped a black mask to his face; it covered his nose and mouth. The mask had a hose. The hose ran up to the shadows of the ceiling.

"*Scream Team!*" the announcer repeated. "How does *Scream Team* work, you ask? It's quite simple. The scruff Dogs will scream into these masks. And the masks will channel the frequency of their screams. And their screams will be pumped! Yes, their screams will be pumped directly into ... into this!"

From the shadows of the ceiling, there lowered a ball, a solid ball of glass. The glass was ten feet wide.

"The scruffs have three minutes! They have three minutes to scream as loud and as hard as they can! If they scream enough, the glass will shatter. If they do *not* scream enough, the glass will *not* shatter, and these scruffs will *not* get the organs they need." The announcer paused. "May I ask, what does this scruff need?" He pointed to the bearded man.

"A heart!"

"And what does this scruff need?" He pointed to Hugo.

"A heart," Liv answered.

"Oh my! Two hearts! Two howls! Let's see how they do!"

The EmLights put on their plastic ponchos. They secured their mesh masks.

"Scruff Dogs! You have three minutes! On your marks! Get ready! Scream!"

The bearded man screamed into his mask. Hugo did the same. It felt so unnatural, so forced. But he screamed. He roared. He bore his soul.

Above them, the glass ball made a whirring sound. It collected their screams.

Two minutes passed.

Hugo's throat hurt, as if raked by a fork.

He stared at the bearded man. The man stared back.

They had fifteen seconds.

Each of them took a deep breath. Then they roared like lions.

Above them, the glass ball exploded. Planetary shards shot in every direction. The EmLights were safe, shielded by their ponchos and masks. The Dogs, however, were hit by glass missiles that splintered their skin. Hugo got hit the worst. The explosion knocked him out of his seat. On the ground, he rubbed his head. He could barely hear.

Someone placed a red bucket right next to him. Then they held a sign up to his face. It read:

Part Two
Ninety Seconds
Collect the Glass
Heaviest Bucket Wins

Hugo looked to his right. The bearded man was crawling on all fours, collecting glass into his bucket.

Fuck me, Hugo thought. He used his hands as brooms and swept broken glass into a pile before him, then scooped the pile into his bucket.

The EmLights hollered and cheered. They recorded every second.

Hugo looked at the bearded man's bucket. It was fuller than his.

Ten seconds on the clock.

Hugo stood up. He lifted his bucket to the edge of the table, then swept all the glass on top of the table. He swept it into his bucket. It was a big scoop, a jingly deposit.

The timer buzzed.

They weighed the buckets.

Hugo's bucket was heavier.

"Well done young scruff!" the announcer bellowed. "You have earned yourself a new heart! A state-of-the-art synthetic heart!" The announcer turned to the crowd. "Now! Let us all advance to the rooftop! Let us indulge in tonight's main event: the Vicarium tastings!"

Hugo looked at the bearded man. He was crying and covered in cuts. Hugo hoped that he could somehow donate his state-of-the-art heart to the man who actually needed it. But it probably wasn't possible. The man was probably going to die.

Hugo felt horrible.

He thought about his classroom, his insistencies on civility, decency, nobility, respect. Then he looked at the EmLights. He saw how they snickered and giggled over angles and filters, different lightings of tortured lives. Hugo felt rage. He felt pure rage.

30

The Vicarium Tastings

In New York City, Ruxton stood on the rooftop of the Serdula building. He was so high up, he couldn't even hear the sounds of the city. No cars, no horns, no hustle bustle. All he could hear was EmLights, drunk, laughing, cackling EmLights. They mingled in different groups; some danced around spotlights. The spotlights beamed upward, into the heavens, into the clouds.

Ruxton pointed. "What are those?"
"The chairs?" Anna said.
"Yeah."
"Those are for the Vicarium tastings."
On the far side of the rooftop, there were thirty recliners. They were plush white and situated in a curved row, a crescent shape.

•

In Los Angeles, Sydney stood on the rooftop of the Bashoum building. A cool breeze skimmed the rooftop. Sydney shivered. Eli put his jacket over her shoulders.
"I'm so tired," she whispered.

"I know. Just hang on a little longer."

Eli looked at the EmLights. They hung around spotlights, swapping videos of tonight's Donor Dog games.

Sydney's eyes closed. She started to fall asleep. Eli shook her.

"Hey! Sydney! Stay awake!"

"It's hard."

"You have to stay awake."

"But why..."

"You're a weapon. There's a weapon inside you. You can change all this. You can end all this. But you must stay awake."

•

In Denver, Hugo stood on the rooftop of the Haines building. He was covered in skin-tone bandages that hid his countless cuts.

Liv rubbed her hands together. At this height in this region, the air was very cold. Many of the EmLights wore robes, while all the Dogs shivered.

"Ladies and gentlemen! May I have your attention!"

Everyone turned to an announcer who stood near a spotlight.

"Thank you all for coming. I hope you enjoyed tonight's Donor Dog games. And I hope you are excited for our final event: the Vicarium tastings." He paused. "Vicarium is the future. It is the greatest technological achievement of the millennia!"

Hugo muttered, "It's a pill that keeps you addicted to bullshit."

"When you take Vicarium, you can *feel* the things you see in your Glow Domes. Whether it's a roller coaster ride, a deep-sea dive, or a warm meadow, you'll be able to *feel* it. That's why we call it Vicarium—so you can live vicariously through your Domes." The announcer smiled. "This drug was created, tested, and patented by Axiom. It is completely side-effect free. No ailments, no hazards. This drug is *safe*, and it is *fun*."

The announcer motioned towards the recliners on the rooftop. "If you purchased a ticket for the Vicarium tastings, please approach the recliners on the far side of the deck. Thank you."

•

Sasha sat in a rusted foldout chair. He was on top of a sixty-story apartment building. Five blocks away, he could see the Haines building, the tallest building in Denver. It rose before him like a monolith.

"This took a long time … a long time and a lot of careful planning. But I did it." He chuckled. "I actually did it."

Sasha reached into his backpack and pulled out the crown, the enlightenment crown. He placed it on his head.

"I've got Sydney in Los Angeles, Ruxton in New York, and Hugo here in Denver. That's three weapons—three weapons of mass reflection for this noisy, noisy world."

At the top of the Haines building, the spotlights turned blue.

Sasha sat up in this seat. "It's finally happening!"

•

In New York, the EmLights moved to the recliners. The young EmLight, the one who ruined a pilot, brushed past Anna. "You didn't buy a tasting ticket?"

"Nah," said Anna. "I don't wanna try that stuff."

"Your loss!" The girl giggled and put in her headphones. Every EmLight who sat in a recliner put in their headphones. They wanted the full experience.

A waiter walked up to Ruxton and handed him a rose.

"Remember," Anna said. "There's a mic inside."

Ruxton twirled the rose under his nose.

"Exactly sixty seconds into the tastings, the mic will remotely hack into the headphones of all the EmLights trying Vicarium. When it does, say the words of the Vastus meditation. But say them into the rose. Don't let anyone else hear you."

•

In Los Angeles, Sydney twirled the rose between her fingers.

"The EmLights will hear it?"

Eli nodded. "It's a small mic with a small transmitter. Its reach is short and brief. But the EmLights should hear you."

Two security guards approached Eli.

"Excuse us, Mr. Soto, but we have to remove your Donor Dog from the party."

"What? Why?"

"We have reason to believe her papers were forged. She's an undocumented Dog."

"What? That can't be!"

"I'm afraid that's the case, sir."

The spotlights turned blue.

"But look!" said Eli. "The tastings are starting. They're starting right now! Can we deal with this later?"

"I'm afraid not. This is a very serious security issue."

"Oh, come on. What is *she* gonna do?"

Sydney looked up shyly, holding the rose.

"I'm sorry sir, but we have to take care of this."

The guard grabbed Sydney by the arm.

•

In Denver, Hugo lifted the rose to his nose and smelled it. It was real.

"There's a mic inside?"

"Yes," Liv nodded.

"When do I say it?"

"Exactly sixty seconds into the tastings. No sooner. No later."

At the far end of the rooftop, the EmLights were seated in the crescent row of recliners. Behind them, there stood a massive digital screen.

An announcer addressed the EmLights. "In a moment, your Vicarium pill will appear to your right. We ask that you wait until the spotlights turn blue. When the spotlights turn blue, you may take your Vicarium pill." He paused. "Once you take your pill, you can turn on your Glow Domes, and your Glow Domes will show you a wide array of human experiences. Fun things! Cute things! Thrilling things! When the drug hits your system, you will be able to *feel* those things!"

The announcer turned to everyone else. "For those of you *not* taking Vicarium, you may watch the big screen. It will show you all the things that you *could* be feeling."

•

In New York, Ruxton walked to a corner of the rooftop, away from anyone who could hear him. He stared into the rose. Then he glanced at the EmLights.

To the right of each recliner, a hole appeared in the floor. Then a pedestal rose from the hole. It stopped at armchair level. The pedestal presented a blue pill and a short glass of water. The EmLights giggled with glee.

Every spotlight on the rooftop turned blue. It was time for the Vicarium tastings.

Each EmLight put the blue pill in their mouth. Then they sipped the water and swallowed the pill. On cue, the recliners leaned back, and the EmLights turned on their Glow Domes.

Behind them, the big screen blinked on. It showed a roller coaster ride from the front seat point-of-view. The EmLights smiled like toddlers as the coaster inched upward. It inched towards the top, the top of the first drop.

•

In Los Angeles, Eli followed the security guards into a stairwell.
"This is ridiculous! You're ruining the party!"
"Sir, you can stay at the party. We just need the girl."
The security guards dragged Sydney down a flight of stairs.
"Stop it! I need her up here!"
Eli looked over his shoulder. The spotlights turned blue.
"No, no, no." Eli looked at his watch. He set a timer for sixty seconds.

•

In Denver, Hugo stood by himself, holding the rose.
At the far end of the rooftop, he saw the EmLights in their recliners. They smiled as their Glow Domes pumped fun into their eyes. Behind them, the big screen flashed every few seconds. At one point, a racecar hugged a cliffy curve.
Liv looked at her watch. Fifty seconds in. She nodded at Hugo.
Hugo tried to speak, but his voice was shot from the screaming game.
He looked at Liv with panic as he rubbed his throat.
Liv understood. She grabbed a glass of water and rushed it to him. He chugged it and cleared his throat. He found some sound.

•

In Los Angeles, Eli shouted at the guard, "Who is your superior?"
"Sir! Please back away!"

One of the guards dragged Sydney down another flight of stairs.

The other guard stood in front of Eli.

"Please go back to the party!"

Eli's timer went off. Sixty seconds were up.

Eli hauled back his arm and punched the guard.

"Hey!" The other guard let go of Sydney and rushed up to Eli.

"Now, Sydney! Now!"

Sydney held the rose. She took a deep breath.

•

In three different cities, at the exact same moment, Ruxton, Sydney, and Hugo held a rose to their lips. They whispered the words of the Vastus meditation: "Smile at your chances. / Chuckle at your tomb. / Laugh at your chances. / Cackle at your doom."

All the EmLights sat up in their chairs. They blinked several times and turned off their Domes. Some of them breathed heavily. Some of them twitched. The silence was in them. It was deep in their brains.

One of them screamed. Then another one screamed.

For the first time in their life, they felt silence, vast, eternal silence.

They couldn't handle it. Some of them ripped off their clothes. Some of them attacked each other. One of the EmLights grabbed a tabletop. He whirled it around his waist and hurled it at the big screen. It cracked the glass.

Security guards rushed in. Medics rushed in. They tried to help, but they couldn't help. Every EmLight who took Vicarium was in a feral state. Horrible things haunted their vision. Crawly things went under their skin. They were in withdrawal. Their minds sweated out the noise, the noise they had been addicted to for so, so long.

The EmLights ran around the rooftop. They craved an escape. Eventually, they made for the edges. All of them hopped the railings. But the actual edge of the rooftop was buffered by barbed wire. It was meant to stop jumpers, but it did not stop the EmLights. Every single one of them swam. Arm over arm, leg over leg, they swam through the barbed wire. No one knew what to do. No one knew how to stop them. As soon as the EmLights reached the edge of the rooftop, they threw themselves over.

•

Sasha leaned forward. He heard the screams as he watched the specks, the falling human specks. As they fell to the ground, Sasha smiled and said: "Open the floor and let them drop. / Satan's throat will fizzle and pop. / He'll swallow their guiltless grins and they'll die. / They'll die and they'll writhe in hell's awareness. / They'll wear eternity's dress."

•

On the ground, at the bottom of all three buildings, people screamed. They jumped left and right, as bodies fell from the sky. And many bodies fell. They fell to the pavement. Each of them ended their existence with a quick, loud splat.

31
No More Glow Domes

The next morning, Anna and Ruxton left New York while Sydney and Eli left Los Angeles. Everyone met in Denver. They met in a penthouse suite that belonged to Liv.

Liv turned on the television. Every channel was the same.

"Ladies and gentlemen! The country is still reeling from last night's tragedy. At the highly anticipated Vicarium parties, over a hundred people died. All of them were EmLights: internet stars, social media stars, the most famous of the famous.

"Reports are still coming in, but from what we've gathered, a minute into the Vicarium tastings, the EmLights suffered a severe side-effect from the Vicarium drug. It appears that the drug drove each of them into a mad, suicidal rage. Medics and security personnel tried desperately to restrain and protect the EmLights from themselves, but the EmLights were in a very violent and hostile state.

"After the EmLights shouted and screamed for several long minutes, they sought the edges of the rooftops, where they took a fatal leap. Many tall buildings, such as the ones in Los Angeles, Denver, and New York, are regulated to have a lot of barbed wire between the rooftop platform and the edge of the roof. This is to prevent jumpers from harming themselves or pedestrians below. However, this did not stop the EmLights. Every single one of them crawled through the barbed wire and made it to the edge of the rooftop, where they took their own lives.

"Most medical professionals agree on one thing: For the EmLights to do something so drastic and so self-inflicted, they must have been in unimaginable pain—and this pain was caused by the drug Vicarium.

"Videos of the suicides are spreading like wildfire. The public is outraged. Many are asking: How could Axiom have been so negligent in administering this highly unsafe drug? Axiom has not commented with an answer, but the public is already taking matters into its own hands. Thousands of citizens are flocking in droves to Glow Dome clinics. They want their Glow Domes removed."

The screen cut to a group of people who chanted: "No more Glow Domes! No more Glow Domes!" A news reporter approached one of the chanters. "Excuse me, mam. Can you tell me why you are here at this Glow Dome clinic today?"

"I want my Glow Domes removed. This technology has gone too far."

"But ma'am, do you really think removing your Glow Domes is the right decision?"

"Honestly, I do. Axiom lost control of Vicarium. What if they lose control of Glow Domes?" The woman shook her head. "I don't want this shit in my eyes anymore."

The screen cut back to the news anchor. "People are scared. They do not trust Axiom. In fact, Axiom stocks have plummeted. And relatives of the late EmLights are already seeking legal action against Axiom, leaving Axiom rattled on all fronts.

Many people have reached out to Bill Sumzer, the CEO of Axiom, for comment, but Bill has yet to reply.

"No matter his answer, we will never forget. We will never forget what happened last night—in Los Angeles, in Denver, and in New York. What was supposed to be the greatest technological advancement of our lifetime will now be remembered as one of the most horrific and devastating events of the twenty-first century, or as people are already calling it: the Tri-City Suicides."

Liv turned off the television.

Ruxton, Sydney, Eli, Anna, and Hugo stared at the black screen. They stared in silence and in disbelief.

Finally, Sydney turned to Sasha and said: "Are we going to get in trouble?"

"What trouble?"

"I don't know. What if they autopsy the bodies? What if they find the silence in their brains?"

"That won't happen."

"How do you know?"

"Silence is undetectable. You can't measure it. You can't weigh it. When they do the autopsies, the only thing they're going to find in those bodies ... is Vicarium."

"The Vastus meditation," Ruxton said. "It lasts nine minutes. And if you can last nine minutes, you make it to the good part." Ruxton paused. "What if those EmLights made it to the good part?"

"They wouldn't have. They never stood a chance."

Sydney put her hand on her stomach. "I think I'm going to be sick ..." She rushed out of the room; Ruxton followed.

"I need to call my lawyer." Anna left as she dialed her phone.

"I need to get a lawyer." Eli hurried away.

Liv looked dazed, as if hit by a truck. Without saying anything, she slowly stood and walked out of the room.

Only Hugo and Sasha remained. Hugo looked at his older brother, and suddenly, everything fell into place. His whole life, his entire relationship with Sasha made sense. Sasha was strong; he was driven. But he did not care about people. He used them. He lied to them. Every person in his life was a pawn for his sick, twisted games.

"The suicides—those were the plan all along."

Sasha nodded.

"I thought we were going to botch the drug release."

"We did."

"You never said anything about killing people."

"It was a drastic measure, but now we can spread Solosis."

"Why couldn't you spread Solosis in the first place?"

"Solosis requires eye contact. Glow Domes hide your eyes."

"I don't believe that."

"What don't you believe?"

"This was never about Solosis. This was never about making the world a better place. This was about you doing something dark and twisted to get back at Dad."

Sasha didn't answer.

"People died, Sasha."

"They were bad people."

"Their fate is not yours to decide."

Again, Sasha did not answer.

Hugo thought about the last forty-eight hours. He thought about the gruesome deaths that would forever weigh on his conscience. With a detached voice, he looked at Sasha and said, "I never want to see you again."

32

An Ancient Bell

One year later

Hugo coughed as he patted dirt off his shirt. He stood in a desert of northern New Mexico. He was on an expedition with an archeological team. They were hunting for artifacts from a legendary tribe.

"We've got something!"

Hugo hurried into the hole that they had been digging.

"What is it?" he asked.

"Some kind of metal. A copper alloy maybe."

For the next week, Hugo and his team spent countless, meticulous hours unearthing this metal object, one brushstroke at a time. As the days went on and the sun beat down, they slowly revealed a cone-shaped hunk of metal. It was three feet wide, six feet tall, and the inside was hollow.

Late one night, while drinking beers, the team sat around the hole and stared at the metal object.

"Maybe they used it for storage?"

"Maybe they used it for punishment."

"Punishment?"

"You could fit a person in there. And if the thing was upright, it would be too heavy to push off."

"It's not for storage," said Hugo. "And it's not for punishment."

"What do you think it is, rookie?"

"I think it's a bell."

"Why would it be a bell?"

"We're looking for a legendary tribe, a people capable of telepathy, reading each other's thoughts and emotions. That takes focus. Bells make you focus."

"That's a stretch."

Hugo grinned.

The following morning, the team continued to dig, but Hugo decided to take a day off so that he could go on a solo hike. He told a colleague where he was going and how long it would take. This desert was unforgiving; one had to play it safe. Hugo packed snacks and water into a backpack, then he tightened the laces on his boots. Finally, he put on his hat and went out for an eight-hour trek in the middle of nowhere.

As Hugo walked, he thought about a lot of things—his dad, his brother, the suicides. For the past year, he had blamed himself for the people that jumped, and the guilt was so bad that he had developed psychosomatic symptoms—abdominal pain, nausea, headaches, insomnia. And he couldn't exactly go to a therapist. What would he say? *I whispered the words of the Vastus meditation into a red rose and all those people killed themselves.*

It was a hard thing to hide, and it was even harder just to feel okay. But as time went on, Hugo felt better. He was in a decent place right now, not perfect, but better. The desert stretched before him and he thought: There's nothing that time can't heal.

Hugo thought more about time. He thought about ancient tribes and forgotten societies, how they speak to each other through the eons of time. He thought about how hard that actually was. He imagined living in the past, discovering a nugget of wisdom, not a thing, but an idea. How would he pass that idea down to future generations? It's a tricky thing to do. After all, languages evolve and die in the blink of an eye. Statues and buildings crumble. What vessel is left? How do you preserve an idea over thousands of years? Maybe you turn that idea into an experience. An experience between people is better remembered than a thought had alone.

Hugo checked his watch. It was time to head back. As he walked in the direction from where he came, he could see heatwaves rising from the desert floor. He suddenly felt tired. When he saw a rock, he decided to sit down and take a break. The sun beat down as he chugged water from his canteen. A beetle crawled by his foot. He chuckled.

"If you can do it, I can do it."

Hugo stood up and finished the trek back to camp.

When he returned to the dig, there was a lot of commotion.

"What's going on?"

"Words!"

"Words?"

"We found words, an inscription on the metal."

"Really?"

"Come check it out."

Hugo was exhausted, but this was far more important than dinner or rest. His colleague led him into the hole. They squatted near the bottom of the object. His colleague pointed. "Right here, right on the lip. Do you see that?"

Hugo squinted. "Oh my gosh, those are letters." He ran his finger across them; it felt like ancient brail.

"Tom's been working on it all day."

"Any luck?"

"He said he might have one or two words."

Hugo crawled out of the hole and headed for the main tent. That's where he found Tom, the on-site linguist.

"You think you've got something?" Hugo asked.

Tom was poring over notes. In the middle of his desk, there was a photograph of the inscription on the metal.

"It's a shot in the dark ..."

"But?"

"But I think I've got two words."

Tom pointed to the photograph. "See these two? They're the same. I think they mean: *eyes*. And the last one, the one on the end, I think it means *gift* or *present* or *prize*."

Hugo smiled. He couldn't believe it.

When the sun set and the team turned in for the night, Hugo snuck back into the hole and sat for a while. As he stared at the bell, he imagined the people who built it. He imagined their struggle, their urgency to find meaning in their short, brief lives, then preserving that meaning for thousands of years. They had no idea if it would work; they had no idea if it would reach anyone, but it did. Through vast stretches of darkness, they passed a torch, they carried a light.

Hugo put his hand on the bell. "Thank you."

33

The Flower Café

"Let's go over the checklist one more time."
"We've already gone over it ten times."
Sydney shot Ruxton a glance.
"Okay, okay. One more time."
"The cooler is stocked."
"Check."
"All the food is labeled."
"Check."
"Utensils are organized."
"Check."
"Sanitary products?"
"Check."
"Oven, griddle, microwave—all in working order?"
"Check."
"Plates, bowls, silverware?"
"Check."
"Trash bags?"
"Check."
Ruxton grabbed the clipboard from Sydney.
"Let's do your half now." He looked at the list. "Lilies?"

"Check."
"Daisies?"
"Check."
"Spider mums?"
"Check."
"Irises?"
"Check.
"Solidago?"
"Check."
"Roses?"
"They ship from South America. They'll be here Friday."
"Vases?"
"Check."
"Ribbon?"
"Check."
"Fern leaf?"
"Check."
"Lemon leaf?"
"Check."
"Good enough."

Sydney slouched over the counter. Ruxton and her had been working for months on starting their own business: The Flower Café. Earlier in the year, they decided to merge their skillsets into one brick-and-mortar store. If customers ordered an omelet, scramble, or a stack of pancakes, it would come with a complimentary bouquet of flowers.

On the window of the café, it said: *A beautiful way to start your day.*

"Let's get some rest," Ruxton said. "We've been working non-stop."

Sydney looked at the dining room. There were a dozen small tables, each with a pair of chairs. On the walls, they had painted bumblebees. Behind the bees were dashed lines, curves and loops that noted where they had flown.

It made Sydney happy. It made her forget about last year.

"Okay," she said. "Let's take a break."

They left the café and walked to a nearby park. Once they got there, they sat on a bench. The sky was blue and the trees were green. Everything seemed calm and serene.

"I'm stressed," Sydney said.

"Hey, we're resting right now."

"But Ruxton..."

"What?"

"This weekend is our opening weekend!"

"I know. It's gonna be great."

"Aren't you stressed?"

"Not as much as you."

They sat for a moment in silence.

Ruxton carefully watched a couple that sat at a nearby bench.

"What are you looking at?"

"Those two."

"Why?"

He didn't answer at first. He just smiled. Then he said, "How many people have we gotten this year?"

Sydney counted her fingers. "Nine. Why?"

"I think it's spreading."

"How do you know?"

"Look."

Sydney looked at the couple on the other bench. It was a man and a woman. They faced each other; they stared intently into each other's eyes. From the distance, it was hard to see, but Sydney could see it—their irises moved; the color swirled around their pupils, if only for a few seconds.

34

Open to Heal

Six months later

Hugo woke up with a smile on his face. He had slept soundly, more soundly than he had in a long time. He wasn't sure why, but it felt good. He got out of bed and took a long, hot shower. As the steam rose around him, he hummed the tune of his favorite song.

After his shower, Hugo dried off. He put on a pair of linen slacks, along with a linen, white dress shirt. It was his new favorite outfit; it made him feel like a real archeologist.

Hugo left his apartment and went for a walk in downtown Albuquerque. The weather was perfect: seventy-five degrees, not a cloud in the sky. Hugo strolled down the street as he whistled notes up and down a scale. When people passed him on the sidewalk, Hugo noticed something interesting, something different. No one was on their Glow Domes. No white circles; no white rings; no recording of any kind. Every stranger on the street had a colorful pair of eyes—blues, greens, golds, and browns. The windows to their souls were open.

Hugo stopped on the sidewalk as he looked across the street. Rising before him was the tallest bell tower in Albuquerque.

The tower was made of big, blocky stones, and the top of it sharpened into a pyramidal point. It was a formidable structure, but people rarely paid attention to it. Every bell tower in America had been decommissioned for over fifty years. With modern technology, no one needed a bell to remind them of the time. But, Hugo wondered, what if bell towers didn't signify time? What if they signified empathy? What if they reminded people to search for something deeper?

Hugo continued down the street. In two blocks, he found Sydney and Ruxton's place: The Flower Café. In front of the café was a wooden patio with a few small tables.

"Hi Sydney!"

"Hugo!"

Sydney rushed to Hugo and gave him a hug.

"How are you?" he asked.

"So busy!" She waved her hand to the café, to all the flower arrangements on the counter, shelves, and tables. "Every egg dish comes with a complimentary bouquet of flowers." Sydney laughed. "Ruxton makes the best eggs in town, so I'm always making flowers."

"Is there anything else you'd rather be doing?"

"No. I love it!" Sydney smiled. She was getting older, more mature, like a wise matriarch in the making.

"Ruxton!" she called to the back. "Look who's here!"

Ruxton stepped back from a stove and waved to Hugo.

"Hi Hugo!"

Ruxton's eyes were bright, and his smile was pure. All his dark edginess had transformed into a goofy cheerfulness.

"Hi Ruxton!"

"Can I whip you up some breakfast? I have a mean special today."

"Oh yeah?"
"It's a mushroom and sausage omelet, with parsley on top."
"Does it come with hashbrowns?"
"Extra crispy!"
"I'll take it."
"Coming right up!"
Ruxton cracked an egg on the edge of the stove.
"Can I make you a flower arrangement to go with your eggs?" Sydney asked.
"Sure thing!"
"Is there any particular flower you're into these days?"
"Hmm, the flowers don't matter. But aesthetically, I like when things are blue and gold."
"Blue and gold ... blue and gold ..." Sydney looked at all the flowers in the cooler. "I can make that work!"
"Where should I sit?"
"Take that table on the patio." Sydney pointed. "It's the only one open."

Hugo thanked Sydney and walked to the empty table. When he sat down, he noticed he could see the bell tower two blocks down, across the street. The top of the tower pierced the sky.

Hugo thought about getting out his phone and checking the news, checking his email, checking any little distraction. But then he decided not to. He decided to simply sit and enjoy the warm weather as he waited for his eggs.

A woman walked up to Hugo's table. She looked a few years older than him, and she was very pretty. She had rich, red hair and a splash of freckles on just one cheek.

"Hi there!"
"Hello."
"I'm Piper."

"Nice to meet you, Piper. I'm Hugo."

"Listen, Hugo, I know this is forward, but would you mind sharing your table? I've been wanting to try this café since they've opened but it's always so busy!"

Hugo nodded. "We can share."

"You're sure?"

"Please, have a seat."

Piper slipped into the chair across from Hugo.

"So, Piper, tell me about yourself."

"Well, I'm really into history."

Hugo's eyes widened as a tingle ran up his spine. "What kind of history?"

"I like ancient tribes, really obscure ones."

Hugo chuckled.

"What's so funny?"

"I used to be an anthropology professor."

"You did?"

"And the young couple that owns this café—those are my former students."

"Did you teach here in town?"

"At the community college."

"What was your classroom like?"

"Meh, stark."

"Did you have any art? Any photos of tribes?"

"Just pictures of owls—great horned owls."

"Why owls?"

"It was a bit I used to do with my students."

"A bit?"

"Every time the news dropped a story about people acting crazy, I said to my students: When will owls fly in flocks?" He smiled. "It means: When will wise people be the most common people?"

Piper tilted her head and stared at Hugo curiously.

"What's wrong?" he asked.

"Nothing ... it's just ... are you one of them?"

"One of who?"

Piper waved her hand in dismissal. "Never mind."

"What is it?"

"Ever since the suicides, the world is changing. People are putting down their phones. They're taking out their Domes. For the first time in a long time, people are looking up. They're looking into each other's eyes."

Suddenly, there was a loud gong. Across the street, the bell tower rang. It rang for the first time in decades. Peal after peal, it rang above the town. And it wasn't just that bell tower. All the tallest bell towers in America began to ring. Everywhere, people looked up. They lifted their eyes and opened their ears. They listened to the ringing of bells, and as they listened, they realized: the feeling of healing was in the air. It was as if the bells had magic, a magic that rang in every direction, a magic that mended a broken species.

Hugo looked at Piper. Piper looked at him.

"Can I try something?" she asked.

He nodded.

"I'm going to say something. It might work. It might not. It depends if you're open—open to heal."

Hugo's eyes welled with tears. This was it. This was Solosis—a brief cosmic connection between two souls, one life funneled into another, all of it, good and bad, flaws and wounds, an understanding, a bond that births a synchronized search for pure solutions.

"Are you ready?" Piper asked.

"Yes," answered Hugo.

Piper took a deep breath. She smiled and said: "When eyes meet eyes, we find the prize—a reason to live, a reason to thrive."

Glossary

Ancient Meditations

The Solosis meditation: a bond between two souls; one life flows through another for pure understanding, pure healing.

The Vastus meditation: a cleansing of the mind; a vast, eternal silence.

The Maxis meditation: the attainment of greatness; the unlocking of one's full potential.

New Technologies

Axiom: a social media conglomerate and the creator of Glow Domes.

Glow Domes: contact lenses with all the technology of a smartphone.

Vicarium: a pharmaceutical drug that keeps one addicted to Glow Domes.

Scrolling Centers: a workplace where employees scroll through the news using Glow Domes; employees get paid for their opinions on the news.

Societal Classes

LowLights: people who do not have Glow Domes; mostly lower socioeconomic status.

Glowers: people with Glow Domes; most work in Scrolling Centers.

EmLights: social media celebrities; mostly Glowers whose clips obtain one billion views or more.

Wanderers: people who are homeless by choice; no Glow Domes or smartphones.

Cultural Phenomenon

Skezz: the act of recording someone losing their cool; recording someone in pain or distress and sharing it online.

Donor Dogs: human pets at upscale parties.

Acknowledgements

I would like to thank my wife Allison for her support, encouragement, and delicious meals through this entire journey. Thank you to my closest friend Julian for reading my drafts and encouraging my crazy ideas. Thank you to Alan Zepp for his thorough notes. Thank you to my mom for raising me to be a fierce and fearless Czech. Thank you to my dad for instilling a love of art and music. Finally, a big thank you to the folks at Vine Leaves Press, to Amie McCracken and Jessica Bell. Thank you for professionally turning this dream into a reality.

Vine Leaves Press

Enjoyed this book?
Go to *vineleavespress.com* to find more.
Subscribe to our newsletter: